The Sacred Mountain

The Sacred Mountain

A California-Indian Family Anatomy

by **Charles Brashear**

Books, etc
www.charlesbrashear.com
ISBN 0-933362-26-9

Acknowledgments:

Several parts of this book have appeared in literary magazines. An earlier version of Chapter 1 appeared as "The Invasion of Alcatraz" in *Callaloo*, 17:1 (Native American Issue, 1994) 309-317.

Earlier drafts of Chapters 9 & 10 appeared as "A Cup for Fresh Rainwater" in *American Indian Quarterly*, 3:1 (1997) 37-50.

Earlier variants of Chapters 20, 21, 22, & 23 appeared as "The Vision Quest of Charlie Stonecrist" in *Blue Cloud Quarterly*, XXII;2 (1976) 3-23.

And versions of Chapters 26, 27, 28, & 29 appeared as "The Battle of Wounded Thigh" in *Denver Quarterly*, XIV:4 (Winter, 1980) 54-77.

ISBN 0-933362-26-9

CONTENTS

Foreword: The Anatomy as a Form of Fiction

In *The Sacred Mountain*, I have tried to write an anatomy, not a novel. My degree of success is, of course, not for me to decide; that is the reader's and critic's privilege. But I thought I might say a few words here to inform interested readers about some of the ideas that guided me while writing; for the anatomy differs from the novel in several important ways.

Most reasonable people would think it unfair to curse a turnip for not being a good potato, or a radish for not tasting like a carrot. Yet, this kind of cursing has been all too frequent in the reading public's reception of long fictions. The romance (not the paperback love-story), that turnip among our fictions, was long thought inferior because it did not taste quite like a novel, our everyday potato. But taste is capable of being educated, and readers are capable of enjoying immensely both romances and turnips when they taste them for what they are.

In earlier times, writers sometimes provided their fictions with prefaces in which they tried to sensitize their readers to the subject or form of their story and thereby to increase understanding and enjoyment. Thus Nathaniel Hawthorne prefaced *The House of the Seven Gables*: "When a writer calls his work a Romance, it need hardly be observed that he wishes to claim a certain latitude, both as to its fashion and material, which he would not have felt himself entitled to assume, had he professed to be writing a Novel." And he went on to distinguish the romance from the novel, because he didn't want his readers cursing his very good romance for being a bad novel, when he wasn't even trying to write a novel at all.

The romance, he said, deals with "the truth of the human heart," but it is at liberty to represent that truth through just about any vehicle the writer wants to. Thus the writer may use events based in curses, magic, witchcraft, fantasy, supernatural or diabolical ideas--anything, in short, from either our real world or any imagined world.

Generally, the romance uses these extreme and/or non-realistic developments to represent psychological, moral, ethical realities. The magic or supernatural surface becomes a metaphor for the archetypal, primal, innate, perhaps subconscious nature of man. Romances like the literary horror story and the science-fiction fantasy are, at their best, psychological allegories.

The novel, on the other hand, deals with an essentially dramatized presentation of people in their public capacities, usually in social groups, interacting with one another according to their codes of manners, morals, and behavior. This kind of story is usually organized by the structure of experience and explained by motivation.

The novelist expects that readers will splash on the insides of their foreheads the images of his persons, places, and plots. In other words, the novel is a kind of private, interior movie, in which readers imaginatively recreate the experiences which the novelist invents. As Henry James noted, the novel lives on this "illusion of reality."

The anatomy also deals with people in public, but in their representative rather than their experiential capacities. In *Gulliver's Travels*, Jonathan Swift gave us (among other things) men arguing about the big and little ends of eggs, but we are supposed to recognize that they represent the arguments of the political parties during Queen Anne's reign.

He shows us a man carrying a huge sack of objects around on his back and exhibiting one or more of these objects when he wants to communicate with others, but we are supposed to recognize that he is referring to the Royal Society's silly proposal that language be legislated, so that each word had a direct correspondence to the object it referred to.

He shows us Hounynyhms talking about Yahoos, but unless we realize that these are men ruled by reason talking about men ruled by appetite, we miss the point. Characters exist in the anatomy to make a point.

The anatomist, of course, tries not to sacrifice life-likeness. But whenever we see a person as a representative of a group and identify him/her as a type, we see him less experientially, less as a motivated individual, and have begun to see him as the vehicle for a set of ideas, which is every bit as true to life as the experiential, but different. When our minds see a character as a type, the character starts to represent our analysis of group behavior and may even tug at the kind of knowledge we used to call "universal" truths.

Truth-to-Life-ness, presented through this typal concept of character, is central to the anatomy. While the details of presentation can never escape the experiential (since no one can paint a generalization, only a particular), you are supposed to respond to people in anatomies for what they represent.

If characters represent ideas in anatomies, it follows that plots will have to represent the impact of ideas upon one another. Thus, theme and organization will be tied to intellectual history. Swift tried to give us a cross-section of his time, to satirize every major absurdity he saw. We respond to Swift and value him highly because he gave us an anthology of the irrationality around him.

Joseph Heller, on the other hand, tried to exhaust a linear, historical subject for us, to delineate military madness. We respond to *Catch 22*, not because it presents an engaging personality involved in conflict and resolution (the book's personalities are generally absurd caricatures, and it has almost no conventional plot), but because it gives us an encyclopedia of military insanity during World War II.

In both approaches, encyclopedic completeness of subject, rather than characterization, is crucial— which is to say anatomies are theme-driven.

This urge toward encyclopedic completeness has allowed the anatomy, historically, to contain many different kinds of writing in addition to scene, summary, and dialog: poems or lines from poems, formal and informal essays, quotations from other writers, sketches, drawings, maps, lists, allusions, parodies— anything, in any situation, that some writer has devised or may devise.

This variety is possible because ideas usually "drive" the story. In the novel, character or plot usually drive the story, but the anatomist is more interested in meanings than in experience. Representational characters, referential actions, if they are understood, necessarily generate ideas by their representations and references.

The subjects, then, of anatomies are ideas that have existed; that is, historical facts. Stories made of these subjects can be organized in a number of ways. Narratives like the "non-fiction novel," the documentary novel, and the historical novel, all of which focus on real events and real people and delineate a time and place, are forms of the anatomy.

Such stories are usually organized by the structure of historical event and gain at least part of their effect from "factuality"; that is, the reader's aesthetic response to fact is blended with and enriches his/her aesthetic response to narrative.

The anatomy is not limited to historical event, however, only to historical facts, ideas that have existed. The anatomist can, if he/she wishes, represent intellectual histories with fantasies— talking horses or six-inch giants. That is, if the anatomy is true to human realities, its characters can be, but need not be realistic; they only have to be representative.

A type that represents a historical existence carries the same intellectual truth as the historical existence; indeed, it focuses upon the principle behind the performance. The principle is "truer" than specific performance because it applies to far more (is typical of more) cases than the specific. Because of its generalizing and universalizing power, the type (and the symbol it generates) may be truer and more important than any one of the individuals that gave rise to it. The Greeks in Classical times thought so.

Similarly, the anatomist has a certain latitude in selecting his "plots." Swift and Heller, for example, often juxtapose events for ironic comedy or satirical comment— which is to say, the principle of organization is the author's intellectual purpose, not the motivations of the characters. Theme is the controlling factor. Heller also uses details of memory, amnesia, repression, and such psychological syndromes in structuring Yosarian's discovery (or is it re-discovery?) of Snowden's secret— a sequence which is more aesthetic than realistic, being more akin to theme and variation in music than to the temporal sequence of narrative.

Mythical or historical patterns, parallels, analogies, allusions, processes, are all available to the anatomist. In truth, he/she can use all those devices, essayistic and otherwise, by which the human mind organizes intellectual experience; for his/her subject is the realities of public, human experiences— that is, mankind and its doings.

Writers may present man and his doings as worse than they are, better than they are, or as they are. The satire tries to correct existing ills by showing them as worse than they are, thereby pointing up the absurdities and suggesting remedies. The utopia offers a vision of how the affairs of man might be made good or ideal, thereby pointing up a goal to strive toward. Anatomies have been written in both these modes.

I know of no anatomy, however, that takes the third possible view of intellectual history: to represent ideas as they are, or have been (with historical documentation if desired). Some non-fiction novels come close, perhaps, though the most famous examples, *In Cold Blood* and *Compulsion*, were both written to explore the private motivations of the characters, not those communal and/or historical forces that produced such aberrations. Whichever mode the anatomist chooses, he asks his readers to contemplate the ideas behind behavior. The anatomy lives on this "reference to reality."

Our anatomies have not often been appreciated for either their fiction or their essential realism. *Gulliver's Travels* has frequently been shelved in our libraries among "satires" or "other prose works"— whatever that is. Yet it should be obvious that the Hounynyhms and Lilliputians are invented characters representing public realities, they play out invented situations of historical probability, and they do it for a coherent purpose. Swift's insistent concern with the real issues of his time is no longer in question. What more should we ask of a fiction?

The same blindness has led to a gross under-valuation of such talents as Addison and Steele, whose perceptive inventions in *The Spectator*, etc., include country gentlemen, milkmaids, foolish gentlemen and ladies, coffee shops, operas, and sundry comments on man's doings about town.

Even in our time, acceptance has been slow. Aspiring writers are fond of remarking (I don't know how true it is) that *Catch 22* went to 54 (or was it 64?) publishers before it was accepted, and that *Lord of the Flies*, a very good modern romance, went to 21.

Confessions, or pseudo-autobiographies, (e.g. *The Catcher in the Rye*) seem to face fewer problems of taste and acceptance. Perhaps this is true because Augustine, Rousseau, Ben Franklin, and others had established the form on biographical (that is, narrative) grounds, even before the novel was well developed as a form.

But the selectivity in such confessions is no less— and no less creative— than in the novel. It should be clear that the purpose is not to delineate facts, nor just to entertain readers, but to instruct them in a religious or social or personal philosophy. Perhaps the "personal experience" angle makes them palatable, as much news and gossip are made palatable. I think of literary confessions as the carrots of our fictional fare— not quite as staple as potatoes, but certainly a standard dish.

Anatomies are more like radishes— sometimes sweet and juicy, but often spicy and sharp, tending even to burn. A mature taste perhaps, but one full of its own rewards!

The anatomist offers an essentially intellectualized presentation, usually in dramatic form, of people in their public capacities, focusing upon the philosophies and historical and ethical movements they represent and participate in; a comprehensive view of public, mental (rather than outward, social) experience. The writer relies more on the reader's ability to understand than on his imagination, for the references of the anatomy abide in the realm of the history of ideas. Anatomies are intellectual adventures.

I realize that not everyone likes intellectual exercise. To me, that is a pity. But it is better a reader dislike an anatomy because he has no taste for intellect, than that he curse it unfairly for something else. Then the failing is in that reader, not in the literary work.

Publishing patterns in recent years, shifting as they have toward history, philosophy, sociology, psychology, etc., indicate that the reading public does, indeed, like and require the kind of intellectual stimulation anatomies deal with. If it is accepted on its own terms, the anatomy can satisfy an appetite. Indeed, because of its power to assimilate all forms of intellectual experience, it may be the most important form of literature we will ever have.

Charles Brashear

1. Dawn's Invasion of Alcatraz

Grandmother Doe-in-the-Dawn is not in the house when I get home from the school where I teach sophomore English and American History. I don't think much of it, though I peek into the garage and see that her '53 Studebaker Champion is gone. I just smile. She's still pretty active— in fact, hasn't slowed down at all, even though she is seventy-eight years old, weighs less than a hundred pounds, and is bird-like.

The phone rings. It's my Uncle George, Granny's oldest son, who will soon be sixty. "Georgie!? Where's Mother?" he demands.

"I don't know," I say. "I just got home. Her car's gone, so she's probably at the grocery store."

"Naw!" he almost shouts. "I've been by there. Her car ain't in the parking lot."

"Well, I wouldn't worry," I offer. "She can take care of herself in Colusa."

"That's just it," he barks. "I don't think she's in Colusa."

"Not in Colusa?" I ask weakly, knowing he thinks me a lame-brain.

"NO! God-dammit!" he shouts. "You know how silly she's been lately about that Alcatraz mess. I think she's going to try and get in on that crap. I think she's trying to run away from home!"

Instantly, I know he's right. When Secretary Hickel ordered the Interior Department to cut off the water and electricity to Alcatraz last week, we all began expecting a crisis, maybe even violence. Granny would think she has to be a part of that. That would horrify the rest of the family, so I temporize, thinking maybe I can throw Uncle George off the track. "Maybe she went up to the Reservation at Stony Creek.

She's been talking about seeing if she could find any of our relatives up there."

I don't know whether he believes me or not, but he says, "I'll check it out," and slams the phone down.

I run to the closet under the stairwell.

Her sleeping bag is gone. She's taken her old sleeping bag, the Coleman stove, and both the lanterns. She has gone to join the Red Power Movement.

I can picture her in her parti-colored Studebaker which was once Sea-mist Green, but has had doors and trunk lids and even fenders added from other cars. It looks more like a harlequin than a seventeen year old classic car. I can see her, chugging along the Embarcadero, looking for a place where she can see Alcatraz Island, looking for a way to get there. I smile in wonder and astonishment, but not real surprise. It's just like her to do something like this.

In my mind, she's leaning forward, almost touching her face to the steering wheel, as if she thought her body english could urge the machine forward.

She has run away from home, to become an Indian activist!

-< * >-

Uncle George's words haven't faded from my ears before I know what I have to do. I have to go at once. I'm no activist, but if she wants to be there so badly, I have to go and help her— because she is my grandmother and because I love her dearly. I just wish I had some faster vehicle than my beat-up, old-fashioned VW camper, with the hinged doors on the side. If George knows where to go, he can drive there and return before I get half started.

I run back to the phone and call the principal at the school where I work. I explain that I need a couple of days of personal holiday and ask could she get a substitute.

She won't just let it go. Wheedles me till I say that Granny is in trouble.

"Mrs. Stonecrist?" she exclaims. "In trouble?"

"Well, not trouble," I try to explain. "She's gone down to San Francisco, and I have to go help her." I mentally kick myself. Uncle George and Uncle Ben will now be able to track me.

"Well— It's so close to the end of the term— " She lets her voice hang. "And you in your first year—"

"Get Mrs. Watson to fill in for me a few days," I order. "My tests and lesson plans are all prepared. They're in my desk drawer." She finally agrees.

As soon as I hang up, I dial Sara Ann's number in San Francisco. She's my girl friend from college days at Berkeley, but she used to be an old-fashioned, southern girl, from Chapel Hill, North Carolina. That's why the two names. She's now working part time and attending Hastings Law School.

Yes, she has heard from Granny. Doe-in-the-Dawn wants her to go out to Alcatraz with her. "She said you wouldn't help her."

"It's not that I won't help her," I say. "It's just that I don't know that her invading Alcatraz is going to do anyone any good."

"She thinks it will," says Sara Ann. "She thinks the *Chronicle* will put her picture in the paper and sway public opinion." She stops. But before I can say anything, she goes on.

"Is there anything dumber than Walter Hickel, or his idea for a 'Bay Area National Park'? With Indian employees? The Indians think he wants them to be the janitors! He's cut off the water and electricity to the island and used the Coast Guard as a blockade. What does he think the Department of the Interior is? His private Kremlin?"

"Look," I say. "See if you can find her. I'm on my way down there. If you can locate her, meet me at 'The Old Fisherman,' that restaurant where we went last time. I'll see if I can hire her a motor boat."

"Good for you!" says Sara Ann. "That's the man I love."

"I love you, too," I say, and hang up.

-< * >-

Since last November, Grandmother Doe-in-the-Dawn has perched in front of the TV news, as if she is part of the invasion of Alcatraz. She is there with Richard Oakes when he claims the island by right of discovery, since it is unoccupied land. She giggles with glee when Oakes offers the U.S. government twenty four dollars in glass beads and red cloth for the island, suggesting that the price is a long-established precedent in American traditions.

When Wallace Mad Bear Anderson, holy man of the Tuscarora, speaks of greed, intolerance, acquisitiveness as the primary sicknesses of white society, she nods silently.

And when she sees women there— Grace Thorpe, LaNada Means, and others— she begins trembling with energy, like a kettle about to boil.

Most of the invaders are clearly mixed-bloods, like herself: urban men and women who have obviously eluded the Reservation system and the BIA schools. Many have gone to college, all speak English well, and some of them fought in Korea or Viet Nam. The girls wear T-shirts with militant slogans and baggy, faded jeans; they are strong and liberated. The men say they want, not assimilation, but justice and fair play and what is theirs by birthright.

The rest of the news is tiresome.

The My Lai Massacre in Vietnam and Lt. Calley's trial— no interest.

Vice President Agnew's absurdities—

George Manson's murderous madness—

Colonel Kadaffi's power grab in Libya— nothing.

Apollo 12, with Pete Conrad and Alan Bean walking around on the moon for 31 hours— switch channels.

She wants to see and hear the Indians of All Tribes' proposals for a Native American Culture Center on Alcatraz.

She wants to talk about an Institute for the Study of Indian Religion and Medicine, and a center for the study of ecology and the Indian view of nature.

She wants to help build a museum and a job-training center.

She leans toward the screen as young Indian men and women in braids and headbands and beaded vests complain of their soul's hunger; she bangs one thin hand into the other when they suggest in one, swift gesture that change is possible— and maybe even justice.

She writhes in agony when Secretary of the Interior Walter Hickel pontificates on the necessity of repressing the invasion. "There's the enemy, Georgie," she says, dragging me in to watch. "There's the enemy!"

She boos when Herb Caen writes in the *Chronicle* that the Indians are just a savage band from *Lord of the Flies*, and she cheers when the *Chronicle*'s "Question Man" surveys his readers, who ask "Why not let them have the island?"

She is delighted when John Trudell is interviewed on TV: "The whites wouldn't have much trouble getting us off here. We're unarmed. Besides"— he shrugs for the cameras— "we believe it would be wise of us to make them look foolish."

"You hear that?" she asks in her slight Boston-Irish accent. "You hear that?"

"Yes," I say. "He *wants* a confrontation."

"Of course, he does. That's why they're there."

"You watch, Granny; it'll be the same old pattern. Negotiations will break down, the cavalry will attack, they'll force a treaty on the Indians, and then confine them to a reservation— where they'll be considerably worse off than before they started. Unless, of course, they can manage a little massacre. Then there'll be this huge outpouring of sympathy for the corpses. That will surely do those corpses a lot of good, Granny. That'll sure do them a lot of good."

"You are impossible. I just don't know what I'm going to do with you." She turns back to the TV.

Watching her gazing at the cathode ray tube, I see the young Indians cease to speak to the world and start communicating to Granny— to her, personally. Their words become sacred. The newspaper reports are holy writ which she doesn't even have to memorize, because her heart recognizes the truth of them from the first utterance.

It is like a vision quest— except there is no long journey, no long waiting, no period of gestation, just a sudden blue flash of insight.

She had been lost— and is now found.

She had been famished— and is now fed.

She had been naked— and is now clothed in a robe whose fringes are the standing rainbow.

She feels a personal and original relationship with the universe, and it calls her to her work. Sixty years of acculturation evaporate, and seventeen years of her youth suddenly appear again. It is a rebirth.

-< * >-

I have little trouble finding Doe-in-the-Dawn's multicolored car at Fisherman's Wharf. I find Granny, clutching her purse and leaning over the metal rail to talk with a pudgy man in a white boat.

She wears one of her pale-blue shirtwaists, which is hardly adequate in San Francisco's wind, even if we are in the last days of May. Her cardigan sweater is fastened at her throat with her turquoise brooch, but the sweater is not enough. She is shivering.

I sometimes tease her about that brooch: our Koru tribe did not have turquoise. Turquoise is a southwest desert stone, never found in the alluvial drift of the Sacramento Valley. She usually ignores my teasing, then touches the stone with a thumb and two fingers.

When I come up to her, she smiles slightly and, with two fingers, wipes the hair out of my face, as if I were a little boy again and we were safe in some long-ago time and place. Then she demands, "Where's Sara Ann?"

I'm more than slightly taken aback. That was about the last question I expected from her. "Why, I guess she's at home. At her apartment."

"Well, call her. That girl knows how to stand up for herself."

"So you're on her side now, huh?"

"Just call her."

"Okay, okay. But first, give me your keys, and I'll go move your car. If I could find it so easily, George and Ben would spot it, too. I'll see if there is a parking garage to put it in. At least, that'll get it out of plain sight."

When I come back from parking Granny's car, Sara Ann is with Doe-in-the-Dawn. Dawn is bundled in Sara Ann's too-big, too-long parka, and Sara Ann looks gorgeous in a burgundy, long-sleeved turtleneck and tight jeans. Her dark hair is parted in the middle and pulled down over either ear to form braid-like pony tails. She's wearing the Zuni Thunderbird necklace I bought her last summer. So this Irish girl, Sara Ann Murphy, from Chapel Hill, North Carolina, looks more Indian than my Indian grandmother.

"They've stopped the ferry," she says, giving me a hug and a kiss, but continuing her report through it all. "The Coast Guard, or somebody. Something about insurance. And all the people with launches are holding back because of the trouble. These boats are all fishermen." She dismisses the marina at Fisherman's Wharf with a wave of her hand. "Either they're out to lunch, or they don't want anything to do with 'that mob' on Alcatraz. I'll tell you, honey: either these people have no principles at all, or they have no principles at all. I couldn't find a boat."

"Well, we've got to find one, or this safari is bust. Did you go to that marina down a ways, where all the private yachts are?"

She shakes her head. "Just up and down among these fishermen." She looks at Granny, and Granny nods. She's still freezing.

"Okay, here's the plan. You and Granny go into 'The Old Fisherman' to keep warm, and I'll run up there and see if I can find a water-taxi or something. I'll come back as soon as I can. In the meantime, you can call the *Chronicle* and the *Examiner* and all the TV stations. See if you can drum up any interest. Let's make this a media event."

They both nod and turn toward 'The Old Fisherman'

restaurant. I watch their backs a moment— these two women I love most in the world— and marvel at what allies they have become.

I turn and jog toward the yacht harbor, hoping to find someone with a boat big enough to help us escape over the choppy waves to Alcatraz.

-< * >-

Doe-in-the-Dawn hasn't always been such a woman warrior. Though her features are thin and straight and her complexion the light olive of a fair Latina, she is a half-breed Koru Indian, granddaughter of an Indian chief. She was born on a sandbar of the Sacramento River— which sandbar, which willow thicket, we don't quite know for certain. She grew up with the Koru tribe, rarely aware of the culture of the town of Colusa, which had replaced her grandfather's village.

At age seventeen, she knew hardly seventeen words of English, when she married George Stonecrist, my grandfather. She apprenticed herself to the 'civilizing' influences of his grandmother, Sarah Stonecrist. Over the years, she and George had six children, including my father.

Through it all, she has guided her children to white culture. Her oldest, George Abelhard Stonecrist, IV, took over great-great-grandmother Sarah Stonecrist's farm, where year after year he raises enough sugar beets and alfalfa to put him among the top farmers of the county.

Aunts Sarah and Elizabeth Jane both married highway engineers; one lives in Scotland, one in Saudi Arabia.

Uncle Ben Stonecrist is a creative carpenter in our town, Colusa, much in demand for his old world craftsmanship and industrious work habits.

Only Dad and Aunt Ruthie, the babies, are problems: Dad's a drunk, and Aunt Ruthie is still trying to live the fast life at forty-five— thinks she'll someday strike it right and become a famous country singer.

For sixty years, Granny has cooked and sewed, nursed the ill, corrected the naughty, taught us all gardening and frugality.

For sixty years, she has pretended that her first seventeen years of life didn't exist.

For sixty years, she has given no indication that she ever lived in a different rhythm. And she might have gone gently to an afterlife beyond the rim of the western sky— if the Indians of All Tribes had not invaded Alcatraz.

-< * >-

I am no more successful at finding a water taxi than Sara Ann had been. There are plenty of boats, and even a fair number of men who know how to run them. But they are out of gas, or the waves are too high, or they don't have the time. Only a few say honestly what is behind their refusal:

"I jist don' wanta get involved."

"I hear the Coast Guard's gonna ram boats."

"Last week, yes... maybe. This week, I don't wanta get in any trouble."

Last week, three ferries were running to Alcatraz on schedule, like tour busses on Market Street. This week, everybody is scared off by the possibility of property loss. How much more American can you get?

When I return to 'The Old Fisherman,' Uncle Ben is standing out front with Sara Ann. She glances at me contritely. In a moment, Granny and Uncle George come from behind some parked cars. Granny is walking fast, trying to escape from George.

She turns and scolds: "You leave me alone, George Stonecrist."

"Mother," he pleads, "be reasonable."

"There's nothing reasonable about what you want."

"Mother, Mother. Can't we talk this over?"

"No. My mind's made up."

"Well, Mother, you'll just have to unmake your mind. I'm going to take you back to Colusa."

"George Stonecrist! When did you ever talk to me that way? I'm your mother!" She moves slightly toward him. For a moment, he backs off, the way a 250-pound son will back off from his 98-pound mother. Then he gets control of himself and stops.

"I'm taking you back, Mother. Whether you like it or not, I'm taking you back."

"You can't talk to me like that!" she scolds.

"Yeah, I can," he says, apologetically, even rubbing his nose with the back of his hand. "I'm bigger and stronger than you are, Mother. I'm sorry to have to do this to you, but— "

She moves toward him again. He is hesitant enough that, when she pushes her purse into his face, he loses his balance and plops backward onto his butt. Granny turns and runs, right toward us.

Before I can begin to move, Uncle Ben has grabbed a wad of my jacket front and slammed me up against the restaurant wall. He lifts me up. My feet are dangling, so I can do nothing.

Uncle George gets up and chases after Granny. He grabs her shoulders, rather gently, but firmly, right in front of us.

Sara Ann hesitates only a moment, then lunges, forcing her right shoulder into Uncle George's midriff, like any good left tackle. He huffs, loses hold of Granny, slings Sara Ann aside, and grabs Granny again, this time less gently.

Granny looks astonished: stopped and paralyzed by the fact that her oldest son is hurting her.

Sara Ann is up quickly and charges again. George sees her coming and swings out a big arm, enveloping her and Granny in one big bear-hug together. Sara Ann's momentum causes them to fall over, but George holds on. He rolls over, straddles and pins them both, like a wrestler. It's over, almost as quickly as it began. George isn't even breathing hard.

A crowd hasn't had time to form. A few people are standing, freeze-framed where they were when it began and gawking like owls that don't know which way to fly next.

"Now, you listen to me, both of you," says George, shaking Granny and Sara Ann by the collars, as if getting the attention of a pair of rag dolls. "This nonsense has got to stop. You understand?"

Granny says nothing. Just stares at him with those dark Indian eyes. Sara Ann is wide-eyed, like she can't believe what's happening.

"Now, this is the way it's going to be," says George to Granny. "I'm going to let you up, and you're going to behave, and I'm going to take you back to Colusa with me. We can't afford to let you run around just everywhere, Mother. You gotta understand: we got too much invested in the community. You gotta stay at home and behave. You understand?"

Still Granny says nothing.

"Dammit, Mother, this is the way it's gotta be. You've been crazy as a loon ever since all this crap started. Everybody says so. It wouldn't be hard at all to get you declared incompetent and put your estate in a conservatorship. You gotta quit acting so eccentric. We want you to act like a regular American."

Still Granny says nothing, but I can see in her eyes that she has given up. George has won.

George sees it, too. "Now, I'm going to let you up, and you're going to behave. Okay? Give me your word."

Granny nods.

"Word of honor?" demands George.

Granny hesitates, so George repeats: "Word of honor?"

"Word of honor," mumbles Grandmother Doe-in-the-Dawn.

George stands up and lifts both the girls to their feet in one huge motion. He starts to brush off their clothes, but now they're female again, and his mores won't let him touch them. Sara Ann's nostrils are flared from the adrenalin rush and her body is tight in her burgundy pull-over.

"You won't get away with this," says Granny. "We'll get you next time."

Uncle Ben lets me down gently and even straightens my jacket front. "You wanta give me the keys to her car and the parking stub? So I can drive the Studebaker back to Colusa?"

I nod and hand them over.

He smiles. "You know, your camper wasn't any harder to find than her car would've been." Uncle Ben doesn't even hate me. It's just a game we play, like touch football, and we just happen to be on opposite teams. He clasps me on the shoulder as he turns to go. He joins George and they walk away, each of them holding one of Granny's elbows firmly, like a couple of cops escorting their criminal away to jail.

I don't even have to think hard to imagine the stories they'll tell in the beer halls and other service stations of Colusa. They'll laugh and re-enact Granny's drive to San Francisco, step by step; then they'll brag about how they managed to figure out the puzzle and catch her before she made a splash in the TV and newspapers. I glance at Sara Ann. She's biting her lower lip.

She and I drive up to Telegraph Hill to look at the bay and watch the day die. The wind brings tears to our eyes, but I know it's not just the wind. I avoid looking at Alcatraz Island for a long time.

I repeat for Sara Ann some of the conversations I had at the marina. Repeatedly, upper middle class yachtsmen had professed support for the Indian cause, until I asked them to ferry us out to the island. Then they became strict conservatives, talking about loss, insurance, arrests; they're not about to get involved in any civil rights demonstration.

"Granny said we'll get 'em next time," says Sara Ann, shivering. We forgot to get her parka back from Granny.

"Yeah? Well, I wonder what she'll try next."

Sara Ann unfastens my coat and rolls herself into it, laying her forehead against the crook of my neck, as if she's never had a liberated thought in her life. She wraps her arms around my body. "It's ironic, isn't it?" she says, muffled. "All those lip-service liberals are too cowardly to act on their beliefs. And you, you old cowardly stick in the mud, you're out acting on issues you don't even believe in."

Charles Brashear

2. Embroidery

Grandmother Doe-in-the-Dawn says, again: "I know you don't feel like an Indian, Georgie. All that education does that to you. All those books cut you off from your roots, from what you really are. But I'm going to make an Indian out of you yet."

"Look, Grandmother," I respond. "A bunch of kids went to an Indian sing over by Reno. An anthro lady says to one of them, 'Anyone can write songs like that. You just think up a line and repeat it.' So he wrote four 'songs' in Pomo while driving home in the car. Is that what you want me to do?"

She refuses to answer when I press her like that.

"How can we believe in Indian culture," I ask her, "when Indians themselves go around copying tourist versions written by and for Anglos? Is that the kind of Indian you want me to become, Granny?"

"You'll see some day," she says and turns away. "You know too much, not to see... some day."

I don't let her dodge so easily: "Why weren't you half this anxious to brain-wash me when I wanted you to?"

"Well, now it's time," she says.

She clamps her thin lips and tilts back and forth in her rocking chair, stopping occasionally to stab at an embroidery the size of a sheet of plywood. She is putting the finishing touches on it in her sitting room. Behind her on the wall is a large embroidered silk panel, in which a mounted horseman in a red jacket gazes across a pond toward a manor house and proclaims

"HOME IS WHERE THE HEART IS."

I think she believed that once.

In the wide upstairs hallway of our old Victorian house, near the triple French windows that open onto the balcony, Granny's quilting frame contains a nearly-finished embroidery the size of a bed spread. It depicts in detail the Koru People's first encounter with white men, when Ewing Young shot three Koru women in 1832.

For almost sixty years, she has obsessively embroidered useful things with daisies, loop-stitching and shade-stitching and French-knotting more dish towels and bed spreads and large, silk wall-hangings than a whole tribe of great-granddaughters will ever be able to use— even if they had the inclination. Too many electric dishwashers and K-Mart wall prints.

Nowadays, she concentrates on large tapestry-like panels portraying "The Renewal of the World," "The Emergence of The People from the Third World," and the like.

She is working now on a five- by eight-feet embroidered silk panel depicting an event in Koru mythology, "The Death and Transfiguration of the Spirits." With it and others she has made, she hopes to draw public notice to the Indian cause, maybe even sell some to a museum or a rich collector and raise money for the newly-formed American Indian Movement.

All through my childhood, I begged her to tell me everything she could about our Indian background, about her own life on the Reservation, about her mother, Cia, and about her grandfather, Sioc; but like the turtle who pulls in her head and legs at the first sound of distant thunder, she refused to volunteer anything.

I have lived here almost all my life, and my grandmother has been my surrogate mother and father, my sibling and playmate, as well as a friend and confidant. In 1950, when I was three and my parents decided to give up the pretense that they had a marriage, they left me here with Granny. Dad went off to Des Moines to become an insurance salesman, and Mother moved to Woodland to work for an optometrist.

Dad refused to have me in Des Moines with him. He is the only one of Granny's children with brick-red complexion and is often mistaken for a Sioux. He said he didn't want to subject any kid to that kind of prejudice. Besides, I would have gotten in the way of his serious drinking.

In 1955, my mother married a livestock auctioneer. He was a man on the move who didn't want any moss or children growing under his boots.

And so, the homeless stray was left with his Indian grandmother.

I found my roots at the University at Berkeley, in the Lowie Museum and those marvelous old records the anthropologists collected at the turn into the twentieth century. By study, I learned much of the tribe's history and folklore. I learned the rudiments of the Koru language from Professor Barrett's interlineal translations of texts and Professor Sapir's essays on neighboring languages. I even listened to Barrett's primitive recordings from 1906 to get the pronunciation right.

But I had to confront Granny with the stories in detail, before she would confirm or deny anything. I had to beg her to tell me the legends of her childhood.

It left me with an appetite to know, to understand, to try to live by humanistic principles. But I have no compulsion to storm the barricades. Even at Berkeley in 1964, I didn't feel the impulse to become an activist. All that effort of the Free Speech Movement seemed to me wasted.

"For principle," my friends said; but it seemed to me they were fighting to be fighting, not developing their minds, not coming any closer to the principles of an open society. And they condoned all that waste and destruction. There's not much respect for the earth or empathy for its people in that.

-< * >-

For weeks, Granny has been trying to get me involved. Because I am her grandson and read books, because I teach school and am not ashamed to argue with people in public places, because I have the exterior of an Anglo but an Indian heart (she insists I have an Indian heart), she is determined to make me a warrior of Red Power.

"You've got to know about *it*," she says. "You've got to feel it, the way it was. The way *it* is. Why aren't you at Alcatraz with the Indians of All Tribes?" She interrupts her embroidery to bang her thin fist into a bony hand.

"How many times do you suppose I've told you that?"

"Well, you never say the right things!"

"I don't want to wear beads and feathers. I've told you a dozen times. What attracts me to Indian culture is the idea that principles other than greed and envy and power can have their puppet strings on the human ego. Maybe even honesty and altruism and concern for the earth."

She refuses to answer. She reaches to turn on the TV. "Maybe they'll have some news about Alcatraz," she says.

"All this talk of buffaloes and blankets is retrogressive thinking. It's just another power play. You've heard those activists. Their main tune is 'We've got to preserve the old ways.' There's a whole lot of backward-looking and greed and envy in that. To gain their psychological identity, these warriors of Red Power have set their heads firmly on backward. That's no way to walk into the future."

She is not convinced. "A lot of good men and women are right now working to create a new day for the Indian," says Granny, pointing her needle at me, as if she could stitch me into the fabric of her designs. "And you're not even going to be up to watch the dawning."

"What do you want me to do, Granny? Scarify my cheeks with a raw flint and paint the wounds with vermillion dye? Would that make me a warrior? Would that enlarge the Sitting Bull in my personality? Or diminish the brutal and egomaniac Custer?"

I admit that I am baffled and confused. What should I feel? How can one have a coherent attitude toward whites, when they range from William Penn who was honest and supportive, to Helen Hunt Jackson who was honest but destructive, to General Sheridan who, in his kindness, once remarked that the only good Indians he had known were dead, to Colonel Chivington who came to believe, honestly, that the greatest kindness he could do the Indian was to exterminate him? By what twist of mind can one be coherent about both Squanto, the first sell-out, and Geronimo, one of the last hold-outs?

Just what can any present-day, rational, self-respecting, English-speaking, reasonably intelligent, twenty-two year old human being, including a descendant of patriotic and credulous Native Americans, believe and feel?

Granny has been good and loving to me: she has nursed me when I needed nursing; she fights fair, when we have to fight; and I would do almost anything in the world for her.

Almost anything.

Except become an Indian.

3. Scottsdale Arts and Crafts

"There," says Grandmother Doe-in-the-Dawn, shaking out her sewing for me to see. "It's finished. We can go to Sacramento now."

On a Saturday morning, in the steel and glass modernity of the American West Savings and Loan Association in Sacramento, the Scottsdale arts and crafts trader looks at Granny's embroidery, *Transfiguration of the Spirits*, cocks his head to one side, and says, "No go," with the assurance and finality of a pawn broker.

We say nothing. We're too shocked to say anything. Too shocked even to taste the frustration. We expected surely that anything sixty by ninety-five inches, and so remarkable, would be worth a serious look.

Even the savings and loan manager looks disappointed. He had hoped the trader would buy something and let him exhibit the purchase here in his branch. He gets a lot of publicity in the quality travel magazines by exhibiting some of the arts and crafts the traders buy and sell.

"You understand, it's not because it ain't a nice piece of work," the trader goes on to explain in our silence, stopping to suck on a tooth. "There's no market for it. Can't sell embroidery. It's not Indian." He looks at me and says, "Do me a sand painting on a sheet of plywood or particle board; okay. Do me an orlon weaving, or a clay pot, or a basket; okay. Even textile prints are okay nowadays, or a watercolor. But not oils— oils are too expensive, they don't sell so well. And no embroidery. Embroidery ain't Indian. That's a pioneer art."

"But my tribe embroidered!" protests Granny, lifting her hands, as if she would beat him with the umbrella she does not have in her hands. I think she learned the gesture from watching 'The Beverly Hillbillies.' "My tribe embroidered," she repeats. "Ceremonial capes and headdresses. And baskets. We embroidered a lot of baskets with feathers."

"Yeah, I saw some of those baskets in a museum," says the trader; then he looks at me. "You get me some genuine old baskets with feathers, 'n I'll get you a really good price."

At that moment, the savings and loan manager suggests, "Maybe we could treat it as a pioneer arts exhibit."

"With all those Indian figures in it?" says the trader.

"Well, yeah. I guess you're right," says the manager. "It's just that it's so—" He stops, searching for a word. "So—heroic."

"Yes," admits the trader. "A real museum piece, but— "

"But what?" says Grandmother Doe-in-the-Dawn, too loudly, too frantically. "What do you want?"

The trader continues explaining to the manager: "Y'see, these figures here— they have some of the qualities of a Sioux robe painting. See? They're sort of stiff in outline, but at the same time they're full of activity. Only, they ought to be flat colored, not shaded 'n rounded the way these are. I've been getting some real nice stuff lately from Taiwan, stuff with heavy, black-line figures and flat paint. Looks more authentic."

"But this— " begins the manager, then stops.

"I know what you're thinkin' and wishin'," says the trader. "But it just won't go. It's too Indian to be a pioneer piece. For a pioneer piece, you want a hunting scene with hounds, 'n men in red jackets, or a landscape with a lake and a castle in it."

The manager leans forward to finger a part of the silk panel. Granny watches him closely, as if she sees a kindred spirit. Her body english silently encourages him to look closer.

"I know how you feel," says the trader, "but take my word for it. It just ain't standard."

He leaves without wishing us luck, or saying goodbye, or thank you.

Granny looks at the manager and quickly folds back the big embroidery to reveal another under it— another sixty by ninety-five inch panel depicting the *First Encounter* of the Koru with Anglos:

In the foreground, several women in tule aprons are standing and squatting at the edge of the river, leaching acorn meal in little sand pits. In the middle distance, a line of canoes makes its way up the river— The Ewing Young trapping expedition of 1832. In the background is Onolai, the tribe's sacred mountain, partly obscured by the smoke that is rising from the white men's rifles, which they have just fired.

One of the women is crumpled in her own blood; another is falling, stiff, like a tree. A third has turned and is looking at the observer; she has an enigmatic smile on her face. The babies, who have been playing in the edge of the water, look up, amazed. To me, the whole picture screams with protest and a curious resignation.

The manager is taken by surprise. He steps backward, stammering, "Why, that's— that's—"

"It's a historical event," says Grandmother. "Some of Young's party killed three Koru women, for the fun of it." She pauses, then adds, "or for the target practice."

"But— That's mur— You mean that really happened?" says the manager, pointing at the embroidery and sputtering. The shading and coloring are quite lifelike, and the perspective puts the viewer right in the picture with the women.

"Yes," admits Granny. "It was a murder. We can document it if you like. Would you like to hang it here, along with a story? My grandson, Georgie, has written one."

"Oh, no. No," says the manager, suddenly as smooth as a waiter at a posh restaurant. "We couldn't possibly— Why, it would offend the customers." He doesn't have to add that it would offend him.

-< * >-

Charles Brashear

We take the river road back to Colusa. The banks are high, earthen levees nowadays, and cottonwood thickets crowd the flood bottoms, but here and there we can stop among trees and rest from our disappointments.

Granny's *First Encounter* keeps popping into my memory. I see in my mind, again and again, that enigmatic combination of protest and resignation in the woman yet to be shot.

Normally, the Koru people feared death and were immensely superstitious about it, but this woman is not smiling in fear. Nor is she happy. Her face contains a bittersweet agony of expected transfiguration, which grew out of Koru cosmology.

Once upon a time, back in the days when all the people on the earth were deities or pure Spirits ("*Saltu,*" insisted Grandmother Doe-in-the-Dawn, demanding that I relate to the concept in her first language, the language of The People, which I understand imperfectly), Katit the Red-tailed Hawk and Old Man Coyote made a fence of elder sticks on the sacred mountain, *Onolai.* They peeled the bark off ten of the sticks, and they left ten other sticks rough.

Katit and Coyote gave each other advice about how to build the fence, say the printed versions of the story. Coyote wanted to use only the rough sticks. Katit wanted to use only the smooth ones. They argued and quarreled a long time about how to build the fence, but neither of them could prevail upon the other. Finally, they built the fence of both smooth and rough elder sticks.

The next morning, the smooth sticks had become kind people, and the rough sticks had become mean people. Thus, Katit and Coyote created people on Onolai.

When Katit and Coyote heard voices behind the hedge, they knew their world had come to an end. Katit said, "We have made people. We will have to go away now. The time has come for the transformation of all the Saltu."

Katit called the Spirits all before him and changed

them, one after the other.

Dahlam, he made into the large, spreading oak tree.

Pinole, he made into the seeds of the grass on the western plain.

Koto, who was very large and strong, he made into the big river.

Others he made into birds, deer, acorns, salmon.

All the things we see in this world were once pure Spirit.

Anus, the Mud Turtle, stood beside Katit, and, as Katit changed the Saltu, she told each of them what use that Spirit would be to the Koru people, who were approaching from the hedge.

Hlo and Ii, the long and short acorns, would be food for Koru. So would Pinole, the grass seeds of the western plain. Koto, the big river, would wash them, inside and out. Hur, the salmon, would swim in Koto and be food for Koru.

Old Man Coyote stood beside Katit and prescribed how the Koru should treat each thing. Coyote informed each of them how they would be prepared and cooked by the Koru people, who were approaching.

Then the Saltu went to the western rim of the world where the sky comes down to the ground. Katit lifted up the edge of the sky with a digging stick and all the Saltu, except Coyote, crept under. They wait there still. Just beyond the sky. They wait there still, for Koru. They will give Koru their next world.

Thus, it came into being.

Thus, the Saltu created this world for Koru.

Thus, the Saltu gave the ways of living to Koru.

Thus, it was transformed. It is finished. It is transformed.

-< * >-

The Koru knew the world had been expanded and remade three times, each time making way for a new people. And they anticipated a great cataclysm of fire and quake, which would destroy the fourth world, their world, when a new race of people appeared. As the women in Granny's picture gazed at the white men on the river, they must have believed their death and transfiguration had come.

There on the river was the new and strange race of people, squirting fire and quake from sticks. The women expected the sky to fold up and the earth to collapse.

What do you do when your world is being destroyed? What can you do when you have seen the new spirits of the fifth age?

You wail in ambiguous anticipation.

For yourself.

For your confused spirit.

You wail for your death and transfiguration.

But the world did not end in 1832. That was the greater confusion for the Koru. The rifles belched fire and shook the ground, but the string of boats passed on up the river, out of sight. The woodpecker, in flickering wave-motion flight, came back to renew his hammering attack on the oak snag. The cottontail stirred again in the fallen leaves. Insects buzzed in the trees. Life went on; nothing apparent happened.

But confusion fell quick upon confusion that year. First, the people fell sick. Red and yellow spots broke out on their skin, and they began dying.

The medicine men built fires in the sweat houses and danced to the destructive north, to the nurturing south, to the west where the dead and the Saltu are, to the east where creativity and the Saltu came from. He bit the red spots. He washed the evil with the waters of Koto. He applied *yom* poultices, which would cure an arrow wound or a grizzly bear's bite. He sweated the people in the dance house and bathed them in the river.

But the people died.

In October and November, it rained for twenty days and nights, and the great valley became a sea of soft, stinking mud, in which the Indian villages stuck up on slick knobs.

Most of their stilt houses, where they stored dried fish and grain, were ruined or washed away, and the people went hungry. They had almost no fresh water to drink, for the river was muddy and filled with the smell of death and the dead.

And still the people were dying of spot-face rot.

Then, as if the heavens themselves were giving a final sign, hundreds of meteors flamed toward the earth and crashed on November 12, 1832, making that California's "Year the Stars Fell."

-< * >-

In Will Green's *History of Colusa County*, published in 1880, Colonel J. J. Warner, who was a member of the Ewing Young party when it passed through the Sacramento Valley in 1832 and returned in 1833, described the smallpox epidemic:

> The banks of the Sacramento River, in its whole course through its valley, were studded with Indian villages, the houses of which, in the spring, during the day-time, were red with the salmon the aborigines were curing. At this time, there was not . . . within the valleys of the two rivers, any inhabitants but Indians. At the mouth of the Kings River, we encountered the first and only village of the stricken race that we had seen after entering the great valley. . . . We were encamped near the village one night only, and . . . the cries of the dying, mingled with the wails of the bereaved, made the night hideous, in that veritable valley of death.
>
> On our return, late in the summer of 1833, we found the valleys depopulated. From the head of the Sacramento, to the great bend and slough of the San Joaquin, we did not see more than six or eight live Indians, while large numbers of their skulls and dead bodies were seen under almost every shade tree, near water, where the uninhabited and deserted villages had been converted into graveyards.

The new race of people had been seen, and they were spouting fire and quake.

Mad-Woman Water had come down from the North, fiercely transforming, and the world was empty.

The stars were falling out of a folded sky.

Surely, it was the end of the universe.

How in the world did Granny manage to embroider that on a bed spread?

4. The Colus Rancheria

"See? You know what to do," says Grandmother Doe-in-the-Dawn. "You know what's right. Why don't you just act on it? You're such a laggard! I just don't know what to do with you."

"But," I protest, "why should I try to be an Indian now? After all, I'm seven-eighths white. I look white. My colleagues and neighbors treat me as white; I'm reasonably educated, live modestly on my teacher's salary; at peace with myself. Why should I open myself to the slings and arrows of Indian outrage?"

Grandmother Doe-in-the-Dawn does not compromise herself enough to respond when I'm in this kind of mood. She just wrinkles her mouth a little and rocks stiffly back and forth in her sturdy oak rocking chair, which was brought across the plains by my Boston-Irish great-great-grand-mother, Sarah Stonecrist.

"Or maybe you want me to flagellate myself for what the presence of the Indian did to the white man's psyche? Heaping all that shame and self-loathing on the poor white man for the genocide he was executing. Look, Granny, it was none of my doing. I want neither praise nor blame."

"For Cia, then," she says, focusing those dark, Indian eyes on me, as if they, too, were a message. "And me."

"Yes," I admit, averting my blue eyes. "What I do, I do for Cia and for you. But I can be enraged for Cia without being outraged for 'the Indian.' After all, she was my great-grandmother, not a symbol of Indian ravishment. I am not obligated to let her rage— or yours— shape my life."

She ignores all my protests. "We'll be going now," she says. "Bring your camper around."

I see in her glance that her craving will be satisfied; she admits of no other possibility. No placards, no sit-ins, no list of unnegotiable demands. Just the tenacity of a beaver after bark. Or a trapper after beaver.

It is as good as accomplished. I must take her to what is left of the Colus Rancheria. It's summer, and she wants to see if any remnant of our relatives survives there.

"Just what do you think you can achieve at the Reservation, Granny? Sioc has been dead a hundred and twenty years. Cia has been dead about sixty. There *is* such a thing as hopes being absurd."

"Maybe there's still someone there who knows something about them. Or knows of other relatives," she suggests, a bit lamely.

"I'm just afraid you'll be badly disappointed out there, Grandmother."

"You don't have to go," she says. "You just have to take me."

I understand the distinction, but I don't believe for one second that she means it. I know she intends me to be her mouth-piece.

Granny is quickly up from her rocking chair. Her arms are as skinny as elder twigs and her dress flaps flat. But once her sinews catch, she leads the way to my old VW camper. "You have no call to feel guilty, or embarrassed, or penitent," she says, letting it drift over her shoulder. "You ought to be angry!"

My mind flashes: Sara Ann and I talking to an angry teenage girl in the summer of 1969 in a uniform of the Navajo Tribal Band, sitting on the hood of a Ford pick-up in a used car lot in Gallup, New Mexico. "You're not going to catch me doing anything for them," she raged in perfect English.

The "them" was the Gallup Chamber of Commerce. Lots of people said they were the only ones that gained anything from the annual Gallup Indian Ceremonial.

The girl's boy friend came up with two pieces of apple pie. "What the hell?" she demanded. "Didn't they have any ice cream cones?"

"Nope," he answered. "All sold out. Only thing left is apple pie."

So she put away her clarinet, sniffed the pie, and they ate. "I'm not going to march in any gunky parade that exploits Indians," she growled between bites of apple pie. "I'm going to get even with 'em for what they did to our ancestors."

-< * >-

The road from the highway to the Colus Rancheria is rut-strewn. I dodge several puddles and a sour chuck-hole where someone was stuck recently. Those gaps could easily take a wheel off my old VW. The air is sticky and hot and abuzz with flies.

Koru, "a person," and *Korusi*, "The People," were mispronounced as Kolu and Kolusi because of that pre-Bering Land Bridge confusion between "R" and "L." It was then made English as Colus and Colusi, then finally as Colusa.

"Rancheria" is what Californios called the villages of the native peoples of California. In 1851, when the Reservation was described in a treaty that was never ratified, the U.S. Indian agent thought he was saving and perpetuating something that "really belonged to the Indians" by calling the thirty-thousand-acre Reservation "The Colus Rancheria."

It's been moved seven times since then; each time an enterprising white man has found a profitable way to use Reservation land, a way has been found to move the reserve.

Each time it has moved, the Colus Rancheria has shrunk. Now, when Doe-in-the-Dawn and I are going to visit it, it is a thirteen-acre triangle, nestled beneath a levee on the west bank of the Sacramento River, about seven miles north of Colusa, California, the town that was the principal village of the Koru people until 1850, the town where white men have lived since, the town where Granny and I live now.

The Reservation ground is soggy and moldy from river seepage. It smells like a place where ringworm would thrive.

Certainly no place for a little old lady of 78, even if she is half Indian. Even if she is strong enough to outwalk three grandsons to Grandpa's grave and back.

I stop my camper in front of the most prosperous building I see, thinking it may be the headquarters. It is a pleasant, small, wooden frame house with a fair roof and greasy-yellow paint no more than three or four years old. A well-fed man comes around the corner of the house. He is carrying a gunnysack with a ten-pound wad of something in the bottom. He is surprised to a guilty standstill by our presence.

Grandmother pokes me in the back, egging me to get out of the camper.

I ask him, "Are you the Chief around here?"

It's awkward, I admit; but then I don't play this role well. I have guilt reactions when I have to probe a stranger, especially an Indian. I can't even buy a two dollar necklace from a Hopi child without feeling the hot saliva of shame.

"Are you— " I begin to repeat.

He only shrugs, sniffs, and shuffles his gunnysack behind him.

"This *is* the Reservation, isn't it? We're looking for the Colus Reservation."

Without looking directly into our eyes, he points behind him and to the right, across the river.

"But the map shows it's here. Right here."

He only glances furtively at the VW, at Granny, at me. He's trying to figure us out. Are we from the Welfare Agency? The Sheriff's Office?

"We're looking for some Indians. Are you an Indian?" That was badly said, I know. Awkward. Insulting. I'm getting worse.

He shuffles and mumbles "I guess so," so quietly we can hardly hear it.

What kind of answer is that? Doesn't he know if he's Indian or not? Am I wasting my embarrassment?

"Look, we're looking for some Colusa Indians. Are you a Colusa Indian?"

He muffles the same reply: "I guess so."

"Were you born around here?"

"My wife was," he offers tentatively, rubbing his nose with the back of his hand.

"Is she around?"

He begins to make a gesture toward the house, where we hear vague stirrings, like children staring from behind curtains, then he changes.

"In town. She's getting groceries."

He's lying, I know. We're not getting anywhere. What can we try next?

He glances at my old VW again. He still hasn't looked straight at me. "You from the BIA?" he asks.

"Me? No. No, heavens, no." Do I sound relieved? "We're just some people. Grandmother Doe-in-the-Dawn here just wants to locate some of her relatives, from the old days, if she can."

Slowly, reluctantly, he strolls over, peers into the dark of the camper— and relaxes. Lets the tension lines in his forehead fade, and begins to smile.

Why did he relax? What can he see? She wears a plain, gray shirtwaist and her turquoise brooch at her throat, which she touches with a thumb and two fingers. Her coarse, gray hair is in short, thin curls that won't hold, but keep frizzing out into a mop. Her nose is straight and thin; her skin has only a hint of coloring, like a Latin beauty.

Can he see in the texture of her hair or the pallor of her skin that she is the granddaughter of an Indian chief?

A Papago chief once did that to Ishi— felt the texture of one of his braids and pronounced him "a high-grade Indian."

But maybe you think I'm attributing too much clairvoyance to the Indian mind? (Is there such a thing as *the Indian mind*?) Maybe you don't think they can perceive and communicate by a magic that you and I never had?

I ask him, "Do you have any very old relatives around here? Were you born here?"

He swings his gunnysack forward and becomes voluble.

"No, no," he says. "I was born in Hawaii. I'm a Kanaka, full-blooded. You won't see many full-Hawaiians any more."

I can feel Grandmother Dawn's heart speed up.

"You!" she says. "You! You!" She's sputtering like a bit actor and moving as if she were about to attack through the open window. "You! Are you one of the Kanakas that John Sutter brought to California? Are you one of those murderers?" I touch her extended arm, trying to calm her.

"No. No," says the man, baffled by her excitement. "I came here about three years ago and started raising beans." He holds up the sack for me to see into. I can smell the fresh beans. "Aren't those nice beans? Premium. They'll bring twenty cents a pound, and I got thirty-five acres of 'em. I'm gonna clean up this year. If nothing happens to the harvest, I'm gonna make it this year."

"Do you farm here?" I ask. "On the Rancheria?"

"Naw. Won't nothing but moss grow here. Too wet from the levee. I leased forty acres across the river. No bridge down here, so I have to drive up to Princeton, to get ferried across. Sure is a long way out of the way, especially when I have to move a tractor, but I guess it's better than nothing."

I have to cut him off. "Who's the oldest person on the Reservation?" I ask.

"The oldest person? Well, I don't know. You see, I'm not one of these people. I'm Hawaiian."

"Can you tell us who might know?"

"Go ask at those shacks down there." He points toward a clump of trees nearer the river. "You have to follow the drive, way around behind my house, then stay up close to the levee. Ask for Mrs. Martinez. She's the woman with a whole bunch of little kids. Lives in an old, beat-up trailer house. Masonite painted aluminum. You can't miss it. She knows just about all the men around here, so maybe she can tell you."

I get in my VW again.

"Ever see such nice beans as those? Not a bug in 'em . . ."

-< * >-

The road is as pocked as the moon, only each crater is a puddle.

An elderly man sits on an apple box in the deep shade of an elm tree. I almost drive past before I see him, because he's wearing a dark gray suit-coat from Goodwill and a black, straight-brimmed hat, like Wovoka, the Paiute Messiah whose vision led to the Ghost Dance craze.

I go over and ask the same questions. Are you Koru? Colus? Colusa Indian? I try all the variations. He just makes the sign of no understanding.

Cripes! Why is he being such a turtle? Granted, the Indian has been burned and gouged by whites lots of times, but that's all over, isn't it? He shouldn't blank me out, just because I look like an Anglo. What does he want me to do? Grow my hair long and wear Indian jewelry? I refuse. Thank goodness, Grandmother Doe-in-the-Dawn has also refused. I don't want to degrade us with that kind of crap.

When I come out of the shadows, the sun is so bright it hurts my eyes. Heat dances on the air. Further along, I see an old trailer house that was once painted aluminum. The area smells of old wood-burning stoves. Pepper wood, or mesquite, or something equally pungent.

Mrs. Martinez, it turns out, doesn't know if she's Colus either. She is so busy, our questions confuse her.

"Who? Who are you looking for?"

"The oldest Indian from this place."

"Who? What's his name? Who do you want to see?"

"Someone to tell us about the old days."

"Well, what's his name?" Suddenly, she points to a weathered shack not six steps away. "Grandpa Kahil. You must want to see Grandpa Kahil. That's his house."

5. Grandpa Kahil

The wood of the shack has never been painted. It has turned, not gray, but black in the mildew of the river bottom and smells musty, like cobwebs. It is small, perhaps eight by ten feet. No window in either of the two sides we can see. Just a porchless door above a stoop made from odd sticks and rotting lumber.

Grandmother Doe-in-the-Dawn is with me now, not leading, but pushing, so I step tentatively up to the stoop and knock on the screen door. I can see through the screen that the door is open.

There is no response.

The inside is so dark, even now in mid-day, that I can see nothing. A fifteen-watt electric bulb glares from a bare cord in the middle of the room and blinds my eyes to the shadows. Then I see something. Vague. I guess: a metal stove pipe running up the back wall, which has no window in it either. The screen is greasy with age and fly-specks. I knock again. Still nothing.

Mrs. Martinez yells from behind us, "Did you find him?"

When we shake our heads, she adds, "He must be there. I saw him around this morning. Knock again. He's there."

So I cup my hands to my eyes and lean forward to the dilapidated screen, trying to see into the dark shack. I see nothing. If my activist grandmother wanted to make a bitter simile, she'd say that Americans have been seeing nothing for three hundred years. Grandmother nudges me and says, "Knock again."

I knock and we wait. A long time, so long that I would have turned and left, were Dawn not standing behind me.

Then we both hear, in the depths of the dark room, the

expiration of an old, old breath and the creaking of a cane-bottomed chair, a sound that to most of us now means not just grandfather, but great-grandfather. And Grandpa Kahil shuffles one foot in front of the other, breathing twice between each step, and at last stands a foot behind the unopened screen. There is no sound but the wheezing of his breath.

He is obese, 250 pounds or more and, standing in the house above me, is no more than half-a-head taller than I on the ground. His skin is pale from years in the darkness and shadow. At the same time, it is blue with age, so that his native redness combines to make him a kind of pale purple. A pale purple hippopotamus stares at me through the dirty screen.

What messages have you for us from the heart of your darkness, Oh Pale, Purple Hippopotamus? A theory of the universe, its origins, purposes, and goals? A personal code of ethics and politics? An alternative to the theory of property and its exploitation?

A vision to live by, embroidered on the warp of a culture's artifacts and the woof of its mentifacts?

Was the old way of life really livable? That's the question young Sioux are asking when they sit around in their Hong-Kong beads, listening to transistor radios, watching a squaw-dance or a Heyoka and saying, "That's witch-doctor stuff, man."

Forgive me. All this flashes through my mind as Grandpa Kahil stands above me, wheezing in the heavy summer air.

Grandmother Doe-in-the-Dawn is urging me on, whispering around my shoulder, "Go on. Ask him." She has already primed me with the questions to ask.

"Have you ever heard of a man named Sioc?"

No response. But through the screen, I can now see the beads that are Grandpa Kahil's Indian eyes.

"He was once principal chief of the Koru nation," I offer. "He would have been a bit before your time, but he was once famous among the people. He was Doe-in-the-Dawn's

Charles Brashear

grandfather. Then I put the same question in my stunted, inadequate Koru."

A grunt. The smallest kind of tentative denial. As if the effort to form the full word "No" would be more than the wheezing could survive.

"Go on. Ask him about Charlie."

"Have you ever heard of Tseret? He was Sioc's son and a chief many years after him."

No response.

"Tseret," I repeat, trying to make his name sound like a Koru word. "The white men called him Charlie. Indian Charlie. He may have been chief when you were a little boy."

Not even the tentative denial this time.

I can feel Grandmother wringing her hands in frustration behind me. She's learned the gesture from watching TV. "The Buttes," whispers Grandmother around my shoulder. "Ask him about the Buttes."

"You ask him," I say, grabbing her by the shoulders, lifting her bodily in front of me. "And ask him in Koru. I don't think he understands much English."

She hesitates, then begins.

"Do you—"

"Have you ever heard—"

Now, *she* is embarrassed to be talking to an Indian. Would sixty years of acculturation do that to everybody?

"Speak Koru," I whisper over her shoulder.

"Do you know the word, 'Onolai'?" she asks. But her voice still sounds English. "Onolai," she repeats. "Have you ever heard of Onolai?"

A long silence. Then a tentative wheeze of affirmation. Not a word by any stretch, not even a hissed "yes," but a breath with an intonation that could be mistaken for a positive response.

Grandmother's mood leaps like an urgent sunrise. "Do you know where it is? Do you know where Onolai is?"

"Don't give him the answers in your questions," I whisper over her shoulder. "You've already told him it's a place."

She composes herself. *"Onolai,"* she says, and this time her voice makes it sound like an Indian word.

Again, a half-wheeze of affirmation.

I can feel her getting ecstatic, so I grab her shoulders, to help her hold it. "Wait," I say. "Give him time."

We wait. Flash-frozen. Nothing happens but time passing.

Onolai is a loaded word. If he knows Onolai, he is a Koru. A kindred soul.

-< * >-

When the universal flood that destroyed the first world began to subside, Katit the Red-tailed Hawk, Anus the Mud-Turtle, and Sedu-Sedit the Old Man Coyote were floating on a raft made of tule-stalks. They were not then in the forms they have today. They were Pure Spirits. Deities. Souls. Ghosts. *Saltu.*

For eons, they floated on the waters. For eons, they were content. Then Anus the Mud-Turtle, who is the Earth-mother among them, became curious about what was under the water.

Because she wore a water-proof dress, Katit and Sedu-Sedit tied a string to her hind leg and lowered her into the water.

In one version of the story, she demurs; refuses to go down into the water until she has made herself a waterproof dress and some fingernails. She spends a millennium making even one fingernail. Katit gets impatient with her, so when she has finished the nails for her hands, he breaks them in half and puts the other parts on her feet. And that's why Turtle has short, square toenails.

Finally, they lower her into the water.

She was down there for eons. For eons down there she was.

When they finally pulled her up, she embraced some mud.

In one version of the story, she demurs. Plays it coy. Won't say what she found— in fact, insists she found nothing— until Katit and Sedu-Sedit discover mud under her blunt fingernails.

This mud they made into a patty and placed on the raft. Instantly, it began to expand. It expanded until it became a mountain.

Turtle went down again and again, each time piling the mud on the raft, until great, spontaneously-expanding mountains stuck up from the water and became the earth we know.

"We shall call this place *Onolai*, 'where we sit,'" said Katit.

"We shall call this place *Onolai*, 'our sitting place,'" said Sedu-Sedit, who was always trying to compete with Katit for top spot.

-< * >-

Travelers, moving across the floor of the Sacramento Valley today, are often surprised when they suddenly notice mountains in the middle of the valley floor. They are called the Marysville Buttes, or Sutter's Buttes on the maps, but they are known locally as just "The Buttes."

There are several of them and they are not just hills. They have out-croppings of igneous and metamorphic rocks; they are dotted with oak, sumac, and a few scrub pine; and they tower suddenly two thousand feet above the prairie.

The center of the world?

No, you will say, smiling at me for making the suggestion, for both you and I know better. We are not fooled by perspective. We know, in our civilized way, that although these mountains stick up far above the horizon, that little blue line that is the Sierra Nevada is far mightier, and more important in the geology and ecology of the region.

Still, they are remarkable Buttes, jutting far, far into the noon sky, where clouds drift like lazy dogs.

The Buttes soon lose their significance from the air. It is easy to climb above them, so that their trees are no longer dots, and, like the Indian, they seem only a flat patch of wildness on the regular pattern of the roads and farms of "progress."

Returning from an air tour, as the Buttes again took shape on the land, I was struck by them in quite a different way. They seem an afterthought. And I understand how the tall tales of the early white settlers grew. When Paul Bunyan had finished building the Sierra Nevada and the Coast Range (they used to smile and say), he had one wheelbarrow load of dirt too much and just dumped it in the middle of the valley.

In another version of the tall tale, when Paul Bunyan had finished digging San Francisco Bay and making the mountains, he stopped there in the valley and scraped the mud off his boots.

I suppose the white man's mind (is there such a thing as "the white man's mind" or "the pioneer's heart?") found it necessary to belittle all in sight, to dominate all, to make The Buttes an afterthought, dwarfed by the imagination long before the airplane and the automobile made us forget how a pebble feels and taught us our perspective of mountains.

Still, they are curious Buttes, and although they are not as spectacular as, let us say, Ship Rock or Mount Sinai, there are still places on them where only Spirits have sat. They, too, have been the center of the universe.

Standing at the foot of the mountains and looking up at the giants, one begins to understand why the Koru, who lived in the mountain's morning shadows, invested Onolai with reverence.

If anyone had spoken that strange and confusing line from the Sixth Chapter of Genesis to a Koru, "There were giants in the earth in those days," the Indian might have answered, "Yes, I know," and looked toward the mountain, toward Onolai, where the great Spirits once lived, the mountains which were the first land in the creation.

-< * >-

"Where is it?" Granny demands. "Do you know where Onolai is?"

Grandpa Kahil slowly, ponderously, lifts his arm and points a stubby, crooked finger in approximately the right direction.

I can feel the volcano of ecstasy in Grandmother Doe-in-the-Dawn, so I hug her shoulders in my hands to help her contain it, while we are waiting for Grandpa Kahil to speak.

His words are as heavy as Sisyphus's rock, and he is slow in getting them to the top of the hill.

"Up," says Grandpa Kahil, "by . . .

We hear a distant stream-born jet liner.

". . . Grass Valley."

Grandmother goes taut, wooden. Grass Valley is on the slopes of the Sierra Nevada, over a hundred miles distant. At least two tribes away.

So Grandmother's expectations dissolve in shambles. I expect her to cry, to collapse— I already taste the bitter copper of her disappointment— but she only lets out a long, baffled sigh and stands in a stiff daze.

"Where were you born?" I ask Grandpa Kahil. "Did you come from around here?"

The same reply. Spaced out. "Up. . . by. . . Grass. . . Valley."

-< * >-

Back in the camper, Grandmother Doe-in-the-Dawn is still in her stupor. "*Lu-mas*," she whispers. "They are all dead. Or transformed. Or faded into . . ." She lets her voice trail off, unwilling, like her ancestors, to talk about death.

When a Koru died, or, as the Koru people used to say, was "about to die," he or she had to run west to the place where the sky comes down to the ground. There, he had to lift the edge of heaven with a digging stick and slip through the hole, to be accepted into the world of the Great Spirits.

In the burial, the dead one was given food, tobacco, water, his weapons, including a digging stick, and a package of medicine-tricks which would help him escape from Coyote. The dead person's greatest task was to elude Coyote on the western plain, for Coyote was the spirit of evil and of death.

If Coyote caught the dead one, he could make the dead

one into a slave, could even make him or her haunt the living. All the burial night, the dead one's relatives sat around the grave and wailed, shouted incantations to keep Coyote scared away.

After that night, the dead one's name was never spoken aloud again, and his or her relatives tried to forget him; for the survivors could never be sure whether the dead one had reached the world of the Great Spirits or was a captive of Coyote. Speaking his name would call up that evil that had caused his death, and it might call up Coyote, too, which could bring that evil upon the living.

If someone who was ignorant of a death asked about the dead one, the one who was asked would lower his head, perhaps brush his nose, and hurry away, whispering almost inaudibly, "*Lu-mas*," which means, "He is dead."

"*Lu-mas*," whispers Grandmother Doe-in-the-Dawn again.

It was not people that she was looking for, you understand, but a way of life, a cosmology that established values and prescribed a way for treating other people, the mountains, minerals, animals, the very air.

In the beginning, God gave to every people a cup, a cup of clay. And from this cup, they drank their life.

They all dipped in the water, but their cups were different. Our cup is broken now. It has passed away.

(Spoken by Ramón, a California chief, and quoted in Ruth Benedict, *Patterns of Culture*, Chapter Two.)

"*Lu-mas*," whispers Grandmother Dawn.

The road to and from the Reservation is only poorly graveled. A few miles away, the county paved an asphalt driveway right up to the road-commissioner's house, but this public access road is only an Indian trail.

Well, that's as it has been through the whole Indian/White encounter. Why begrudge a small man his small pleasures?

Maybe we should, you say? Or at least maybe you think it? We have to begin somewhere to rectify.

Though Dawn is too numb to respond, I stop my VW on the highway and take her in my arms. "I will help you, Grandmother," I say. "I will help you."

I recite a prayer-chant I heard years ago.

> Make me, O Great Spirit, thy instrument complete;
> Thy shield and thy spear, make me.
> Make me the wind that brings you the scent.
> Make me the path that leads to the hunt.
> Make me the bow that propels your arrow.
> Make me the fire that cooks your food.
> Enter me, O Great Spirit, thy servant complete;
> Thy will and thy way make me.

6. The Water in the Empty Basket

Late in the fall of 1852, my great-great-grandfather Sioc, chief of the Koru people, waded the Sacramento River at Salmon Bend for the last time in his life. As he climbed the gentle slope of the little hill toward the sprawling cottonwood and live-oak trees where his home had once stood, he carried his little daughter, Cia, on his infirm arm.

He was searching for Will Green, the eighteen-year-old white man who had been generous to the old chief. Green had even bothered to learn a few words of the Koru language, enough to act as interpreter when the U.S. Indian Agent had presented his unilateral treaty to the people at Colusa. Sioc was going to ask a special favor of his friend, Will Green.

Sioc was exactly six feet tall, muscular and straight, even lean, according to historical reports, and his recorded speeches show that he could be eloquent. But in 1852, Will Green reported in his *History of Colusa County*, the old chief was feeble and broken-hearted. He was about 50, not especially old for a Koru chief, still reasonably handsome in a breech clout, but dealing unsuccessfully with the invasion of his people's land had aged him beyond his time.

His voice was halting as he told Green, "Bad times come. Me. 'The People.'

"Wife dead.

"Children scattered. Dead, except Tseret and Cia.

"Many relatives, old people, dead.

"'The People' die hunger. Disease.

"No medicine. No one know how to treat."

The huts and shacks the white men called the town of Colusa were built among the oak trees where Koru village had once stood. In my mind, I see Sioc becoming even more disconsolate, gazing at Green's "Colusa Hotel" (it was a one-room

Charles Brashear

shack with a communal sleeping loft) and telling (*telling*, said Green, not complaining) how the Koru tribe had become dissolute and disobedient.

The men and some of the women lay drunk in the paths over half the time and would not hunt.

Their families were suffering.

They were disrespectful and rebellious.

The old chief could do nothing to stop it.

The obsidian-tipped spear Sioc carried was both the emblem and instrument of his office. He once had the absolute power to strike men dead with it, but now, said Green, he confessed he could not control the people as he once did.

His authority was broken.

His will to live was broken.

He expected to die in a short while— and would be glad of it.

He asked Will Green would he take care of Cia, who was about two years old. Would Green feed and protect the little girl and help her to grow up in the white community? For that, the old chief had concluded, was the only way anything Koru would ever survive.

The old man was deeply scarred from smallpox, which had nearly killed him twenty years earlier, and he was so earnest that Green could not refuse him. Green took the naked child from the old man's arms. She was quiet, for she knew Green from his visits to the Indian camp across the river.

Then Sioc gave Will Green a little basket. "For Cia," he said.

Hardly two inches across, it was woven from plant fiber as gossamer as angel hair and so tightly wound it would hold water. Delicately embroidered with woodpecker and yellow-hammer feathers, so that their tufts were a raised, fuzzy surface, it depicted in its red, yellow, and black designs the inhabitants of the earth: the two-leggeds and four-leggeds, the feathered people, the people with fins and shells; above them the sky, and below them the earth. It was a ceremonial basket that Sioc had used many times in the annual Hesi Dance.

"For renewal of life," Sioc said in Koru.

Green took the basket and let Cia hold it.

-< * >-

The Koru people performed the Hesi Dance during the Moon of Budding Leaves to reaffirm the existence of Spirit and welcome the earth back to life. In Sioc's time, it was a four-day dance, which recounted the psychic history of the universe: events back in that remote time when all beings on the earth did not have their present forms, but were deities, Pure Spirits— *Saltu.*

At one place in this ritual, which old timers call a "Big Time," everyone is practically dead from the Universal thirst and famine. Over in one segment of the dance house, Old Man Wasp has been buzzing and complaining about being hungry and thirsty, and he's tightened his belt so many times that he's permanently pinched his middle down to almost nothing.

Then, this little Hesi basket near the fireplace in the center of the dance house— this little, two-inch, embroidered basket— this little feathered basket spontaneously fills with fresh rainwater for Old Man Wasp to drink his salvation, his life. The water is ambrosia, the sustenance of gods.

But, before Old Man Wasp can drink, Coyote jumps up, grabs the basket, and tries to drink it dry.

As he empties it, the basket refills. Coyote drinks and drinks, but each time he puts it down, the basket refills. Even if everyone tried to drink it dry, there would still be a full drop left for Old Man Wasp.

The basket is the universe. It has the attributes of the universe. Inexhaustible. Always provident. There's always one drop left for Old Man Wasp.

-< * >-

After giving Will Green the basket, Sioc turned and strode off into the willows to die. We do not know that anyone ever saw him alive again.

-< * >-

Grandmother and I pore together over old letters, old pictures and histories, interviewing everyone we can think of, trying to weave a robe of the artifacts that will contain the mentifacts, trying to recreate the warp and woof, the web of a culture. But Grandmother seems to know more than I can understand, something I can't get in the books.

"It's in the blood," she says. "You have a memory in the blood. It's a blood and cell memory."

I have my doubts. Maybe we do have a non-logical, non-literal way of knowing, but I suspect it's more connected with the archetypes of the psyche than with blood and cells.

What frustrates me so much is why the Indians mix up and confuse things. Take that little Hesi basket; it's a beautiful metaphor for the necessary nourishment of the psyche; why mix it up with some child's fantasy about a wasp's belt, or a turtle's toe-nails?

I can see that the Indian was always close to the things of his world. He thought of himself as one of the growing things and saw that his fate was tied up with the fate of all things. If the animals, the trees, the air and water were healthy, man was healthy; so it was in man's interest to nurture the earth that nurtured him. This close participation in his destiny gave him his sense of power with the great mysteries of the universe.

I'm not talking about the power of shamans, who seemed to transform themselves into Grizzly Bear before one's eyes.

Rather, I mean the living miracle of living; the power in Indian potatoes and wild onions; the force in the fruits, the gift in the grains of the prairies. There was so much power in such knowledge that one's voice couldn't help but quaver and his hand shake in collecting and bringing home these astonishing blessings of the universe.

Each food the Indian dug up or gathered was taken lovingly and with an unerring sense of its worth and dignity.

Truly, they ate the health of the prairie in those days and knew nothing of the degrading insides of supermarkets with their tin cans and styrofoam packets.

All this I can see. But when I look into the basket, I cannot see the water that is not there.

And that is exactly what Grandmother Doe-in-the-Dawn wants us all to see— the water in the empty basket.

7. The Indian Problem

When Sioc gave Cia to Will Green, Green was a teen-ager, unmarried, inexperienced. Cia was a problem to him. He hardly knew what to do with a small child. After a few weeks, he found a family, the Blanchettes, who had a little girl, an only child, about the same age as Cia. They were delighted to gain a playmate for their Suzie, even if she was copper-skinned. With them, Cia grew to be a handsome, healthy child.

She followed Suzie to school and, when she showed considerable academic ability and when the public conscience was right, the cultural leaders of Colusa sent her away to Sacramento Normal School, where she was trained in Latin grammar and Greek mythology in translation.

Then she returned to Colusa where, year after year, in the Blanchette backyard, a pleasant, secluded yard with hollyhocks and hedges, she tutored a long line of valley boys in their college-prep studies of *Commentaries on the Gallic Wars*.

Years later, in the 1890's, while starving on the Reservation, Cia managed to keep a small journal in school-girl Latin and transliterated Koru, but almost no English. She was a close observer of detail and she had a sense of style, sometimes even quoting the words people said. We, of course, have had the Latin translated and have pieced it together with the Koru; because this log book and Dawn's memories are all we have of Cia.

She wrote:

> I never realized, I simply always knew, that I was Suzie's toy. I knew no other existence. From

the time my father left me with Mr. Green and he, in turn, left me with the Blanchettes, it was not meant that I should be any thing but Suzie's servant, her companion, her victim.

The Blanchettes did not intend to send me to school, but Suzie cried when she could not have her toy. The teacher never put a book before me; she never spoke to me, never explained the lesson; she simply looked through me as one might ignore a puppy; it was not meant that I should go to school.

But I learned. That must have made them angry, for Suzie was and is dumb. I looked on others' books, I picked up their pencils and paper, I overheard the teacher's instructions. The teacher did not test me, but I thought that was because I knew all the answers. In spite of them, I absorbed their knowledge.

They must have hated her for that.

In the third year, when Suzie was still in the primer, Cia tutored the older boys and girls, those who were about to leave school and marry or take up work. She taught them to read in their own language, which they knew imperfectly.

The community didn't know what to do with her, so they sent her away.

"No," says Grandmother Doe-in-the-Dawn, who never went to school, but has acquired a fair education. "They sent her away, so they could take credit for her."

I had never thought of it that way. But that must have been it. She was smart. I had never thought of that either, but she was smart. She had absorbed their eight years of school and more, in less than three years, and they wanted to take credit for her being smart. So they sent her away to prep school. They sent her away to learn Latin grammar and Greek mythology.

They did not do it for her. They were not trying to give her a start in life, a training, a profession that she could live and

Charles Brashear

be proud by.

"No," agrees Granny, "they did it so they could brag about their brilliant little Indian princess."

By creating a scholarship and sending her to their Teachers' College, they could make themselves feel good and also claim they discovered her. When she had learned and mastered their Aeneas, their Caesar, their Tullius, their Dante, their Greek in Latin translation, they could claim credit for educating her.

She was their token. Their payment for the hundred thousand slain. She was their thoroughly civilized Indian princess, with which they hoped to expiate their guilt, and she was too much caught up in Hera and Achilles and Marcus Aurelius and *Commentaries on the Gallic War* to see it.

They had told her to go, and she went. They told her to go home, and she went home.

Back to Colusa, back to Suzie.

It never occurred to any of them that she might actually teach, that she might use the brain they had trained; for none of them offered her a job. None of them ever assumed that there was a job anywhere in the world for her. So she went home.

Home to Suzie.

"Yes," says Granny. "Home to sweep Suzie's floor, comb her hair, lace her corset. Home to the servility that she had accepted from the beginning of thought as her lot."

Suzie and she were 19. Then began that string of parties, where Cia was dressed in a modest, white party gown and sent to chaperone Suzie; forced to sit at the side-bench while Suzie danced and flirted; forced to watch in the willows later as Suzie threw off her satins and seduced the young men, one after the other; forced to see secretly them enter her, one after the other; forced to hear her cry "More! More!" for she was not fulfilled even when they were spent; forced to keep her pretense of virtue, for Cia was guardian of Suzie's virtue!

Cia wrote:

The Sacred Mountain   61

And she was barren. She can thank her god of appearances for that. Then we were 23 and the parties tapered off and ceased. Suzie was plain and dull. Her eyes were vacant, her jaw slack, her hair coarse and lusterless, though we tortured it into a thousand curls.

Suzie grew fat, and even the young bucks that had once hopped her thighs so readily were no longer attracted. She beat Cia, forced her to bathe her, so that her hands would caress her skin. Suzie loved those Indian hands, as a nymph might love a satyr, because they were dark, animalistic.

"Oh, Cia. Love me," she pleaded, but I would not, could not. And when she tried to touch me, I froze and would not let her.

A new pretense began when a man approached Mr. Blanchette and asked if Suzie would tutor his son in Latin, for he wanted the boy to have a chance to get into Harvard. So they sat in the parlor, or the garden, or Suzie's bedroom, and Suzie yawned into an open *Godey's* or *Police Gazette*, while Cia drilled boy after boy in his vocabulary, his declensions, his translations of *Commentaries on the Gallic War*.

When one of their pupils of several years began to develop whiskers on his chin, it occurred to Suzie to seduce him. She told Cia to help her, to plan it. So Cia began translating from *The Satyricon*. On the pretense of acting out a scene, Suzie unlaced her bodice and told the boy to remove his shirt.

He looked at Cia, unwilling to do so. "Oh, don't mind Cia," Suzie said. "She's just an Indian, and she won't say anything. She'll never tell a soul, will you, Cia?"

Cia could not answer, for she had accepted Suzie's conspiracies as her own.

Their saturnalia, their lesson in Roman decadence, was not satisfactory, for Suzie did not have the power of culmination. It was not the inexperience of the boy; she simply could not achieve zenith. She tried six more, over the next year, but without fulfillment.

Cia nursed Mrs. Blanchette through her final illness. Bathing her, carrying her bed-pan, laying out the body for burial— while upstairs Suzie tried lesson after lesson from *The Satyricon*, without success.

> Then I was 32, and I was asked to be an Indian. With Mrs. Stonecrist and Mrs. Jackson preaching about America's "century of dishonor," no family in Colusa wanted to be dishonorable. I, who, to my knowledge, had not seen an Indian in the thirty years since my father had left me with Mr. Green, was asked to instruct town leaders in solutions to "the Indian problem."

It took her a while to realize that they wanted her to dress in beaded and fringed buckskin, and scream and stamp about incoherently while someone beat a tom-tom. She went to my great-great-grandmother, Sarah Stonecrist, who introduced her to some of the Indian people on her farm— at Somé and Katsil, two of the old Koru villages. They taught her a few songs and let her take back a few baskets, a turtle-shell rattle, a bow and arrows.

Then Cia was actually asked to teach school. She was given a job. So she told elementary school pupils about Pocahontas, the first Thanksgiving, and the egalitarian ideals of American Democracy, while living the double life of a pupil at Somé, where she learned a few words of Koru, where she began to see how her mother and father had cooked and hunted and died. For five years, she lived two lives, learning to weave tule mats and telling the blanched-truths of white culture.

Near the end of it, she even had a suitor. A middle-aged bachelor lawyer with a purple caul-mark on his face called with the pretension of discussing *Commentaries on the Gallic*

War. They walked in the garden, conversed in bursts of school Latin, and Suzie was furious. She tried to steal him away from Cia, but one ride in the gig with her sent him whistling back to his office, and he never called again.

Then it was suddenly not good to be an Indian. It was 1890 and talk was everywhere of Indian uprisings. The Ghost Dance had swept across the plains and mountains from Nevada to South Dakota. The cavalry called for and got reinforcements, missionaries were evacuated, editorials preached that the only solution to the Indian problem was extermination, since the Indian would not be civilized.

When Sitting Bull was killed in December, 1890, Mr. Blanchette's true self emerged: his was exactly that terribly popular mind-set that transformed General Sheridan's "The only good Indians I ever saw were dead" into "all good Indians are dead Indians."

Hysterically, he waved the newspaper in Cia's face and screamed, "See? See what you get for raising hell? See what you deserve!" Suzie slapped her and stabbed her with a hat-pin.

What could she do? Her copper skin and angularity, which had always been her hiding place, were now beacons guiding the onslaughts.

Just after Christmas, 1890, the news of Wounded Knee was her undoing. None of them had ever heard of Wounded Knee, but that news unleashed Blanchette's glee and violence as never before. He came running into the room where Cia was combing Suzie's hair, getting ready for the New Year's Eve party. "See?" he screamed, laughing. "See! They have quelled the uprising. A whole tribe of Indians attacked the cavalry, but the cavalry surrounded them and wiped them out! What do you think of that! A whole tribe! Wiped out! Haha!" He was screaming in Cia's face.

Suzie pulled Cia's arms behind her and screamed over her shoulder, "Make a whore of her, Daddy! Give her what she deserves!"

At first, Blanchette did not understand, though his eyes

were flared and crazed. Suzie released Cia's arms, reached around her shoulders, and ripped open her dress. Then a demon personality took over Blanchette's body. And it wanted vengeance and violence.

Cia didn't know what to do. These were the people she had trusted most in the world. She was astonished, didn't understand.

Suzie ripped Cia's under-bodice from behind, and Cia felt her clothes falling about her hips. She turned and slapped at Suzie. In the midst of it all, Cia noticed a ray of winter sun streaming through a chintz curtain and bathing parts of the pine floor and hooked rug.

She didn't want to fight. But she grabbed Suzie's bodice, just above her bosom, and tore it open. She felt Mr. Blanchette ripping her drawers from her hips. She spun again.

Suzie grabbed Cia's arms and held them behind her. Cia sank into the ball of her clothing, to hide her nakedness. Suzie pulled her over and stretched her arms out on the floor, above her head. "Get her, Daddy!" she screamed. "Fix her good!"

He clawed away her clothing as he clawed open his own. He drew her legs out straight and pierced her privacy. Cia noticed that his fat flesh felt like cold lard. In the wallpaper, angels with silver trumpets floated on white clouds.

"Harder, Daddy! Harder!" cried Suzie. Her chest lay across Cia's arms, but she was not looking at Cia; she was mesmerized by her father entering Cia. Cia turned her hands and dug her fingernails into Suzie's flesh. "Faster!" Suzie cried. "Don't stop!"

Suzie's bosom felt like bread dough. Cia ripped and ripped. She could feel Suzie's blood in her fingernails, and still Suzie cried, "More! More!"

Suzie was no longer lying on Cia's arms, but had pushed up slightly on her hands. Her body twitched all over as she gazed. Cia quit digging her fingers into Suzie's breasts. But still Suzie twitched all over, crying, "Harder, Daddy! Faster!

Deeper!" Blanchette's nose was fatter than Cia had ever noticed before.

As he pumped his seed into Cia's belly, Suzie's eyes went round and fixed. Her breath burst out in great, aspirated, guttural, twitching gasps.

Cia's reaction to the rape was not hysterical:

> I was not angry at him. In a sense, he had done nothing, goaded on by his women.
>
> If he had said, "I'm sorry," I would have forgiven him.
>
> If he had said, "Forgive me," I would have loved him.
>
> If he had said, "Get under my thumb," I would have removed to his bedroom and accepted my concubinage as easily as I had accepted my servility from the beginning of memory.
>
> But, he said none of these. He said, "Get out of my house! Never let me lay eyes on you again!"

Cia fled. Out the back door, into the alley. They did not even let her take with her the rags they had ripped from her body.

She was alone in the world. Naked. With no destination. An Indian without a tribe, her heart was full of rejections. A culture without a population, her head was full of Latin. She sought refuge in Latin.

> I came to the river. It was swollen with high water. I saw a dead sheep floating in its swirls, not unusual at that time of year. I think I would have drowned myself, had I not found a pile of dry leaves under a tree, where I burrowed myself for warmth and maintained my sanity by repeating aloud to myself everything I could remember, beginning with "Omnia Gallia in tres partes divisa est."

Charles Brashear

8. The Birth of Dawn

Cia was unclothed, alone, cold; everything she had known since her memory began had just collapsed. Though she could speak only a few dozen phrases of the Koru language and knew next to nothing of Koru culture, she went to live with the Indians.

Legends in the tribe say that she rapidly became notorious and feared, for she was quick to attack anyone or anything, viciously, and she went around with her hair and body dirty and in disarray, railing and raging at people in a language no one could understand. She refused to understand or speak English, for she hated everything white, everything her life had ever been.

But, as her belly began to swell, she began to change. When she felt the life quicken within her, a new life quickened in her spirit, too. She softened, began sitting quietly by the river, contemplating her own amazing chemistry. She even softened toward the whites and, by the end of her term, her fury had dwindled to a dull indifference that she could live with, as long as she had nothing at all to do with the whites.

She learned about her father, too. About his leadership, his strength and coherence in the face of destructive trials, his love and wisdom. She developed the idea of having her child as near as she could manage to the spot where she thought Sioc's bones had been scattered by coyotes. It became an obsession. So, as her time came on, she went to a sandbar in the willows— to lie in labor amid the gifts of the universe.

The baby came with the first light of dawn on a warm September morning.

Cia arranged her baskets in the sand, built a small fire to

warm the water, got the rabbit-skin blanket ready, laid out the tule mat. Then she stripped off her clothes and went into the river to bathe, scrubbing gently each part of her body with sand.

When she came out of the water, she told her daughter later, a curious thing had begun to happen. She was covered with chill bumps, felt the gentle breeze that contracted her skin with cold; but, with her hands on her belly, she could feel also the fever in the fetus, burning already with life. She could feel the heat in and around each chill bump. Then she ceased to feel hot and cold; she felt only the tingling of sensations as they ran across her skin and along her backbone.

She began to hear and see things, too. The night owl, the moving leaves, the rush of the water, of course, but more. The death-thrashing of Sioc, the stride of her ancestors along willow paths, the grating of the stars in their orbits. She felt the darkness with her fingers, saw the sand and pebbles with her toes, tasted the milk inside her swollen breasts. Smelled the branches, the sap in the rocks.

The labor pangs were almost continuous then, but she did not feel them as pain. Rather as music, singing through every atom of her universe. She had planned to lie on the tule mat, but, on impulse, she spread her feet wide and squatted above it.

With her hands on her belly, she felt she was pushing the earth, fondling the round earth. Tasting and smelling it, too, along with the fire ashes and smoke. Earth, air, fire, water, she smelled them, tasted them, felt, heard, saw them all, as she pushed and grunted, and the child splashed out onto the tule mat.

It was a girl.

Cia's arms, her legs, her womb encompassed the world as she stood above her crying child, the umbilical cord still attached at both ends. Suns and planets tied in their umbilical orbits, moons in their movements, she and her child *were* the universe. The very stars whirled in her.

It was dawning. When Cia looked up, she saw a doe, not ten feet away.

She stared at the doe, and the doe stared at her.

And there, staring at the doe, Cia, who could hardly speak Koru because she had spoken and lived only English and Latin in the 39 years since Sioc had left her with the whites— Cia, whose name translates as "woman-without-basket"— Cia spoke with the deer in the language of the basket that is always full.

The deer, she told her daughter, showed her how fire belongs above wood, the sky above water, and the earth under. From the union of earth and sky were born the two-legged and the four-legged spirits; those with shells and those with fins; those that were trees, grass, rocks, hills; all.

As Cia watched, they all emerged from the earth's basket and stood along the path, waiting for Cia, the woman without a basket. And the deer beckoned.

She picked up her baby and, with the umbilical cord dangling, walked into the basket.

-< * >-

After that, Cia became more Indian than the Indians. She avoided all contact with the whites and protected her daughter from knowledge of them. Those around her on the Reservation were a ragged lot at that time, and much that the tribe had once known had been forgotten. But she started seeking out old men and women who harbored some secret fancy for the way things once were. She learned the traditions of the Koru as she and her daughter were learning the language.

She spent the rest of her life at the task and came, in the end, to the same conclusion her father had come to in 1850, the year of Cia's birth— that there was no hope for the Indian way of life.

Anglo culture was insatiable, without compassion.

The only hope for individual Indians was to join the Anglo culture, to live like white men, to assimilate.

And so, one day in September, 1908, when Cia thought she was dying, when it was too late to teach her daughter either Latin or English, she sewed her Doe-in-the-Dawn a white party dress with pink lace at the collar and tiers and tiers of red ric-racked ruffles, gave her the small journal she had kept when Dawn was a baby, and sent the seventeen year-old girl, who could hardly speak seventeen words of English, walking from the northwest end of Market Street, into Colusa, with a letter of introduction addressed to my Boston-Irish great-great-grandmother, Sarah Stonecrist, and instructions to forget, absolutely forget, everything she had ever known— to begin a new life.

-< * >-

Dawn almost did it, too. That's the wonder of it, to me.

Grandfather George Stonecrist was almost twelve years older than Dawn and already a successful merchant, a haberdasher, in Colusa. They were married at Thanksgiving, 1908, and, though they lost a first child, they began in 1910 producing the string of acceptable children that a couple was supposed to produce in those days.

Dawn was not poor nor dirty; nor did she live in a shack at the edge of town or the soggy part of the river front; and she soon spoke fair English with a slight Boston accent (thanks to Sarah Stonecrist); so she was invisible.

In 1917, though they had four children, Grandfather Stonecrist did his patriotic duty and enlisted. He was gassed in France, but lived on, a semi-invalid, until 1934. By the time of the Depression, Uncle George, though only 19 years old, was already an accomplished farmer, who converted the farm to food production for those hardest years. So, with food from the farm, clothing from the store, and shelter in their sturdy old house, they survived the thirties. They were fortunate in finding a good manager for the business, a man-and-wife team who continued with Dawn until the beginning of World War II.

Dawn and Aunt Ruthie managed through the war.

Somehow, they expected that his U.S. Navy experience would bleach my father and instill in him the motivation to sell clothes to pale housewives. It didn't happen.

Dad tried it only long enough for me to be born, 30 Sep 1947; then he started courting the oblivion he found in a bottle— I never knew for sure whether it was to quench the vision of his shipmates boiling into the sky on the crest of a fiery, kamikaze eruption at Ie Shima, or to insulate himself from the bigotry that followed him to the hospital, and later followed him to his attempts to find work in the city, even to his choice of bars to drink in.

After Sarah died in 1912, George and Dawn owned the farm northwest of town, his store, and a nice Victorian house, though somewhat square and plain, on a quiet side-street. They were not exactly wealthy, but certainly well-to-do. With the aid of cotton print dresses and a parasol to keep her from tanning too much, Dawn became exactly what her mother and grandmother-in-law had told her to become— a respected, upper-middle-class housewife.

-< * >-

The second major wonder of Dawn's life, to me, is how she again became Doe-in-the-Dawn. How in the world did she remember so much? After having repressed it all those years?

She will say it was her blood and cell memory, but I think it's more than that.

It was not just the awakening that followed the invasion of Alcatraz by Indians of All Tribes, because it started before that.

It erupted, I think, one Sunday when she and I had gone to Davidson's Drug Store to get an ice cream. A dark, pudgy woman was there with two children, a boy and a girl. They were keeping off to themselves and trying to pass as Mexican, for they were speaking Spanish to each other.

The children were playing with the water fountain, holding their fingers over the nozzle, trying to spray each other. Just as we were passing, a shower doused the front of Granny's dress.

"Oh, Barn-owls!" cried the boy in Koru, forgetting in his surprise and haste to use Spanish. "Look what you did to the lady," he accused the girl.

"Barn-owls, yourself," said Granny, as if she had used Koru every day of her life. "You can't blame others for what you do. If you pass the burden for your acts to others, I'm going to tell Coyote to come and get you."

The children stopped, freeze-framed in surprise at hearing Koru come from the mouth of a woman in a print shirt-waist. Maybe they were hypnotized by the threat of Coyote catching their spirits. They gazed at Granny for a long moment, like owl babies in a nest when a snake is creeping up the limb toward them.

Granny released them with a little gesture. A flip of the wrist.

Then they broke and ran to their mother.

"What is the matter? What is the problem?" the mother asked, but the children weren't talking. Nor did they look back. They squirmed their hands into their mother's, one on each side.

Water was still dripping out of Granny's thin hair and running across her powdered forehead. She ran her hand across her brow and wiped away the make-up, then looked at her hand strangely.

Dawn was like a person who has walked across a wet field and comes to the porch with mud caked on her boots. She kicks at the foot-scraper to dislodge the dirt with the force.

But each bit of the mud flying forward with momentum turns into a blossom, a little pink flower. And each little pink flower is a memory, a life experience of long ago.

"You've been practicing your Koru every night, haven't you?" I say.

She only looks at me, not yet admitting it. She wipes her forehead with the other hand, removing the face powder. Her skin is darker when her hand comes away.

"You whisper to yourself in Koru when you're alone, don't

you? You imagine long conversations with people you don't know. You make sure you dream in Koru. Don't you?"

She finally admits it. "Yes."

"Why?" I ask.

She is slow to respond. "Yes. I talk to Cia. I talk to Mother in my sleep."

"Does she answer?"

"She used to. But for a long time, she didn't. Now, she talks to me again. I'm afraid to forget her. If I forget her, I might as well never have been born."

"Weren't you afraid for her spirit? Weren't you afraid the ghost of Coyote would catch her spirit and turn it against you?"

"Mother? Oh, no. Mother is much too strong for that! Coyote is the one who has to worry. Besides, Mother always has her protection with her. Her medicine."

"Her protection?"

"Yes. Her guardian *Saltu*."

"Guardian?"

"I thought you knew. That doe in the dawn. She goes with Mother everywhere. That visionary doe in the dawn."

9. Look At Me! Look at Me!

In the spring of 1833, Sioc, the new chief who had yet to gain the confidence of the people, sent messages to all the villages of the Koru nation: all the people of the Turtle and Hawk should come to Koru village in the time of Wanhini-bo, the moon of first leaves; for it was time to rejoice.

Over two-thirds of the people were dead of face-rot spots. Three-fourths of the food supply had been lost in the winter floods, and the people were lean and weak with hunger. No man dared trust his neighbor or share with him, for men and children had been bludgeoned for a mouthful of food. And Sioc sent word that it was time to rejoice, to come to Koru village and dance the Hesi, the dance of world renewal.

And now, at Thanksgiving 1970, when The American Indian Movement has called for a day of mourning at Plymouth, Massachusetts, Grandmother Doe-in-the-Dawn has invited every Indian she could contact to come to our house for a kind of Red Power re-enactment of her grandfather's 1833 ritual in our "sitting room."

In 1948, Uncle Ben, Granny's carpenter son, made two large rooms into an even larger room by transforming the wall between them into a fourteen-foot arch. At the front, double sliding-glass doors open onto the entrance hall. At the back, a door opens onto the screened veranda outside the dining room. At the same time, he updated the 1920's style bathrooms.

There is where Grandmother Doe-in-the-Dawn will dance the Hesi.

Sara Ann has come up from San Francisco for the holidays. She'll help me with the back-stage support. We've been working for days on the arrangements. I had to learn a bunch of drum accompaniments to rituals.

Grandmother and Sara Ann have made themselves fringed Blackfeet maiden's dresses of that pale blue combed-cotton denim that looks like doe-skin, and Dawn wears a headband decorated with angular Aztec symbols. Though Dawn is beautiful, even radiant, I tease her: "What have we to do with Blackfeet and Aztec habits?"

"Come on, 'n get with it, Georgie," she says. "We're all the same now. Since we've been detribalized, we're all the same under our skins."

"Begging your pardon, Mrs. Stonecrist," says Paul Winslow, a tall angular Apache sitting with others on the carpet near the fireplace, his feet crossed under him. His hair is parted in the middle and pulled back into two braids. He wears a white dress shirt, the collar open and the cuffs flipped up twice. "Begging your pardon, but that's just what Big Brother Robber has always wanted us to think. He's used 'Indian Unity' as a weapon against us."

Sam Mitchee, a Navajo with a tight copper skin and a straight nose, agrees. "That's right, man! They've insisted on unity and unanimity till they've paralyzed us." He tosses his head to throw his breast-length hair back over the shoulders of his faded-blue work shirt, so that his inlaid Thunderbird necklace is exposed, then he mimics: "'Just let us know what all you Indians of the Rocky Mountains, and on the Plains, and in the deserts and swamp-lands, want, and we'll give it to you. Just one thing. That'd be fair to everybody.'" He relaxes so that his hair falls forward again. "Then they start fanning up and catering to tribal interests, until we're all raging with competition again."

A general murmur of assent goes around the living room. "That's right." "Yeah!" "Better b'lieve it!"

Only a man of about 35, who has changed his name to James Hawk, pursues the issue. He is a regional leader in AIM, the American Indian Movement, and speaks like a man being interviewed on film. "That's the way they've made us 'invisible' Americans all right, and I think they'd like to keep it that way. They'd like us to stay 'forgotten' Americans. But we can't let 'em get away with it any longer.

"We've got to band together and fight together, or we won't get anything. We've got to make Uncle Sam let us pick our own leaders. We've got to get a good Indian in as BIA commissioner. We've got to get back our rights under the Treaty of 1868. We've got to get back the right to control our own destinies. We're all making noise, but we're not being heard.

"The only way we'll ever be heard is to all yell together. We've got to unify, set our priorities, and yell. The BIA has been a dictatorship, and the Reservations have been concentration camps ever since they were created in 1852. They've stolen our languages, our religions, our right to educate our children in the important things, and we're discriminated against in every— "

He is interrupted by the door bell. Sara Ann lets in Ed Baer, who hasn't yet determined if his grandmother was a Tlingit or a Kwakiutl, but he wears a Kwakiutl blanket depicting whales, birds, and many-toothed dogs of the sea. He is a clown, what the Koru called a Moki, a contrary, whose ceremonial function is to belittle the high seriousness of the high priests.

Right away, he sizes things up from the silence and a quick glance at the way others are looking at James Hawk. He grabs an imaginary shovel and, with exaggerated motions, starts digging his way in. I see that he's welcome relief to several around the room. He digs only a couple of shovels-full before he straightens up, wipes the imaginary sweat from his brow, and asks, "Gollee, Man! Who laid all this shit on yo'all po' sweatin' Injuns?"

James Hawk says nothing. Most tribes apparently had clowns who served this function, and even a man who has changed his name knows that he is not permitted to answer or even acknowledge the clown's antics.

Abruptly, Ed changes. Now, he's the Seneca or Iroquois in

the pollution-control commercial on TV. He's paddling across the pristine Eastern woodlands lake, beaching his birch-bark canoe, standing at the edge of a freeway where passing Anglos— they have to be Anglos— throw a sack of garbage at his feet. Ed intones, with mock seriousness, "Some people have a deep, abiding respect for the clean air they lay on other people. Some people don't." Some of us laugh at James Hawk.

Grandmother Doe-in-the-Dawn chides him. "Teddy! Can't you ever take anything seriously? You're worse than my Georgie, I swear."

"Well, I don't know," says Teddy with deep solemnity. "I always thought he was a little worse than me. Why, I wouldn't put it past him to mock his own Grandmother." Teddy squats, Indian-fashion, with the rest of us.

Dawn's smile is frozen on her face, and she says nothing more. Nevertheless, in a few moments, she begins her enactment of the Hesi.

She picks up a leg-bone of a chicken and an empty juice can with both the top and bottom removed. Both of these, she has painted with straw-colored Tempera and decorated with red and yellow dyed feathers. "These were supposed to be the leg-bone of a hawk and a basketry 'cylinder of the world.' The leg-bone represents the power of the skies, the power of the Gods, and the cylinder is the world of the people, much like the Sacred Hoop of the Sioux."

She stands in the middle of her living room and lifts the fetishes to the western sky. Suddenly, she sings the Hesi invitation song, loud and clear:

> wer-eti, weni,
> wer-eti, weni,
> lo-iba wer-eti,
> ser-iba wer-eti,
> ilain wer-eti,
> eu bala weni,
> wer-eti, weni,

tcen-wer, tcen-wer

apatcu, weni,
tatcu, weni,
Lantcu, weni,
mile ilain
mile lo-iba
mile ser-iba
eu bala wer-eti,
    tcen-wer, tcen-wer

eu bala weni,
eu bala huyalis,
matapan olel weni,
matapanma olelbe wer-eti,
topi bole weni,
eu bala huyalis—
weni, wer-eti, weni
    tcen-wer, tcen-wer[1]

Mary Barnesfish lets her breath out audibly, saying, "Hey! That's really cool." The rest of the room is silent. I glance at Sara Ann; she is as rapt as Mary Barnesfish.

Dawn lowers her hands, crosses her wrists in front of her, and leans her whole body toward the west. Four times, she screams a long, drawn-out "Heeee," the last one trailing off into silence.

She holds the silence and the pose for fifteen or twenty

---

1.   Come on. Arrive/ Come on. Arrive/ Girls, come on/ Boys, come on/ Children, come on/ At this eating, arrive/ Come on. Arrive/ Come down. Come down...

My mother's brother, arrive/ My father, arrive/ My younger brother, arrive/ You children/ You girls/ You boys/ At this eating, come on/ Come down. Come down.

At this eating, arrive/ At this eating, assemble/ Grandfather above, arrive/ Grandfathers above, come on/ All you spirits, arrive/ At this eating, assemble/ Arrive, come on, arrive/ Come down. Come down.

                                            Charles Brashear

seconds; in the old days, the Hesi singer might have held it twenty minutes or a half hour, as if continuing the song into its silent, more-important part.

When she has completed the silence, she turns toward the South, lifts her bone and basket to the sky, and repeats her Hesi invitation song. Then she repeats the ceremony to the East and, finally, to the North.

When she has finished, she places the cylinder of the world on the carpet and stands the decorated leg-bone in it. It is a visual prayer: may the power of the Gods enter the hoop of this tribe.

"I'm very sorry we couldn't do this really right," she says. "The singer is supposed to be totally naked, and all visitors are supposed to remain at their camps just outside the village until they hear the invitation song. Then they come in, single file, to be greeted and welcomed. In Grandfather's time, they always puffed bits of acorn powder at each other as part of the greeting."

She unties a little pouch from her belt. "I don't have any acorn powder," she says. "Though I *do* know how to fix it. Mother and I fixed it many times when I was a little girl. We'll just have to do with white flour." She holds up a pinch on her fingertips and puffs it in the general direction of the group. "*Wile wilak,*" she says. "That means 'healthy world.' May you have good health and a good life."

She nods to me. My signal to wheel in the serving cart we have prepared and parked on the screened veranda.

"In the old days, I would have given you food as a part of the greeting. Pinole cake and acorn gruel, cooked in a basket with hot stones. Well, I don't have any acorn gruel or pinole cakes; so I'm going to give you chicken soup and sesame crackers. It's supposed to be served in a turtle shell, like this one." She holds up a turtle shell she has kept buttons and pins in these many years; she uses it as a serving ladle. "We're going to have to serve in styrofoam cups."

Sara Ann stands beside Granny, handing her the cups one at a time. Granny gives each person a bit of the chicken soup and a sesame cracker, repeating to each person, "*Wile wilak.* Welcome to my dance-house."

Dawn sends me away with the serving cart and speaks to the whole group again. "Next is a period when you may talk with one another. Greet old friends. Make new acquaintances. Visit. Get to know to each other."

She puts on the record of Natay, the Navajo singer. I love it when he sings "The Zuni Morning Song." I think that's my favorite Indian song. She turns it down low, so that it's just in the background.

In a few minutes, the room is buzzing with small conversations. Sara Ann and I are picking our way around and through the crowd, collecting styrofoam cups and offering people peppermint candies that look like little pillows. I catch snatches of conversations.

". . . learn some of the old-time ways. They were a more natural way of life."

"Hogwash! That's Romantic hogwash! You can't go through life with those old values. You've got to live in . . ."

"It is our duty to treat the earth with respect, for it belongs to the seventh generation of our descendants."

". . . strike at the women and children. That was their way of striking at the roots, at the reproduction, of a people they were trying to efface. . . ."

". . . went to the city council and said the Flagstaff Pow-Wow was sacrilegious. These dances were not meant to be performed like a side-show, in front of white people. And they're not supposed to be performed for money. The council said, no, they wouldn't stop the dances. So the group from AIM asked if they could have a microphone at some time during the dances to explain their beliefs to the audience. Again, they were told flat no. So, when the Yei-Be-Chai dancers were coming on for their Sunday night performance, about twenty of the group from AIM walked in quietly and sat down in a circle. Just that. Nothing else. A couple went up to the announcer's booth, but the mike had already been turned off. So seven of the Indians were arrested for inciting a riot.

Can you imagine that? Inciting a riot! They were thrown in jail under $20,000 bail. One of the guys, a Navajo from Tuba City— his name's Andrew Kelly, Jr— is a Viet Nam hero. Silver Star, Bronze Star, Air Medal, wounded three times. And not one of the Arizona newspapers mentioned any of that when they reported how this herd of wild Indians took over the Flagstaff Pow-Wow. . . ."

". . . a true Indian will always remain an Indian . . . "

". . . not one of the 191 Reservations that hasn't been cheated in some . . ."

". . . really like what that woman said on Alcatraz: 'It's no worse than on the Reservation where we lived.' No water, no natural resources, the population has always exceeded the land base . . . "

". . . It is not necessary for the eagle to be a crow. . . ."

I've collected about all the styrofoam cups. I pause and look back over the crowd. Sara Ann comes up beside me. I say, "Hooooey!" and wipe imaginary sweat from my brow.

"I know what you mean, honey," she says. "It's hard to keep up with the Indian wars these days. If it's not a logging company in Oregon or Washington blitz-logging a Reservation and ruining the land for sixty years, or more, it's an electric power or gas company that's reneged on the royalties they promised to pay."

"Or the students," I add, "in some red-neck high school in California hating and taunting "Red Niggers." Or their parents who run the town's businesses refusing to serve them or let them swim in the public pool, or a dozen different other predicaments. I can see why a lot of people are attracted to the primitive; life was so simple then. Sometimes simplicity is a good thing to have. I wish I had some right now."

She pretends to pour 'simplicity' into my cup.

"Just a half a glass, please. Thanks. No more. Don't want to get into the habit."

On impulse, I turn off the phonograph, pick up my drum, and sing, as loudly and as clearly as I can:

Daybreak people are chirping:
Above me on the roof,
Alighting, they sing, "tci-tci."

Daybreak people are chirping:
Above me on the roof,
Alighting, they sing, "tci-tci."

The room has fallen silent when I finish. "That was a Wintu Bird Song," I explain, glancing at Sara Ann. Her maiden's dress can't hide the fact that she's got a great figure. It almost throws me off. "The Koru word for 'I' or 'me' was, is, '*tcu*.' I've always wondered if that little bird up there on the roof wasn't saying, 'Look at me! Look at me!'"

10. A Cup of Fresh Rainwater

My interruption, it turns out, came at the right time. Grandmother Doe-in-the-Dawn is ready with the next stage of her Hesi.

She comes in through the sliding glass doors. Naked to the waist, with bold, white, horizontal stripes on her face and down her chest. The sides of her rib cage and her back are painted black. She wears a long, net skirt that is decorated with red, yellow, and brown dime-store feathers, and on her head is a basketry headdress with feathers arranged in a sunburst halo, with four cardinal feathers sticking forward over her forehead. Making soaring and little bird-like motions, she really does remind one of a red-tailed hawk. I tap the drum slowly, irregularly, to echo her movements.

She is carrying a ceremonial bow and arrows in a quiver. The bow and arrows are from her great-grandson's fiberglass archery set, though she has removed the rubber cups from the arrows. The quiver is a bit of red cloth, simply wrapped around the four arrows.

She has a little prefatory speech:

"My grandfather, Sioc, called the people to a Hesi dance in a time of great crisis and danger, because he had a beautiful vision. That vision became a part of the Hesi. People still spoke of it, in 1900 and 1903, 1905 and '06, when I was a young girl and my mother was taking me to Hesi dances. Sioc's father and mother were killed by smallpox in 1832. That made him *Sektu Koru*, the one who leads the people.

"But, at first, he didn't do anything. He just sat in front of the dance house and gazed at the trees, the water, the sky. This caused a lot of gossip, of course. And it spread all through the tribe.

"Then one day— they still told this story in 1905— he got

up and took a *kimir* in his hand; that's a stone that's pointed conically on both ends and has a hole in one end, so it can be worn on a thong around the neck. '*Kimir*' is the word for 'thunder,' and it meant 'the power of the gods.'

"This particular stone that Sioc had that day once belonged to a medicine man who had been discredited for treating smallpox by having people dance in the sweat-house. Well, Sioc walked to the edge of the river and, with everybody watching, he heaved 'the power of the gods' into the middle of the river. That caused quite a stir, you may believe. I've come to think he did it deliberately, as a staged psychological gesture. He must have known how the people would react."

'Staged psychological gesture' snaps my attention up. I see Sara Ann do the same. I see my grandmother who all my life has looked and sounded like a country farm-wife, carrying bits of trash from an Anglo dime-store, naked as a savage, and talking like the books she's been reading. Sara Ann smiles at me, as if to ask, "Will activism cause such rifts in us all?"

Dawn continues: "Then Sioc disappeared for several days. We knew later that he had gone to *Onolai*, the sacred mountain of the people. And there he had a dream-vision. Katit the Red-tailed Hawk visited him in a dream and told him what lessons to teach the people.

"No one knew exactly when he returned, but, one morning"— she nods to me, to make sure I'm ready to accompany her with the drum— "he awoke the village by standing on top of the dance house, singing at the top of his lungs:

> E-e-e-e-e Yo-o-o-o-o
> All are invited.
> E-e-e-e-e Yo-o-o-o-o
> All the beings to the West are invited.
> All are invited.
> E-e-e-e-e Yo-o-o-o-o
> Katit, our father, is invited.

Anus, the turtle, is invited.
The deer-people are invited.
All the bird-people are invited.
The trickster, too.
The trickster is invited, too.
All are invited.
E-e-e-e-e Yo-o-o-o-o
All are invited.
Heee. Heee. Heee. Heee-eee-ee—e———-e.

"He had aroused a lot of interest by this time, of course. He sent word to all the villages of the Koru nation that everyone should come to Koru and dance the Hesi. While he was waiting for the people to arrive, he repaired the ceremonial regalia, the prayer sticks, and stuff. And he found some help: a person to play the drum, a couple of Tuya dancers, a Moki to make fun of things.

"On the day set, people began arriving and waiting outside the village until they heard the ceremonial call again. They had come from Keti, which was at the present site of Princeton, about fifteen miles above Colusa on the river; from Ts'a, three miles below Keti; from Waitere, ten miles above Koru; from Katsil, six miles from Koru; from Tatno, two miles from Koru to the north; from Somé, five miles north and west from the river; and from Kukui, two miles south of Koru.

"They all came and made their ritual greetings at the edge of the village. Sioc led them, group by group, to the dance house and gave them food, acorn gruel and pinole cakes that had been set aside for use in the ceremonials. It wasn't much, you may believe, because of the circumstances, but everybody was surprised that he had managed to find anything at all.

"Finally, he came to his *Bole Ho* oration. '*Bole Ho*' means literally, 'ghost, yes.' It is the affirmation of Spirit. This is approximately how it was still being sung around 1900." I fall in behind her, like a *tuya*, and tap the drum to the rhythm of her chant, as she acts out the story.

"Listen to me. Listen to me. Listen to me, now.

"I was sick. The people were sick. We were sick at heart.

"I went above. I went above to Onolai.

"I called out above. I called out above to our father, Katit.

"I called on Katit, who is above. I talked with Katit. I talked in a dream with Katit, our father, who is above."

She pauses. She dances four times around the basket and prayer bone that are still on her carpet. Then, she takes up a position beside the prayer basket and continues:

"You must believe what I say. You must believe what he has taught you. Here we should be glad. He said, 'give this speech to all the people, all the people of all the villages, for they are awaiting it. Every one of them is to be saved.'"

"Yes, yes," I chant, keeping her rhythm. The Koru word for 'yes' is '*Ho*' or '*Yo*,' depending upon whether a vowel or a consonant has gone before, and just '*O*' when spoken alone. In the Hesi, the audience is expected to respond with 'yes, yes,' but somehow I don't feel like saying 'O Ho' to Granny just now.

Besides, we want the crowd to respond in English. I hold out my palm to Sara Ann, as if asking for something, and she echoes the "Yes, yes." The others in the room look at her, then at me. I give them the signal and they catch on. At the gesture, they'll soon join me in the response.

Granny continues: "Some people will not assist. Some will not do as they are instructed. Though our father told us this, we see that some people do not believe it. Sometimes we ask what the reason is.

"We must give a dance. We will give it for all the people, for all the people of all the villages. It is for the betterment of the world and for the improvement of the people."

Yes, yes.

Again she pauses, dances around the prayer basket four times, then continues:

"Katit, our father, spoke to me in a dream.

"Katit, our father, spoke to me, saying thus:

"'Do you see these three hills?

Charles Brashear

"'These three hills?

"'These three hills.

"'They are your mother's brothers. They are three previous worlds. But they are not for you.'"

Yes, yes.

"'I call you all to let you know that I am going away in search of the future world. I do not know just where it is, but know I shall find it. Somewhere above. Either in the north or in the west. That is the way I shall look about.

"'I do this for Koru. This I make.

"'This I do, when I look for another world.

"'This I make in the other world: This oak tree I make.'"

Yes, yes.

"'This mountain I make.'"

"'This water I make.'"

"'These rocks I make."

Yes, yes.

(The series goes on to recount most of the animals, birds, and plants of the Koru world. It served to make them acutely aware, once again, of the material and spiritual bounty in which they lived. Each item is answered with "Yes, yes." As the series continues, Granny and her audience get more and more emotional.)

"'I do this for Koru. This I make.'"

The hawks, ducks, geese, woodpeckers, and yellowhammers; the crow, magpie, blackbirds, the doves, quails, owls, buzzards, and sparrows; the egrets, cranes, loons, and terns.

The grizzly bear, the elk, the antelope, deer, and coyote, too. The ground squirrels, jack rabbits, cottontails, raccoons, gophers; mountain lions, too, and badgers, fox, and skunks.

The oak, the maple, dogwood, honeysuckle, and manzanita; the sycamore, the lilac, the willow, the pine, the fir, the leatherwood, the cedar; the sumac, too. The laurel, the nutmeg, the rose, the chestnut, and the box elder, too.

The grapes, the blackberries, gooseberries, huckleberries; raspberries, salmon berries, strawberries.

The soap plant, the hemp, tobacco, peavine, oats, tule, cat-tail, ferns, grass. All the vines and creepers.

"'This I make. This land I make.'"

Yes, yes.

"'This I make. This grass I make.'"

"'This I make. These rocks I make.'"

"'This world I make for Koru.'"

Yes, yes.

"My father called me and spoke to me.

"He called me to hear his counsel.

"I went above and found him in the west.

"He was naked to the waist and seated facing the east. He was glad to see me, and said: 'I called you that you might hear what I have to say. I will look for another place. All the people are to be saved. All the sick people, too.'

"We here should be glad."

Yes, yes.

"We here should be happy."

"We here should make the dance."

"We here should give thanks to our father, Katit."

Yes, yes.

"Thus it was. Thus it was. Thus it was, when I went above to Katit. For this we give thanks. For this we are thankful. For this that we have, for this that our father gives us, we give thanks."

Grandmother dances around the prayer basket four times. She transfers her ceremonial bow to her left hand and takes a bit of white flour from the pouch at her belt. She holds it up on her fingertips and puffs it into the air.

Yes, yes, the audience answers at my signal.

Four times, to the west, the south, the east, and the north, she puffs a pinch of flour to the gods.

"Thus it was. Thus it was.

"Thus it was transformed. It is finished. It is transformed."

She pauses for several moments. Now that she is no longer Katit the dancer, but Granny, her hands keep drifting up to partially cover her sunken breasts, only to flutter away again when she becomes aware of them. She takes from a chair a gray, woolen shawl that one of her granddaughters brought her from Scotland, puts it over her shoulders, crosses the ends over her breasts, and tucks them into her waistband. Then she goes on:

"The Koru thought they had the wealth of the world in the old days. Each item they took up lovingly. They all dipped into the same basket, and it was always full.

"Always, a part of what they had belonged to the gods. The *ciabas*, or women, gathered grass seeds in their conical baskets and stored them for the long winters; but part of what they had gathered was always set aside for the gods. They gathered acorns along the river, but these were not considered theirs until the gods had their share.

"The men caught salmon and perch in the river, and dried them; but no one ate them until the gods were satisfied.

"Sometimes, the men put antlers on their heads, or put white clay on their buttocks, and, taking their bows in one hand and their long arrows in the other to imitate animal movements, they stalked the deer and the antelope. Whenever they killed an animal, the first blood was for the gods, and they offered drops of it to them in the four directions.

"Even in times when the food supply was short, or people were starving, the gods had their share of the bounty of the earth.

"For even gods must be fed. We, today, have largely forgotten how to nourish that part of ourselves which is nourished by feeding the god.

"After Grandfather had sung of his dream vision, the Koru feasted on the wealth of the world, or at least on what was available. The story is that they had lots of fresh perch and a little dried salmon, some deer and antelope, fresh Indian potatoes that some women had dug, and pinole and acorn powder that had been saved through the disastrous winter. And as they ate, they watched the hills and the plains, and they contemplated their world.

"Then, in the deepening twilight, as fires that mark the home were kindled, they heard sounds they had not noticed during the epidemic: the sweep of the wind across the prairie, the rush of water in the river; the mating calls of the insects and birds. And they felt once again that they belonged to it all. The people became aware that they had been hungry, and the land had fed them; they had been nourished.

"The Koru people are virtually gone. Many tribes have vanished from the earth, and I am sick. We are all sick. We are sick at heart. The white man has come upon the Indian both like a flood and like a famine. We live in a time of confusion and crisis. Let us dip into the waters of life and be nourished."

I wheel forward the five gallon stainless kettle we have prepared, and Sara Ann brings new styrofoam cups. Grandmother Doe-in-the-Dawn goes around, giving each person a cup and struggling with her shawl to keep herself covered.

After three or four people have been served from the kettle, Billy Tabe tastes his and exclaims, "Hey! That's clean!"

"It sure is," agrees Mary Barnesfish. "What is it?"

"Yeah, what is it, Mrs. Stonecrist?" asks James Hawk.

"One of the basic staffs of life," answers Grandmother Doe-in-the-Dawn. "It is pure rain-water. 'Drink and be whole again.'"

Teddy Baer can't pass up the chance to be contrary: "Pass the bourbon, please Suh. This here braanch wahtuh needs a leeetle flavorin'."

"Tell me, Teddy," says Jacky Martinez, a big, dark, and bitter Mexican Indian, "Do you think you're citizen enough to be trusted with firewater?"

Everyone is stunned to a silence for a moment. Mark Ellis, a Cherokee, starts us again:

"Actually, it is a staff of life, you know. I was reading an article in *Science Newsletter* some time ago, in which these scientists had found that there's a tiny, micro-organism

Charles Brashear

related to the B-vitamins living in rain drops. It goes through several life cycles on the way down, feeding on the air through which the rain drop falls. After a few hours, it's dead and gone, but just when the rain falls, it's still alive and very nourishing. That's why fresh rainwater is such a great tonic for plants, far better than just plain water. Here's to fresh rainwater." He salutes a toast with his cup and drinks.

I can see that Grandmother Doe-in-the-Dawn is vexed and divided by what he says. She wants this to be an Indian evening, very Indian, and she is pleased that the Indian way, primitive and instinctual, is proven right, yet she is disturbed that some paleface scientist has found a better reason than hers for drinking rainwater.

"They ought to put some of this in the Yakima River," says Mary Barnesfish. "What with all the factories crudding down the river, and the paleface Sheriffs ripping out our nets, and the boat traffic, and sport fishermen, and seasonal laws on game fish, our people can't hardly make a go of it. Maybe fresh water would help."

"Did you have treaty rights to that water and those fish?" asks James Hawk.

"Oh, sure. But you know how that is."

"Was it ever ratified?" pursues James Hawk.

"I don't know," says Mary.

"Over 200 treaties negotiated in 1848 were never ratified by the Senate. Did you all know that? Over 200 treaties! And there are at least 371 treaties that were ratified, but have been disregarded."

"Ours must be one of them," says Quinsel Law, a Quinault from Taholah, Washington. "My Uncle Bob is our tribal councilman, and he has one hell of a time trying to stop them. They not only ignore the treaty; they've got contracts that give them a license to rob us. Uncle Bob goes to the courts over and over again, but nothing ever happens. The logging company still comes in every year and slash-logs about 2,000 acres on our Reservation and just leaves most of it. They don't even clean up the debris. And they cut young trees just to get them out of the way of the bulldozers. Nothing's going to grow there for a long long time. And what do we get out of it? Say the logging company takes out $10,000 worth of lumber, well, one guy in the tribe will get a nickel, another will get a penny. I just don't know what we're going to do. The courts don't seem to be much of a help."

"We've got to get control of . . . " begins James Hawk.

"Ha!" laughs Quinsel in scorn. "The chief forester up there is an Ottawa. He's partly Uncle Tomahawk, but the other part can't seem to get through the red tape and contracts.

"That's what Red Power is all about," says James Hawk. "Look, we've been discriminated against for centuries in hiring, in housing, in education. We weren't even citizens until 1924 and then only because Congress wanted to make it legal that they had drafted Indians in the First World War. If we want a fair shake, we've got to band together and raise a hell of a lot of noise. We've got a lot of land and money and rights coming to us, but they're not going to give them up of their own free will. We've got to make noise. They're going to hear a lot more noise from now on. Any of you haven't joined AIM, you ought to get with it. That's where the future is. AIM is the only thing that'll stop them from grabbing the food from right out of our mouths."

And so on. He is not even stopped when Teddy Baer gets up, stretches his legs with exaggeration, and says, "Sheee-ut, this sitting like a dumb Indian is sure hard on the legs."

Grandmother Doe-in-the-Dawn stands amid the crowd in a stiff daze, with Sara Ann trying to comfort her. Tears stream across the white bars on her face and fall on her thin chest.

She had not managed to give every person here a cup of fresh rainwater.

11. Bury My Heart at Salmon Bend

Grandmother Doe-in-the-Dawn insists that we now write our chapter: "Bury My Heart at Salmon Bend." If we can't touch our Indian friends, we'll hit the general public, the way Dee Brown did. She has collected books, old pictures, manuscripts, maps, artifacts, anything she could find. And has spread them all over her sitting room, not just on the tables, but on and under chairs, on the mantle of her fireplace, in boxes, on make-shift shelves.

"Why bother," I protest. "It's the same old story of chicanery, dispossession, and detribalization. Everyone already knows it all."

"It is not the same, you hear. This is my story. My story! My grandfather lived through it. I have a right to tell my story. It happened to me. I have a right to claim justice, the same as anyone else who has been wronged."

"But Granny, it's the same old pattern. Red Cloud probably put it best: 'They made us many promises, more than I can remember, but they never kept but one; they promised to take our land, and they took it.'"

Ah, yes. Land. Subject of song, legend, law, history.

> As long
>   *as long*
> As the moon
>   *as the moon*
> shines
>   *as the bright moon shines;*
>
> As long
>   *as long*
> As the river

as the river
Flows
as the dark flood flows;

As long as the sun shines;
As long as the grass grows;
This land . . .

That used to be one of our favorite songs. It's by Peter La Farge, a Hopi songwriter, and it uses the words of a treaty between President Washington and the Seneca Chief, Cornplanter. On Pete Seeger's program, a chorus used to take the echo parts, in the country gospel tradition, and it was just beautiful. Sentimental as hell, but beautiful.

The beautiful idea jerks us around like we were puppets on a string. As long as the moon shines, as long as the river flows, as long as the grass grows, this land, as far west as the eye can see, will belong to the Indian.

-< * >-

But others had other ideas. Imagine an American farmer in the light of a secret candle with his long finger stopped momentarily on a map spread out on his kitchen table.

Myths pass through the mind of this pioneer— big-screen images of immigrants to Texas; reports of William H. Ashley pulling a cannon over South Pass in 1827, the first set of wheels to mark the Oregon Trail; reports by government explorers, like Lewis and Clark; Frémont and Kit Carson; dreams of Texas about to be annexed; dreams of Oregon contested; of California waiting like a peach to be picked; dreams of the United States completely spanning America.

And imagine all these dreams mingled with the sad realities of Kentucky and Tennessee, states for forty years; the realities of crops smaller, the land depleted, families burgeoning with ten or twelve kids, and neighbors closer.

And, worst of all, the quick, infuriating realization that adventure was passing him by, while others were building opportunities in a West that really did seem golden.

The dream pulled the puppet strings of their minds and sent thousands of people west from Independence in a fleet of wagons, the covers looking remarkably like sails, to be banged and battered in the springless wagons for four months or more, to transform the wagons into makeshift boats when crossing streams, or to dismantle them and pull them with ropes up some precipice in the mountains.

With a pistol and a poke, but not a single thought about the Native American, the white man invaded his paradise of dreams.

Movies come to my mind when the actors are playing roles, when they are acting out their unconscious myths, when some archetype has caught their souls and is acting itself out through the puppet strings of their fakery. It's a kind of other-directed thing, a Hollywood. One does what one does to affect another, or make him mad, or to mollify, or celebrate.

OPEN TO WIDE SCREEN, TECHNICOLOR, ESTABLISHING SHOT

The L. W. Hastings party of eleven covered wagons is moving south on the plains a few miles west of the present site of Princeton, California, in August, 1843. The party had wintered in Oregon, then was forced to wait until their crops had ripened before they could continue to their destinations in California. A huge cloud of tan dust rises behind the wagon train and partly obscures the cumulus clouds in a cobalt blue sky.

MUSIC should be expansive, excited, somewhat like "Sunrise" in Ferdi Grofés "Grand Canyon Suite."

We see wagon wheels, grinding through dust. In the foreground, very sparse, very small oat-grass wilted before it made seed. A horse's leg brushes against a brown, leafy bush. Dust falls from the leaves. The four mules pulling the wagon go down into a small, dry water-course and pull the wagon out the other side.

A SCOUT on horseback is loping back toward the wagon train from the line of trees that mark the Sacramento River. He comes up to the wagon and falls alongside, walking his horse.

>   DRIVER
> What about some of these little creek beds? Couldn't we get down to the water in one of them?

>   SCOUT
> Nope. They don't flow into the river. They flow out of it in high water time. The river's cut cliffs under them, same as everywhere else.

>   DRIVER
> Flow out of it? How so?

>   SCOUT
> The river runs on a ridge of silt it's built up over the years. During high water it will flow out and make this whole valley a pond.

>   "SHOTGUN" GUARD
> *(lifting his arm and pointing to a small break in the row of bushes, where we see AN INDIAN scurrying from behind one bush to the next)*
> Jack!

The SCOUT rises quickly in his stirrups and gazes. Very quick zoom from quite wide to quite close: THREE INDIAN MEN, bent over and running in the bush-lined draw toward the river.

>   SCOUT
> *(whipping up his horse, lifting his rifle, and yelling)*

Yaaaa — Hoooo!

"SHOTGUN" GUARD
(voice-over, while scout races toward Indians)
Jack's gonna get him a couple more.

The THREE INDIAN MEN come out of the draw, stand three abreast, and fit their long arrows to their bows, as scout gallops closer. They point them at the scout and draw the bows, making fierce faces and yelling: "Hump! Wump!"

The SCOUT, surprised, reins in, so that his horse skids on his hind legs.

"SHOTGUN" GUARD
(to driver)
Lookit that! They're gonna put up a fight.

The THREE INDIAN MEN. One runs forward three steps, yelling, draws his bow the length of the arrow, but does not shoot. He then goes back into line with the others. A second makes a run forward. All yell and make threatening gestures.

The SCOUT throws back his head and laughs. His hat falls off.

SCOUT suddenly quits laughing, levels his rifle, and fires. ONE OF THE INDIANS clutches his heart and falls. The scout draws his pistol, fires once but misses, fires again. A SECOND INDIAN grabs his thigh, drops his equipment, and hobbles back into the brush. THE THIRD INDIAN goes with him. The SCOUT holsters his pistol, pulls his knife, and whips up his horse.

"CUT! Stop! Do whatever you do to cease this nonsense," yells Granny.

"But it's true, Granny. Or at least as true as I can reconstruct."

"True?" she snorts.

"Yes. Bidwell, in his account, mentions and I quote: 'Some two or three of Hastings' party— their names I do not now recall— were in the habit of shooting at Indians, and killed two or three before reaching the Colusa village, which was the only known point within about 40 miles above and 30 miles below, where horses could be watered from the river.'

"The Indians' behavior in war is taken from Kroeber and Barrett's reports of Patwin war stories, collected near the beginning of the century.

"Repeating rifles weren't yet available, so I gave the scout a single shot rifle— in 1843, it would have to be a muzzle-loader— and a double-barreled pistol, and—"

"That's not what I'm talking about. Why does he come on like John Wayne shooting clay pigeons?"

"But Bidwell says 'in the habit' and—"

"'In the habit,'" she mocks. "What does that mean?"

"Well, it means that, while I am, in fact, simulating reality for this particular event, I can authenticate the behavior of both the Indians and the white men. It must have happened just this—"

"At any rate," says Grandmother Doe-in-the-Dawn, "let's quit pretending to recreate it. Let's just get down to the facts."

"Ah, but Granny, what are the facts? We're all pretending, all the time. Our facts are only myths that tell us which roles we will play. 'All the world's a stage,' remember, and 'each man in his time plays many parts.' And those parts control us. They are our puppet-masters.

"Those men in the 1840's and 50's and 60's didn't have or need John Wayne movies, because their minds *were* John Wayne movies. Those men were the puppets of their own myths. And our minds are the puppets of our myths."

-< * >-

Word got ahead of the Hastings party and the Koru at Salmon Bend were warned. They sent the women, children, and the very old off to hide in a safe place, and the warriors of the tribe were lined up and waiting with their bows strung and their arrows fitted.

Yet, they were taken completely by surprise. None of them got off a shot in the first wave. The Hastings forces simply swept right through them, over them, and on down to the water, where everybody and every animal stopped to get a drink.

The Koru men stood on the slope watching in amazement. The story handed down in the tribe claimed that not a single Koru had been wounded in that first onslaught. That was a kind of victory to them: that they had been shot at and missed.

Grandmother Doe-in-the-Dawn traces her finger slowly on the armchair, following the pattern in the upholstery. "Yes, I say let's call it a victory. They never again had an experience they could remotely call a victory."

One of the young Koru— perhaps one of those wanting to make his reputation, perhaps one of those, slightly older, who had been to Sonoma and had seen that the Mexicans there were not magic or charmed spirits, but just men— someone shot an arrow. It thunked into the side of a wagon.

Who fired the first shot at Lexington? A Briton or an American? Who fired first at Wounded Knee? A Sioux or a soldier?

But a shot was fired. Then everybody shot. For a moment, the Koru men were filled with glee, shooting enemies in a pond. They stuck arrows in a good many mules' rumps and punctured a few wagon sheets.

Then the Hastings men answered with a volley of pistol fire. Two Koru men were hit. One died right there, the other died later in a thicket. The Koru men flushed like a covey of quail.

One white woman jumped from her wagon and tried to prevent the slaughter. She pushed at the white men's rifles, stood in their line of fire, yelled for them to stop it! stop it!

The tribe never identified her, or understood what she was doing. She was Sarah Stonecrist, my Boston-Irish great-great-grandmother.

-< * >-

Ironically, if Hastings had asked permission to water his mules and horses where the hard-packed ground of Koru village sloped gently down to the river, he would have been invited to share the bounty of the world. Such was the Koru custom.

By themselves, by their principles, they could not have conceived the idea of defending their water hole. In fact, they weren't defending it; they were merely meeting a challenger near it.

Grandmother Doe-in-the-Dawn sighs. "For this, they were reported hostile when the Hastings party reached Sutter's settlement." She sighs again, then continues: "So Sutter sent his Kanaka warriors up the river to punish— "

The army crossed the river at Kukui, below Koru. They surrounded Kukui village in the dark and at dawn killed thirty-five people there— men, women, children, old people— all except for two or three that managed to sneak through and run to warn the other villages. When the Kanakas came to Koru, everyone was prepared and had hidden.

"Georgie, how did he get the Kanakas ... to kill ... so ... so easily? ... So readily? ... So happily? They were the natives where they came from. The invaded people. How did he manage to turn them so quickly and completely against us?"

"The old puppet strings, again."

"He kept them like slaves," she goes on. "Treated them like scum. Herded them in at night like chickens or pigs. And they put up with it! They could have revolted. There were surely enough of them— seventy or eighty. He had given them rifles and taught them to use them— why didn't they revolt? Why did they come up the river and shoot us, like they shot deer and squirrels?"

"Why did the Narragansetts fight the Pequots?" I ask. "Why did the Delawares fight the Hurons? Why did the Sioux fight the Pawnee? Or the Arapaho the Utes? Maybe they got a thrill out of killing 'legally.' And status in their self-image.

Maybe their rage at being victims was purged by their making victims of others. One of European man's special talents was getting Indians to fight his Indian wars for him."

Grandmother Doe-in-the-Dawn is suddenly outraged. She strides around the room, slamming furniture into straight rows. "That's it?" she asks angrily. "That's how our people were defeated?"

"Yep, that's it. That's how the Indians of Colusa County were 'pacified.'"

"No broken treaties?"

"Nope. No treaties to break. They didn't even bother to make treaties so they could break them."

"How can I claim injustice for that? How can I claim my heart is buried at Salmon Bend? For that?"

"Well, they took our land. They came to take it, and they took it."

"But couldn't we have had one little massacre? Nothing as big as Sand Creek or Wounded Knee. But a little one, maybe? How can we tell the world of our passion and suffering, when we just— just— stood around?"

"Well, we *were* dispossessed."

"But they wouldn't have had to kill us if they hadn't wanted to. They wanted to, and so they shot us like rabbits, one at a time. But they wouldn't have had to. That's the ugly part, don't you see? That's the ugly part: to dispossess us, they wouldn't have had to fire a shot at all."

12. Staking out Colusa

In the fall of 1850, the Koru came back to Cowpeck village and began repairing the salmon weir at the north end of Colusa. That's what gave Salmon Bend its name. Sioc was in charge, but Bokay, the medicine man, was conducting the ceremony. With each stake to be driven, he'd lift his little symbolic mallet and chant

> wer-eti, weni,
> wer-eti, weni,
> Anus wer-eti,
> Sedu-Sedit wer-eti,
> Katit wer-eti,
> matapan olel weni,
> matapanma olelbe wer-eti
> topi bole weni
> eu bole-ho huyalis—
> wer-eti, weni,
>   tcen-wer, tcen-wer[2]

"He had to hold his arms up to the Spirits," Grandmother explains, "and repeat the prayers to the North, the West, the South, the East. If one didn't call the gods to help, the whole salmon season might fail. And no one in the tribe was allowed to get mad during this time, either, because that might anger Hur, the Salmon Spirit.

---

2. Come on, arrive/ come on, arrive/ Mud Turtle, come on/ Old Man Coyote, come on/ Red-Tailed Hawk, come on/ Grandfather above, arrive/ Grandfathers above, all arrive/ All you Spirits, arrive/ At this affirmation of Spirit, assemble/ Arrive, come on/ Come down, come down.

　　　　　　　　　　　　　　　　Charles Brashear

"Then he'd go to the next stake and cry out, 'Wer-eti, weni! Wer-eti, weni!' and he'd tap the stake with his mallet. Others with heavier mallets had to do the actual work of driving it into the river bottom.

The white men in Colusa came down to the water's edge and yelled things like, 'Hey you can't obstruct boat traffic, like that,' but the Koru paid them no mind. They had to catch a supply of salmon, or the tribe would go hungry. So they continued. That is, they tried to continue.

Late in the season, when they were almost finished repairing the weir, the hulk of a boat that had sunk at Chico Landing in August floated again in the high water and ripped out the weir like a battering ram.

"They never again managed to rebuild it," says Granny, trailing off and looking away. "They caught some fish, from the bridge at Doc-Doc where they speared salmon. But that was never enough for the whole tribe."

ESTABLISHING SHOT, EARLY AFTERNOON

The oak grove at Salmon Bend. In the background, in the shelter of oaks, are several tule huts and brush wickiups with Koru Indian men and women beside them. On higher ground, under shelter, are a number of little stilt houses made of bound tule. In the middle background are two large earthen lodges, the communal dance houses, looking somewhat like huge bread loaves, with grass growing up their sides. On top of each is a pole about six feet high with feathers and basketry objects tied to them. In the foreground is a stack of sawed lumber.

The Indians are all gazing toward the stack. Will Green and Charles D. Semple, his uncle, come on, carrying a heavy plank. They put it on the stack, then lean against the stack to catch their breath.

The screen is filled with Charles Semple's back while he is leaning on the lumber. He is six feet, seven inches tall, extremely slender, with an angular, pointed, well-trimmed beard and blue-gray eyes. He turns around, looks at the sun, takes a watch from a vest pocket and looks at it.

SEMPLE

We might as well start measuring. It's early still.

Semple and Green on each end of a measuring rope. Semple measures, drives a stake in the ground. Two other men, a Mr. HEEPS and a Mr. HALE, are coming up from a thicket near the river.

HEEPS
(a short, red-haired man)
And what is it you'll be doing?

We see Charles Semple, silhouetted against the highest part of the oaks and sky.

SEMPLE

I'm staking out city lots.

HALE
(a tall, coarse-boned man)
Well, dinna ye mind. Mr. Heeps and I were here forst.

In the background, four Koru men, including one carrying an obsidian-tipped spear and wearing a basketry headdress with four cardinal feathers sticking forward, are coming slowly nearer to get a better view of what is happening.

SEMPLE
(lifting his arm and waving in a wide arc)
But I own all this.

The Indians look where he is waving, but see nothing.

HALE

Hoot, Mon! Hoo can ye own it, when 't is ours?

HEEPS

Now, Mr. Hale. Let us not heat up our heads.
Gentlemen we are, gentlemen we should be.
(He turns toward Semple again.)
Is it a hotel ye 'll be abuilding?

Charles Semple, silhouetted the same as before.

SEMPLE

(looking off in the distance)
A whole city.

HEEPS

Ah! a whole city? And what will you call your city?

SEMPLE

Colusa. I'm going to call it Colusa. After the name of
the land grant I bought.

HEEPS

Ah, it's a fine name. Much like the Indians hereabouts.
And will it be a hotel ye 're abuilding in your Colusa?

HALE

We— Mr. Heeps and I— hav a right bonny hotel near
finished. We wunna want another.

INSERT:

*An unfinished shanty, built of cottonwood poles, a scrap of
canvas, a couple of weathered boards, some brush on the roof.*

*We see Charles Semple, again, straightening up from driving a
stake.*

SEMPLE

Listen, you fellows. All this land is mine. I bought it
from General Bidwell and paid for it. I'll do with it what
I like. You can do whatever you like, until I'm ready to

do that, too. Then, I'll throw you off. I've got a map of what I own, in case you want to go off to the other side of my line to set up.

We see Charles Semple's arm only, holding the heavy hammer and pointing north.

> SEMPLE *(voice-over)*
> You go up the river three and a half miles as the crow flies ...

The top of the stake. The heavy hammer comes down and strikes it. Semple raises his arm and the hammer, pointing west.

> SEMPLE *(voice-over)*
> From there you go west, three miles away from the river...

The top of the stake. The hammer comes down and strikes it.

The four Indians, staring at the stake. Semple and Green move on, measuring off another lot, followed by Heeps and Hale. The four Indian men are left behind.

FREEZE FRAME
SLOW FADE OUT

-< * >-

The four Indian men come closer to the stake. Two of them squat near the stake, but do not reach out to touch it. The Indians look variously at the white men, at the stake, at the sky in the four directions, then back at the stake.

Bokay, the Maleyomta, the principal medicine man, looks at a stake and says, "The white man is building a house for his gods at Koru."

Sedu-netsu-sere, whose name translates as Old-man-related-to-everyone, responds, "Aiiee, always before, they have gone away after a few days. Perhaps these will go away, too."

Sioc looks after the departing men. "Yes, they pass through and change nothing." He stands up and adjusts his basketry head-dress with the four Cardinal feathers sticking forward.

"But these are not passing through," says Bokay.

"They are building a house. Perhaps they intend to stay," says Kapaya-Sel, Bokay's apprentice.

"Do you think they are the world-destroyers, as my ciaba thinks?" asks Sedu-netsu-sere

"They have started to build houses before. They have left them unfinished," says Sioc. "Perhaps they will leave this one unfinished and disappear from our world, as they have always done."

"That is true. It seems they have no spirit in their houses and must leave them unbuilt," says Sedu-netsu-sere

"But they have brought their gods with them this time," says Bokay. "You all saw it, the same as I. Their spirit covers the land with straight lines in the four directions, like a net. They have cast a spirit net upon the land. It will catch all, like fish. Aiiee, they have brought the spirit of the white man into the land this time.

"Do not listen to the white man's spirit," says Sioc. "Do not act in the white man's ways. In the meantime, we must have food, as always. We will move to Cowpeck and net perch."

He takes off his basketry headdress and stands, looking at the ground. "Aiiee! Their gods are lines on the earth you cannot even see."

In the Library of Congress, is a mural. In the center foreground, a mountain man is leading some miners into the wilderness. Behind them, in the right foreground, a farmer is plowing with two oxen. Further back, we see a covered wagon, a stage coach, a pony express rider, three trains, a river full of steamboats, and, in the distance, a wagon train. In the left background, a small herd of buffalo is running out of the picture. In the left foreground, a group of Indians, some on horseback, some on travois, some on foot, are disappearing. Dominating the panel, in a scale that would make her at least a hundred and fifty feet high, is a white goddess. She is clad in flowing white gossamer in the Greek style. A star shines on her forehead and her wavy hair streams back like stripes in a banner. She is trailing telegraph wire across the prairie. The panel is called "The Spirit of Progress."

13. The Treaty That Never Was

Dr. O.M. Wozencraft, the Indian Agent for Northern California in 1851, was a treaty-making son-of-a-gun. He could make treaties faster than John Wayne can shoot. In the summer and fall of 1851, he made at least 38 treaties with Indians in northern California, sometimes including as many as eight "bands" on one treaty and putting as many as fifty tribal groups on one tiny, non-existent Reservation.

He came to Cowpeck, which he called Camp-Colus, on September 1, 1851. In addition to a wagonload of baggage and papers, he brought with him three Spanish bullocks, which he had bought near Princeton. He offered these to the Indians as a gesture of friendship and the good will of the U.S. Government.

Sioc sent word to all the other villages that the people should come to Cowpeck for a feast, and he directed the overnight roasting of the bullocks.

Cheered by how well his gesture was received, Wozencraft sat up late, writing a treaty, in which the Indians relinquished their land on the river at a rate of $1.25 per acre and agreed to removal to a Reservation in the foothills.

When told there was no water in the foothills for at least six months of the year, he said, "Never mind, that's their problem."

He was even happier the next morning when he found eight villages represented at Cowpeck, five from the Koru nation, three from the Maidu. He hoped to have his treaty signed and be on the road by ten for a full day's travel.

He was taken aback, when Sioc refused to sign the treaty. Through Will Green, who had learned a couple dozen Koru words, Wozencraft asked, "Don't you realize how much the United States paid for those cattle? Don't you realize we gave you those cattle to sign the treaty?"

"Why do you talk to me in the voice of a mere boy?" asked Sioc, who had heard of Wozencraft's treaties with the Maidu and Wintu near Chico. "I do not believe that you speak with the voice of the Great American *Sektu,* for your voice is like a mere boy's. You talk of losing your cattle, like a boy talks of losing shells, or of missing a rabbit when he steps on a twig. You said last night that you gave the cattle in peace and friendship. Do you now have another reason? I have nothing more to say to you."

So Wozencraft went back to Colusa and drafted a new treaty. In it, he described a Reservation of almost 30,000 acres which lay along the east side of the Sacramento River, in the Sutter Grant. He further provided that all the Indians living on the Sacramento River from Stony Creek, forty miles to the north of Colusa, to Sacramento City, seventy miles to the south; all Indians living in the adjacent Coast Range; and all those Indians living on the Feather River from Sacramento City to the Yuba River should be included in the said Reservation, and, should any of these other bands not come in, then the provisions of the treaty would be reduced in ratio to the number signing the treaty.

At the treaty conference, Sioc delivered an oration:

"They promise us peace and friendship! This is kind of the American *Sektu,* for we know and he knows that he has little need for our friendship in return, for his people are many. They are like the grass that covers the western plain, while we have become like the scattered trees on a dry prairie.

"Every hillside, every valley, every plain and grove in this land has been hallowed by some fond memory or some sad experience of the tribe.

"Our religion has been the traditions of our ancestors, the dreams of our old men, given to them in the solemn hours of night by the Great *Saltu* who rise inside them. It was written in the hearts of the people and came from a place that was true. And because our knowledge came from the heart, this beautiful land gave us being.

"All this and much more was once all true. But no longer,

for we are changing. Our living are lonely-hearted. I know of no way to fill their hearts again.

"Some of you blame the white man for all this. Some of you think, as the *ciabas* first thought, that he is the world-destroyer. It is true, when the first white man came into the land, the Indian people were doomed. On every side, they have come closer and closer with their guns, and we are isolated among them.

"We are destroyed by a competition we have no means to sustain. Our hearts are so thin, we no longer cast shadows. We no longer know where our dead will be buried.

"I will not dwell upon, nor long mourn, this decay, nor blame the white man for hastening it, for we, too, have been to blame. We have been found weak, when we should have been strong. Evil influences our hearts, too. Some of us have nursed hatred for our own, and manufactured malice. All this has contributed to the destruction of our world.

"You all know this in your hearts, and our white brothers, there—perhaps, they know it, too.

"And now, we must change even more. The white man comes to us and says that we are weak and must move out of the land, or he will send his brave warriors against us. They can destroy us on every side. I see no hope for my people. We are alone. We are defeated.

"Therefore, I think we will accept what this paper says and retire to the Reservation which is offered us. There we will live in peace for a little while. The white man will not be long satisfied with us, even on the Reservation which he has built, for soon one of them will want that land, too. But that does not matter.

"It matters little where we pass the remnant of our days. They are not many. The Indian's night promises to be dark. No bright stars hover in the dawn above our horizon. Sad-voiced winds moan in the distance. Some grim death is on the path, and no matter where the Indian goes, he will soon hear the sure-approaching footsteps of his destroyer.

"A few months, a few more winters— "

The treaty was signed and bears the date, September 2, 1851. On October 15, Wozencraft wrote to Mr. Lea of the Department of the Interior:

I had but little trouble in concluding a treaty at Colusa. The Indians had been previously informed of what I had done for those on the Chico [Creek]. The Reservation given them is on the eastern bank of the Sacramento, opposite Colusa, three miles in depth by fifteen miles in length, unoccupied, and most of it good soil. It is on the Sutter claim. One of the purchasers, however, informed me that he has no objections to their remaining on it.

So! The U.S. Government didn't even have title to the land it used to create a Reservation!

But no matter. The U.S. Congress never bothered to ratify the treaty. So the trade never existed legally. And the Indians were left to hide in the bush to avoid the bullets of the same vicious hunters they had dodged before.

14. The Metes and Bounds of Justice

In the belief that treaties are both meaningful and binding, Grandmother Doe-in-the-Dawn has filed a class action suit in Federal Court in San Francisco, on behalf of herself and any surviving Koru Indians that may hereafter be found, claiming title of ownership to Rancho Colus, a Mexican Land Grant on the west bank of the Sacramento River, embracing the city of Colusa and the surrounding countryside.

Sara Ann in her "lawyer uniform"— a trim, mannish business suit with a ruffled white dicky— is helping us in court, but since she hasn't yet got her license, she can only kibitz as a friend. She has researched cases in the law library and Federal archives and has written out reviews, possible arguments, and strategies as our lawyer's helper. He looks at her work half-heartedly, with little understanding.

What is unusual is that the judge appears sympathetic and, by putting us on the stand, asking us questions, and tolerating long, circuitous, sometimes foggy answers, he is in a sense conducting our case for us. Indulgence is popular among the palefaces this season.

Granny flutters right around the judge's bench to show him the maps and papers we have. The bailiff protests, but the judge motions that it's okay. He even stands, one hand on a hip, and bends over the map beside Granny to get a better look.

It's one of those yard-square county maps with the township and range lines drawn in. It shows clearly the boundaries of the Mexican land grant known as Rancho

Colus, starting about four and a quarter miles north of Colusa, running to about four and three-quarter miles south of Colusa, two and a half miles wide at the north and six miles wide at the south.

"Well, that's very interesting," says the judge, but I can tell by his tone that he is baffled by Granny's sense of evidence.

Sara Ann leans close to me and whispers, "Say something. The judge is getting impatient."

So I start talking, hoping to keep the judge's indulgence alive with information. The defense does not object, and the judge allows it. "Ours was a luxury area," I say, hoping to stir some note of pride in Grandmother Doe-in-the-Dawn.

"Kroeber shows that the Hesi had to originate with the river Patwin and puts the mark on the map right where Koru village was located. He shows that the other tribes were living too near subsistence to have the leisure time, the luxury culture, to invent new forms of religious thought. Before 1750, and possibly as early as 1700, our people furnished northern California with the Hesi form of the *Kuksu* and probably with the World Renewal Cult."

"Yes?" says the judge. Tolerant but baffled as to why I brought this up.

"This should establish, along with the shell mounds and excavations of grave sites and other archeological finds"— I mentally kick myself for that fillip of the tongue. Archeological 'finds,' indeed!— "should establish that the Koru exercised hereditary proprietary rights— "

"The court will accept as established that the Indian was here before the white man."

Supercilious bastard! But I know that we can't afford to get him mad at us. That'd kill our case quicker than anything. A sense of impotence and rage. To know that you must caress the beast that devours you.

"It was such a— So much a— " Granny begins and begins again, toying with a button on her shirt-waist. But the enormity of what she wants to say defeats her. Or is it the vacancy? The vacant feeling one has when he knows there is an enormity to express, but one knows that expressing it will make no difference, utterly no difference at all.

"I want to go and visit my relatives," says Grandmother Doe-in-the-Dawn, fingering the turquoise brooch at her throat.

Some day, I'm going to wring her dumb old neck. She's dodging, playing turtle. I hate it when she does things like this, which come right out of Koru traditions.

This place feels wrong. I am alone in the world. I will go and visit my relatives in some distant place.

"Whenever I dream I have been at a Big Time," a very old Indian told professor Alfred Kroeber in the 1920s, and by "big time" he meant one of the ceremonial dances where shamans transformed themselves into grizzly bears before his very eyes and the great Spirits did not need impersonators in the dance, because they still came to the dance in person— "Whenever I dream I have been at a big time, I feel lonely the next day, and where I live seems wrong. My family notice and ask what is the matter, but I do not tell."[3]

That was the Koru response at the time of the occupation and dispossession, and for over a hundred years after. Anomie— the breakdown and loss of values and norms that once made their society cohere.

Yesterday's promise, today's depression.

Anomie. That's how the Navajo, the Hopi, the Pueblo, the Sioux, the Shoshoni, and so many others deal with that feeling of vacancy that follows broken promise.

I ask for a half-hour recess, and the judge grants it.

"Look," I say to Granny and our lawyer, "we've got to pull our case together."

Sara Ann echoes me: "Right. We've got to get this thing on

---

3. Told to Professor Alfred L. Kroeber and included in his monograph, "The Patwin and Their Neighbors," *University of California Publications in American Archeology and Ethnography*, Vol. XXIX, No. 4., 1932.

---

an even keel. A logical order."

I add: "We're going to lose before we plead if we don't play the game their way."

The recess is over before we've gotten much of a plan set. Sara Ann has been talking with our lawyer, but I don't get a chance to hear what they have decided, if anything.

Granny is calmer, now, however, and talks quietly, evenly. She's telling what the Sacramento Valley looked like before the white men arrived. The judge is listening patiently. Sara Ann is writing notes to our lawyer. I lean back and allow Granny's words to draw pictures in my mind.

I can see that the judge is getting fidgety. None of this is evidence to him. He's beginning to look for a way to dismiss us. It's Friday afternoon. He'd like to quit a bit early, so he could beat the rush-hour traffic on the Golden Gate Bridge. I glance at Sara Ann, but she's busily writing on her legal pad.

The judge shuffles some papers on his desk. "Well, you have certainly given the court a lot to think about. Perhaps too much to assimilate in one sitting. I suggest, therefore, that we recess until Monday morning at nine, and, Counselor, I suggest you get your clients to come to the germane issues of the case soon. He taps his gavel on the desk, gets up, and leaves.

-< * >-

Alone, we all look at each other, as if lost. "So here we are," I say. "Now what?"

"Get on with the case," says our lawyer.

"But what does he want?" asks Granny. "I'm telling him everything I can."

"He wants what you want. Can you tell me again," he asks, turning to me and Sara Ann, "what you want to say? Cut all the history, cut all the extenuating circumstances, all the anthropology. Tell me as simple and straightforward as you can, just what is it you want to say?"

I make the first response: "That the white man unjustly

and illegally took from us everything of value we ever had."

"What we're trying to establish," says Sara Ann, "is that the tribe was exercising proprietary rights by practice, by actually living on and using the land and its resources."

He looks at her, waiting. Like the judge, he does not approve of women at the bar. He regards them as a species of dancing bear— it's not that they dance well; the wonder is that they dance at all.

Sara Ann is not cowed. "It's the same principle as was practiced by the Mexican government," she says. "When a grantee took possession of a land grant under both Spanish and Mexican land grant law, the Alcalde was required to 'cause the grantee to pull up grass, throw stones, scatter handfuls of earth, break twigs, and cry *Viva el Presidente y la Nación Mexicana!'*

"The idea was that such acts were prima facie evidence that the occupant had permanently altered the face of the land. He had possessed it by using it.

"The same principle applies in U.S. law," she goes on. "Those who occupy and use a tract have some presumptive title to the property. And, in cases where there is no conflicting claim to ownership, such title to property has been confirmed to the occupants, and even perfected. In cases of conflict, some cases have been adjudicated by compromising the boundary lines, so that both parties get what the court considered fair."

"Look. You want my advice?" says the lawyer. "Attack the paper. Show up the Mexican Land Grant. Or that Treaty that you say you never made. That's the stuff this case is going to be settled on. Now, you-all sit down and figure out what you're going to say Monday when he puts you on for the last time."

"The last time?" asks Granny.

"Yep. This case will be decided Monday."

-< * >-

On Sunday afternoon, Granny, Sara Ann, and I go to our lawyer and summarize what we are thinking. He's reluctant to buy our strategy.

"You're essentially claiming squatters' rights," he says. "The court and the Congress consistently go against squatters' rights."

"What d'you mean, squatters? We were there first, and we're squatters?"

"That's about the shape of it."

"What about the ninth article of the Treaty of Guadalupe Hidalgo?" says Sara Ann, picking up a copy to read from. "The U.S. obligated itself that people— squatters, if you will— would be 'maintained and protected in the free enjoyment of their liberty and property, and secured in the free exercise of their religion without restriction.' Doesn't that guarantee some squatters' rights?"

"Not good enough. Won't hold up in court."

"What?" I protest. "A U.S. Treaty won't hold up in court? They were systematically detribalizing us, and that won't hold up in court?"

He just looks at me, as if waiting for me to go on.

"They were methodically annihilating us, and you say that won't hold up? They were destroying our customs. Our laws, our means of livelihood, our religion, our very lives—"

"Nope. No value to it."

"No value?"

"Nope. Show it to me on a paper. Show me where you had it, and they took it."

"Anomie has no deed!"

"Then you can't get it back."

"Oh, we've still got that. That's the only thing they never wanted to take away from us."

<*>

On Monday morning, Grandmother Doe-in-the-Dawn shows our photocopy of the Bidwell map to the judge and explains that just because the Koru left their main village and moved to Cowpeck to fish did not mean that they were forfeiting their rights of ownership to the land.

"They looked upon the whole hunting and gathering area as belonging to the tribe— communally," she says. "When the seeds ripened, they *had* to live on the prairie by the lakes. When the salmon ran, they *had* to live at their fishing village. When the winter floods came, they *had* to live on the high ground at Koru village. It was the habit and tradition of the people to move from place to place at different times of the year."

The judge looks at her with raised eyebrows.

Granny flares with anger. "Now, you listen to me, young man! You're not being fair. You're not listening to what we have to say." With a sharp finger, she pecks the photocopy of the Bidwell map which he has in front of him. "Our people lived here!" she declares. "Here! Our people made their living here!"

He is astonished, but does not hold her in contempt. Slightly amused, he says, "Go on."

I see Sara Ann nudge our lawyer, but he does nothing. Abruptly, she stands up and starts talking. "Our contention is," says Sara Ann, "that these practices demonstrate prior vested and paramount rights which the United States is obligated to uphold, by the 'protection of property' clauses of the Treaty of Guadalupe Hidalgo, as well as accepted interpretation of international law, then and now."

"Twenty minutes recess," says the judge. "And Miss"— he looks at his papers to find her name. "Miss Murphy. I understand that you have not been admitted to the bar as yet. You may not practice law in my court." He taps the bench with his gavel, gets up, and leaves.

Granny stands in the middle of the courtroom floor, abandoned. She fingers the turquoise brooch at her throat. I go over and put my arm around her. She looks at me, her eyes glistening.

-< * >-

All this and more, we present to the judge— the Koru had the land in the beginning. They never relinquished title to it. So it is legally still theirs.

After a thirty-minute recess to consider the evidence, he delivers his opinion.

Opinion, hell! It's law! What he says becomes the law in this case.

"I find the plaintiff's case defective on three counts," he says.

As he speaks, Granny begins to rise, in slow motion, an incredulous look on her face.

"First," says the judge, "she has failed to establish that she has a right by birth to make the claim. In light of the romance and legend of her birth in the brush, we could hardly expect any documentation of her origin, but she has also failed to submit any affidavits of persons in a position to know the germane facts.

"However, even if we assume no irregularities concerning documentation of her birthright, she would remain only a citizen, hence she has no right to negotiate with or enter into treaties with the U.S. Government. The United States does not make treaties or 'deals' with its own citizens.

"Further, treaties were discontinued by Act of Congress in 1871, hence I find no way that she has a right, either as a treaty participant nor as a citizen, to challenge the status quo of the property known as Rancho Colus."

Sara Ann has begun to rise, unbelieving, in the same pose as Granny.

"Second," says the judge, "she has failed to show that there was anything irregular about the Mexican land grant known as Rancho Colus. Indeed, it seems this grant was proved by Mexican authorities before the acquisition of the territory by the United States and, therefore, the United States is bound by the Treaty of Guadalupe Hidalgo to honor the proprietary rights vested in it at that time.

"The records show that John Bidwell had assigned his right in the plot to Charles D. Semple and that Semple's title to the grant was affirmed by the U.S. Land Commission created by Act of Congress, March 3, 1851, and confirmed at the June term, 1855, of the U.S. District Court of Appeals at San Francisco, Judge Ogden Hoffman, presiding.

"The conflicts of titles resulting from the superimposition of the Jimeno and Colusa Grants have been adjudicated and, therefore, have the same force as the Treaty."

Our zombie lawyer just nods. I'm not sure if he's agreeing with the judge or sleeping.

"Third, she has failed to show sufficient cause to overcome the precedent that the land has been occupied for over a hundred years by a happy and prosperous people, who have worked innumerable improvements upon it— "

"What?" I scream, jumping up. "You mean you'll recognize the precedent that white men have lived on the land a few decades, but not recognize the twenty-five thousand years the Indians lived on it? That sounds like a lot of precedent to ignore."

"The qualitative difference is the case in point here," he says, tolerating my outburst. "There is no evidence that the Indian improved the land while he had it, while the citizens now in possession have indelibly and irrevocably stamped their personality upon it. We could not, even if we wanted to, return to the situation as it was at the time of the alleged dispossession. It would be absurd, at this late date, to try to enforce the Treaty of 1851, which, as you say, was never ratified. ..."

He goes on and on with gobbledygook, but I don't listen particularly well. "Plaintiff's claims are denied" is too much to hear right now.

My mind keeps flashing on that 16-year-old boy from the Fort Hall Reservation in Idaho. Two days after chatting with members of the Indian Education Subcommittee, among them Senators Walter Mondale and Robert Kennedy, and telling them about his aspirations for himself and his tribe, he committed suicide in the county jail where he had been taken without a hearing and without his parents' knowledge.

He hanged himself from a pipe running across the ceiling of the cell, where two others from his Reservation had committed suicide within the last year.

"It would be grossly unjust," says the judge, "to deprive the present population of the luxury they have attained. Indeed, it would seem they have created from the land a profitable center of progress and civiliza—"

"I want to go and visit my relatives at Koru," says Grandmother Doe-in-the-Dawn.

"But they're all dead, Granny."

"Yes," she whispers. "*Lu-mas*. All of them are dead."

15. Sarah Stonecrist's Nightmare

For many years when I was a boy, a wooden Indian stood in front of Davidson's Drug Store in Colusa. He wore Iroquois buckskins and a Sioux eagle-feather bonnet, he offered a bundle of wooden cigars in his hand, and he was called "Chief Colusa."

No matter that all the details are wrong, everyone called the four-foot-high statue "Chief Colusa." In the early days, they said, an Indian once lost a cow. He wandered among the whites, asking in pidgin, "Cow loose-a? Cow loose-a?" So the whites named him Chief Colusa.

"Preposterous!" says Grandmother Doe-in-the-Dawn. "Utterly preposterous!"

And she's right, of course. This ridiculous ignorance about Indians was one of those absurd and unconscious ways the white man's mind was soothing its own conscience for the genocide it was unconsciously trying to commit.

Still, Grandmother Doe-in-the-Dawn gets mad when we think about "Chief Cowloose-a," but she gets even madder when I point out that no Indian in those days had a cow to get loose.

And she gets even more angry when I remind her that the wooden Indian at Davidson's Drug Store dates from 1891 and was the business of our own Sarah Stonecrist, my great-great-grandmother and Dawn's tutor in American culture.

A newspaper clipping in Sarah's trunk in the attic describes the dedication. All my life, I've enjoyed browsing in her scrap book and among the artifacts she saved, and, now Grandmother Doe-in-the-Dawn has agreed to tell me what she knows about some of the items. I've lugged the trunk down to the upstairs hallway.

"That old witch!" says Grandmother, holding up a dark sweater that is decorated with a bright ring of simple, knitted diamonds at breast level— not terribly imaginative, but apparently Sarah's own design. "She couldn't even weave, she always knitted."

"Knitting is no crime," I say. "You can't hate someone for knitting."

"It's not straightforward, like weaving. It's all tangled up. Just like that old woman was."

"And embroidery isn't all tangled up?"

"That's an art form."

You see, during the last years of Sarah's life, from 1908 to 1912, she and Dawn lived in the same house, this house we live in now. Sarah, more than anyone else in the world, taught Doe-in-the-Dawn to speak English, albeit with a slight Boston accent, taught her to cook American food, taught her to be content with being called "Dawn."

"She was a meddler," says Grandmother Doe-in-the-Dawn, closing Sarah's scrap book with finality, as if putting an end to the whole matter. "We'd all be better off if she'd never lived. Or at least never came to Colusa."

I don't agree, so I defend Sarah: "The lip of civilization was made of riff-raff, loafers, drifters, thieves, murderers, drunkards, and dregs. And you think— Listen, George and Sarah Stonecrist were patronizing, that's true. And that was the ugliest part of them.

"But what do you think it would have been like without the restraining— and civilizing!— influence of people like them, with their good hearts? It would have been even more barbarous. Patronization or annihilation, Granny? Those were the real choices. You and I wouldn't be here today if it hadn't been for George and Sarah Stonecrist."

"I still hated her," says Grandmother Doe-in-the-Dawn, but not with finality. She has found, again, and holds up a white party dress with pink lace at the collar and tiers and tiers of red ric-racked ruffles. "Mother and I made this," she says. And she lifts the hem of her own print dress to wipe a tear from her eye.

-< * >-

My great-great-grandmother, Sarah O'Shaughnessy, was born in Cambridge, near Boston, while William Ellery Channing's "Unitary Christianity" and "The Moral Argument Against Calvinism" were ringing in her father's household. Their remote Catholic background did not put them at a social disadvantage, for they were well-to-do by the standards of the day, and they were Unitarian converts.

At table, as she was growing up and attending grammar school, Sarah heard talk of benevolent pantheism, the universal brotherhood of man, the perfectibility of the human spirit, the ethical duty of good works, the free will that (in a curious hangover from Calvinism) forced every person to earn his own salvation in his own lifetime, if he were going to have it.

She was sixteen as she sat with the family, watching her brother and her sweetheart graduate with the Harvard class of 1837, and listening as Ralph Waldo Emerson charged young American scholars to open their eyes to life, to meet nature face-to-face and "enjoy an original relation to the universe."

Thus, Sarah's mind, like the New England Renaissance, was shaped by the forces that gave nineteenth century America much of its ethical fervor. Her Idealistic background gave her a conscientious and principled outlook—and the courage to stand by it—and her Irish background gave her a sympathy and understanding for victimized minorities.

Sarah O'Shaughnessy and George Stonecrist had been married hardly a year, when, armed with a few Daguerreotypes of their families, they set out for the dark and distant reaches of the West, convinced it most needed the moral illumination they were prepared and anxious to give the world.

"That's reason enough right there to think we'd have been better off without them," says Granny.

Because an early snow covered the passes, the wagon train was forced to winter in Eastern Oregon. The next spring, these pioneers had to plant vegetables and grain to re-provision themselves, and, in mid-summer, continued their journey to California.

That is how Sarah Stonecrist, aged 22, wife for just two years, mother for just six months and already five months with child, came to be in one of those wagons of the Hastings Party that blitzed through the Koru men that hot, dry day in August, 1843. Sarah wrote to her mother:

> Our scout reported natives lined up to defend water. Wagon boss suggested attack, running all and wagons right thro' them, for the ground is hard packed and a gentle slope right down to the river. Could we not parlay first, we asked, for perhaps some peaceful way can be discovered to acquire water, which we and our animals most urgently needed. Guns are the language the Indians understand, was the reply. Formed a cavalry skirmish, women and children told to scream and beat pots, the men to fire into the air. The party attaining the water, the men would immediately form a defense line to ward off attacking Indians. Piteous little flares, we made no glow in the darkness of their souls, these men who twisted their minds to believe they were justly defending women, children, and property against the perfidious attack of Indian invaders.

She had managed to keep her baby quiet by holding her in her arms during the wild attack, but her womb was constricted with terror. As she lay the baby on its pallet in the wagon bed, an arrow zipped through the wagon-sheet, thonked against the sideboard, and fell across the baby with a clatter that made the child shriek with fright.

Sarah grabbed a flintlock from the wagon box, came out

from under the wagon-sheet, cocked, aimed, and fired the rifle all in one motion. It was in the lull after the first volley of pistol fire from the men in the party.

Sarah saw what her bullet hit. Saw a rosette on a Koru man's chest blossom into an aureole, squirting out demitasses of blood, one, two, three, as the man fell.

She didn't faint. She was far too strong-willed for that.

She didn't stand and gaze either, though that image was to change her entire life, was to haunt her to her death.

She jumped out of the wagon. Left her crying baby and jumped out of the wagon. Ran in front of the men-folk. Put her body in front of their rifles and pistols. Screamed at them to stop. Not to shoot. She pushed one back, so that he fell and his rifle fired. The bullet whizzed past her ear. She pushed two others. Shrieked. Then collapsed with the cramps in her womb.

Six days later, in Sacramento, she wrote her mother a long narrative of the whole affair.

> I thought to lose my child in the forced trek. Each jolt of the wagon brought a scream from me. But that pain was as nothing to me, compared to the pain in my soul. I cannot get the man's blood out of my mind's eye. I see again and again, him looking down, amazed, at his life's blood spurting from his chest, until the sentience in his features dissolved and he fell. Doctor here has given me potions to sleep, and says I should not be so perturbed over 'just a savage.'
>
> Calling the Reds around us savages will not absolve us from our duty of treating them like human beings. They are human beings. They walk like we do; communicate with intelligent discourse; organize themselves in proper marriages and social institutions; and they exercise all the proprietary and occupancy rights of sovereign nations. It will be to our eternal discredit and national dishonor if

we fail to recognize their humanity. Our men make beasts of themselves when they shoot them like wolves around camp, and we are the despicable barbarians, invading for plunder.

I took to bed, ill. My milk has gone down and poor Emily is hungry and crying. I think I will lose my milk over this. Perhaps it's just as well, with Emily getting teeth and I in fifth month. This second one coming all too soon and showing signs of being a big child.

"Grandmother, how can you hate a woman whose very mother's milk sours out of compassion for another human being?"

"She was ninety, and fat, and a tyrant," says Grandmother Doe-in-the-Dawn. "And she soured my milk with my first-born. I've always thought that was why the poor thing failed."

"Be fair, Granny. That party dress you and Cia made fits a seventy pound child, not a young woman capable of bearing a child. Your being a skinny little Indian suffering from marasmus, scurvy, and I don't know what all nutritional diseases had more to do with it than Sarah Stonecrist."

"Well, perhaps they did," admits Granny.

16. Ethical Bricks

George Stonecrist's calling in life was to become an enlightened brickmaker. Sounds silly, doesn't it? He was going to make enlightened bricks! Ethical bricks! He opened a tileyard in Sacramento, taking advantage of a building boom.

Partly at Sarah's suggestion, partly because of a labor shortage, George hired Indians to mix the adobe, tend his kilns, stack the bricks; he even taught a few of them to build simple walls. His little company prospered rapidly, and his hacienda soon had a fringe of "tame" Indians around it, subsisting on the settlement by choice, as the Mission Indians in Southern California had never done.

"Economic bondage is stronger than all the guards at San Quintin," says Granny, challenging me. But I say nothing; I know she's right.

Sarah's child-bearing slowed down after its spectacular start. After Emily and Jane, in February and December 1843, came Elizabeth in 1847 and George Jr. in 1850, but George Jr. lived only eleven months. William Ellery Channing Stonecrist— Billy— was born in 1856, completing the family.

Sarah Stonecrist then turned her attention to civilizing her workers. I don't think she ever realized she was making prisoners of the Indians, even as Sutter had done. She saw herself as providing for, not exploiting, them.

During these years, Sarah's letters to her mother are full of everyday descriptions of family life, the changing city-scape, the distinguished and insane visitors that passed through on their way to the mines. Only occasionally did she turn her pen to the Indians. In 1854, she wrote her mother:

I am sorry to report they take but imperfectly to civilization, (she wrote in 1854). Juan Burock, a good man at the kiln, tells me he does not like to live in this place. As a boy, he and family roamed over whole area of the tribe. I tell him of oceans and lands across the sea, but he not interested. Prefers to live in his own country, with his own stars, he says. He thinks they have different stars in China! and he would be lost. I think his experience of place must be very small, but deep. But now, he feels trapped, for none of our local Indians dare leave our protection, for fear they will be conscripted as slaves in the mines, or shot by barbaric white men on the prowl.

A crisis in 1858 raised her ire:

My Indian girl, Maria, came to me and said the constable had taken her uncle for robbery. I rushed out to defend him, for I had guaranteed the loan with which he had bought the heifer in question. But I was too late. The constable had already hanged the poor wretch. I was furious: since when do we hang a man for suspicion of theft? Our men are so stupid; they say only, you never can tell about an Indian.

Only once, in 1861, did she ever doubt the wisdom of what she was doing:

In spite of all our nursing, the savages about us are but poor and puling. It saddens my heart when I think of how noble they once were, striding their native forests, living the unfettered life of a primitive, happy with the stars in their places. Yet that life is broken now; it has passed away; and we must work to make civilization work.

Then came Fort Sumter. Secession. And George Stonecrist mounted his horse in the spring of '62, rode three thousand miles to join the Massachusetts Regulars. Emancipation. Gettysburg Address. Then on November 14, 1864, George Stonecrist stopped a bullet in an insignificant battle in Georgia, his heart producing its rosette, aureole, demitasse of blood, and Sarah was left a well-to-do widow. The description of his death reached Sarah at about the same time as the nation was outraged by the Sand Creek Massacre of the Southern Cheyenne.

> Have wept til my eyes are like boiled eggs, my poor George gone. To give his good heart to a cause, to give his good heart for a cause, and now he has no heart. Is life worth dying for? To die in order to live is a twist of soul I do not understand.
>
> Emily and Jane are sending you daguerreotypes of their children. They are such cheery little cherubs! Oh, how I hope the world can be made decent for them to live in! Betty, as flirtatious as a courtesan, can hardly wait to get in the marriage bed. Billy, thank God, has his wits intact— he asks why men are so cruel? Why indeed?
>
> I have not been well lately. Since George's death, I have been dreaming again of the man I shot at the water hole so many years ago. His heart will not quit pumping out his blood, and I wake in a sweat. Over and over, I see in memory the humanity drain from his face. When I wasted a brother, I wasted myself.

So in 1867, with Elizabeth safely married to a not-quite-satisfactory risk, Sarah sold her brickyard, prosperous though it was, and moved to Colusa. If she were going to get rid of her nightmare, she reasoned, she would have to meet it and master it in its own territory.

She bought land four miles north and two-and-a-half

miles west of Colusa and built a substantial house on a slight rise overlooking the Koru town of Soma, on a slough where a sizeable band of "wild" Indians still survived.

She built of wood, in the "prairie crackerbox" style, two stories with a porch all the way across the front and a balcony above it. In the back, like the leg of a "T," the one-story pantry-kitchen-dining area big enough to serve a harvest crew stuck out with a screened veranda on either side.

She hired a young man to be her foreman and his wife to be her maid and cook. At age 46, Sarah Stonecrist embarked upon the career of a wheat, barley, and vegetable farmer.

It was an opportune time. Petty squabbles over land titles had kept prices down (she paid only $1.60 per acre for a section of prime, loamy land, rich in silt and organic matter, with a small amount of clay to bind it).

Also in 1867, the Oregon-California Railroad was surveyed, and serious people, like Sarah, would soon have the means of transporting their goods to paying markets.

It wasn't long before she took in two Indian girls, one about fourteen, the other about eighteen years old. "They are caught hopelessly between two worlds," she wrote her mother. She bathed them, as she said, with her own hands, dressed them decently as her own daughters, and began praying that they were not infected with canker. She noticed Billy hanging around a little too much and ordered cold baths for him.

"Ha!" says Grandmother Doe-in-the-Dawn. "It's a wonder she didn't marry him to one of them!"

"Why, he wasn't yet thirteen!"

"No matter. She would have loved that. The meddling old wench! He would have been her tithe to the world."

"Well, she never got the chance. Within two weeks, the girls had run off. Disappeared again into the tule marshes."

"Good for them!" says Grandmother Doe-in-the-Dawn.

She and I have been over this point before. We agree, it was better for the girls to run away.

What Sarah had in mind was to teach them to cook, sew, bathe, and converse with correct grammar, after which she would let them go— back to the tule marshes where they would eat roots and grubs, go naked and dirty, and speak only when spoken to.

She could not conceive that anyone who could cook and sew and speak their minds would choose not to. Could not conceive that a whole tribe would not be converted by a small example, for she assumed the inherent superiority of her form of civilization.

"Those girls knew what they were doing," says Granny. "The price of being civilized was too high to them."

"Yet, you paid that price when you came into Colusa, Granny. Why?"

"I didn't know any better, then. With both mother and that old witch working on me, and me such a young thing, I just didn't know any better."

"Ah, so many threads in the warp and woof of each of our lives."

"And she was all balled up in her own mind," says Grandmother Doe-in-the-Dawn.

"Perhaps so," I admit.

Sarah wanted desperately to believe that there was something good, inherently good and noble, in Indian life. In primitivism. All her sentimental philosophizing had told her that.

But, deep down, she had to believe that her own culture was superior. Otherwise, *she* would have been the one detribalized. In order to not hate herself and her own people, she had to believe that her kind of progress was toward something 'higher and better.'

She and her whole crowd, like George Manypenny, Helen Hunt Jackson, and a host of others, could only think in terms of their own culture. They simply demanded that Indians deny everything their soul had ever known and adopt an alien language, an alien religion, and an alien value system that would not even allow them to think of their primitive selves as human beings, much less citizens.

Sarah wanted it both ways. She wanted to perpetuate her wooden Indian as a symbol of sentimental primitivism, and she wanted Indians to live in houses, cook in tin pots, wear collars, and join a church— she was liberal enough to give them a choice of jobs and a choice of churches, but she wasn't liberal enough to leave people alone.

"She was a born meddler," says Grandmother Doe-in-the-Dawn, beginning to put things back into Sarah's trunk.

"Yet, on the whole, wasn't she kind? We can't hate her for having a good heart, can we?"

Granny is silent; so I go on:

"She was kind to individuals, wasn't she?"

"Not to the tribe."

"Ah, I begin to see what you mean. To the tribe, she was finally more destructive than those vigilante parties that went out scalp-hunting. They only massacred groups of people, from which some remnant might survive.

"But Sarah was committing cultural genocide. Sarah was breaking the cup of life itself."

17. Sarah Stonecrist's Century of Dishonor

From 1868 to 1885, Sarah conducted a stalemate war against the vigilante crowd in Colusa that simply wanted to "exterminate the brutes!" Those were the years of the Plains Indian wars, when the Sioux and Cheyenne were severely decimated. The years when the buffalo were all but exterminated. When hundreds of treaties were ignored. The attitude stretched back to before the American Revolution. It was indeed, as Helen Hunt Jackson protested, a century of dishonor.

In Colusa, Sarah Stonecrist did everything she could to frustrate this dominant American attitude toward Native Americans.

In the winter of 1871, she single-handedly saved the Koru tribe from annihilation, or at least the population of Soma. The California Ghost Dance of 1871 was reaching its highest intensity. Because of it, the Indians had been meeting in camps, to dance and sing of their ancestors returning and driving the white man out.

Rain had flooded the river, which reached its highest watermark in over twenty years on the 17th of December. The Indians on the slough just north of Sarah's house were flooded out. Sarah went to them. She understood that most of the scattered bands of Koru were there dancing and praying that all white men would vanish with the first greening of the grass. The ghosts of their ancestors danced with them at their fires. She knew she faced ritual hatred, but they were wet and cold. So she said they could stay in her barn, to get out of the weather.

They accepted. The entire remnant of the tribe was thus in one big building, dancing night after night for the destruction of that building, with a small fire in the middle and one of the loft doors opened a little for a smoke hole.

Just before dawn on December 23, Sarah saw a party of fourteen men, armed with rifles, creeping toward her barn. She was only half-dressed, but for the second time in her life she unthinkingly swept up a gun— her old single-shot, breech-loading rifle— cocked, aimed, and fired it in a single motion. Only this time, she didn't hit a man.

The bullet whizzed so near the leader's head, that he swore afterwards he might as well have been hit; it wouldn't have scared him any worse. He treated it as a joke, so that the truth he told would sound like an exaggeration.

His lieutenant had a similar story. The bullet splintered the gunstock of the third man and flash-froze the whole party. This was not in their script; they didn't know what to do next.

The Indians came boiling out of the barn, sleepy and naked, standing around, gazing in wonder. They would have made excellent targets. But not a one of them was even shot at.

The Indians were absolutely defenseless. And so was Sarah, for she did not have a reload. Her rifle was only so much weight.

Unabashed, she charged the invaders in her under-bodice and petticoats. They flushed like quail. She screamed after them: "I'll shoot the first one of you who comes back! These people are working for me, now! You leave them alone, you hear! These are *my* Indians!"

"You hear that?" says Grandmother Doe-in-the Dawn. "She was a slaver. '*My* Indians!' What did she think? That she owned them, or something?"

"I don't think you should call her a slaver. She was patronizing and stupid and a little insane, but she didn't hold them by force."

"She had a slaver's mentality. She created servility.

Wherever she went, whomever she dealt with, she created servility."

"Having a strong personality isn't exactly a crime, Granny. Ah. I begin to see what you mean. Her strong personality is what made *you* see her as a witch. With it, she controlled you, as she controlled people, as surely as if she had cast a spell on you and them. As surely as if she had hypnotized and enslaved you. And she abused that power!"

"That's just it. She was so strong, she always just assumed that others were weak. Inferior. She made them inferior by doing things for them."

"Ah so? Aggressors create their own victims? The giver's mentality and assumptions create the beggar?"

"Yes, she made beggars of everyone, by being so wise and generous and protective. She made people feel like slaves. That was hardly a favor."

"Aren't there worse things? She knew of worse things, some of which she wrote to a cousin: "In April 1871, vigilantes pursued some Indians into Deer Creek canyon, north of Chico. They finally cornered the band in a cave. The leader of the whites shot almost all of the thirty-eight Indians killed that time with his .56 calibre buffalo gun. Except that he could not bear to shoot the babies and children with his buffalo rifle. 'It tore them up too bad,' he said. So he shot them with his .38 calibre Smith and Wesson revolver.""

"Kroeber and Waterman discovered an old settler in 1916 who had a blanket made of Indian scalps. Scalps he himself had taken, without anyone ever calling him to any account. He was the worst sort of savage. Sarah wasn't a murderer."

"To die was the easy part," says Granny. "To live. That always was the hardest. To live with Sarah Stonecrist, that was the hardest of all."

"Is that why you hate her so much?"

"No. I learned to live with that part, too."

-< * >-

Mention of the vigilantes and the Indians tapered off sharply in Sarah's letters, because the time of crisis had passed. The Ghost Dance was quieting down and the vigilante crews were beginning to be affected by the moral leaders of the country.

The white exterminators were shamed into more-civilized behavior. They went back to a few night hunts for Chinamen who had escaped from the mines and hid in the undergrowth along the river, but mass hysteria no longer supported the insanity of the leaders.

Sarah's attention turned back to her farm. Billy was almost sixteen and doing a man's work. He could drive a six-mule team as well as most men, could lift and pull, with energy making up what he lacked in power.

He was also getting a little wild. Drinking when older men would give him the stuff, smoking on the sly, cursing and joking almost like a veteran.

In 1875, when Billy was nineteen, she caught him in the barn with Antoinette Marques, the 18-year-old daughter of Jacques Marques, a frontier drifter who worked for Sarah one year in the wheat. Marques and his wife were themselves looking for land to take up, so they could become farmers. When Antoinette was five months pregnant, they attended the marriage, then departed into one of the mountain valleys. Then, after two years, they moved farther on, then farther on, and were lost track of.

Antoinette's first child, a little girl, was still-born in 1878. From Sarah's letters to Jeannette, Mildred O'Shaughnessy's oldest daughter, we can reconstruct how Billy felt. He was furious. Felt he had married for nothing. He had been trapped. If the baby was going to be still-born, they might as well not have married. There was no need to marry. He fought with Antoinette, physically, passionately, sexually.

In 1880, a second child was born: George Abelhard Stonecrist, III. Antoinette never cared for the child, refused to name it or nurse it. She let Sarah, who was then 59 years old, superintend an Indian girl who nursed George, along with the girl's own half-breed infant. Antoinette scoffed and read magazines; *Police Gazette* and *Godey's* were her favorites. She kept away from Billy, and there were no more children.

In 1885, Billy was killed in a brawl, by a drunk Indian, whom Sarah refused to prosecute, because she could not find him more at fault than Billy.

Soon after, Antoinette went to Sacramento to "find work." She was an "actress" in San Francisco, for a time. As near as I can figure out, it was in a strip-tease parlor. We have one record of her being arrested for soliciting, and she was fined. She died in 1887, of venereal disease and starvation.

Antoinette was my great-grandmother, you understand. Strange, what threads run through our histories, what passions are funneled into our awareness.

When Billy was killed, Sarah was 64 and tired. Perhaps, his death broke a part of her spirit. He was not exactly what she wanted, but he was all she had. And now, she had only an infant grandson, Georgie.

She rented the farm out on shares, but continued for some years to live in the big house with Georgie. Through that last half of the 80's, she continued to pressure her tenants to hire and train Indians. She often carried a copy of Helen Hunt Jackson's *A Century of Dishonor* with her in the late 80's, remonstrating others to good works. An old woman, vibrating with moral fervor. A blind old woman who never understood the implications of her life.

The allotment policy in the Dawes Act of 1887 gave her one of her most disastrous ideas. She deeded small farms to several Indian men. That was supposed to make them— presto— responsible, integrated members of American society.

She used a great deal of her own land for her "allotments," but she also caused the whole unclaimed area of tule swamp, pond, hunting grounds, everything surrounding Soma village, to be surveyed and conveyed conditionally to Indian families as homesteads.

They hadn't the slightest idea what to do with them.

It didn't take land-hungry white men very long to discover they could acquire the titles Sarah had defined. They either got the Indian drunk, or offered him a tenth or a hundredth what the land was worth, or drove him and his family away with threats of death or actual physical violence, or promised to pay monies or services they had no intention of paying, even in the promising.

Soon, Soma village was diminished to a few fragments amid the gridded metes and bounds of progress, and the few surviving Koru were reduced to even greater poverty than before. Many of them sought refuge in the foothills or along the river bottom. Sarah had made them sand to the whirlwind.

Soon afterwards, Sarah and Georgie (he was now ten) moved to town. Sarah was 70 and getting more and more tired. She complained, "The white man's refusal to recognize root causes and real situations is a national dishonor," echoing the books she was then reading.

In 1891, she bought the wooden Indian. It was supposed to be a memorial to the dead at Wounded Knee and the man she had killed in 1843. She stood it in front of her haberdashery on a main corner in town, where she hoped that people would be reminded of the shameful situation in their midst and the nobility which their insensitivity had destroyed. Later, it was moved to Davidson's Drug Store.

Through the 90s, Sarah slowly grew heavy. She no longer had her energy, and her projects were less spectacular. She tried, for instance, to establish a trade in Indian artifacts. She got some Indians to make clay pots and baskets, which she tried to sell. No one wanted to buy, but she was willing to buy from everyone.

That's how the Blanchettes came to sell Sarah the very Hesi basket that Sioc had left with Cia in 1852.

In the new century, she complained often of bad dreams. She kept seeing the man she had shot in 1843. Maybe her guilt drove her to it, but she began to collect a small museum of her own— baskets, pots, implements made of turtle shells, arrow heads of chert, whatever she could find. She had little else to do.

"Except brainwash George," says Grandmother Doe-in-the-Dawn.

"What?"

"She spent a lot of time brainwashing George."

"What do you mean? She let him choose his own life. Helped him to set up his own dry goods store when he was ready. It seems to me she left him alone.

"Ah. I begin to see. It was no accident that a skinny little Indian girl found a sympathetic haven. Every logic would suggest that Colusa society would have met you with only ridicule, maltreatment, exploitation. But you found George.

"No. It wasn't even that accidental. George was prepared and waiting for you. There were no coincidences. The dead man of 1843, the move of 1867, the haven you found in 1908 were all knitted together. And Sarah was not heroic after all. She was petty, and personal, and guilt-ridden, like us all.

"So that's why you hated Sarah? Because she had brainwashed George. She had made him her tithe to the world and sacrificed him to you. That was her payment for the genocide that even she felt. You hated her because she gave you George!"

"No. Not that," says Grandmother Doe-in-the-Dawn. "Because George and I were happy. He had suckled an Indian breast and felt no repulsion when he touched mine. He was patient. And tolerant. And he cared for me. Not for a sick little Indian, but for me. In spite of that meddling old witch, I loved George from the beginning."

"Then you hated her for sitting in the kitchen, making you repeat the words for "stove" and "plate" and "rocking chair."

"No. Even Indians can learn to like tin pots and rocking chairs."

"Then, what? What made you hate her so much?"

"I don't hate her. Not any more. But I can see that you do. Why do *you* hate her?"

"I don't," I insist. "I don't hate her."

"I can see it in you. Why do you hate her?"

I hope this doesn't sound glib: "For that wooden Indian that stood so many years in front of Davidson's Drug Store, blocking the crossroads of the mind for another century of dishonor."

18. All the Same as Coyote

Grandmother Doe-in-the-Dawn is furious with me. She has kicked me out. Won't let me in the house. She says she can't stand the sight of me. I remind her too much of her loss.

It's okay. I don't mind. In the old days, I might have been primitive and mad about it. But now, I don't mind. This stuck in my mind from Aldous Huxley's *Brave New World:* "One of the functions of a friend is to suffer, in symbolic form, the outrage and injury we would like, but are unable, to inflict upon our enemies."

It reminds me of a story that Old Bill Drannan told in his *Thirty-One Years on the Plains and in the Mountains:*

> We looked off to our right and saw a large herd of horses, driven by seven Ute Indians, who were pushing them at the greatest possible speed. We urged our horses in the direction of camp as fast as possible. As soon as we were in sight of camp, we gave the alarm and every man sprang to his gun, mounted his horse, and was ready to receive them. The Indians did not see us until they had run the herd of horses almost into our camp. Our saddle horses being fresh, we succeeded in killing the seven Indians before they got far away, and captured the herd of horses, which proved to be a herd they had stolen from the Arapahoe Indians the night before, and in less than an hour, Gray Eagle, the Arapahoe chief, came along in pursuit, accompanied by fifty of his select warriors. When Uncle Kit [Carson] showed him the dead Utes, he walked up to one of them, gave him a kick, and

said: "Lo mis-mo Cay-o-te," which means, "All the same as Coyote."

So I'm Granny's coyote, just now. I understand, so I've cut out. I've taken my camper and come here to the Colus Rancheria to camp.

Oooooooo, the night air is thick, and cold with fog, even if it is only September. If I didn't have the VW to sleep in, I don't know whether I'd make it or not, I'm such a civilized tenderfoot. I just get in the van, crack a window at the side and the one at the back, and fire up my Coleman lantern. That way I get light to read, and it warms the place up like toast pretty quickly. I open all the doors to ventilate, just before going to bed.

I haven't tried to talk to anyone yet. I just go down to the river with my pole, catch a few fish, come back, and cook them in mud in the coals of my little fire. That's the way the Koru did it. In his *History of Colusa*, Will Green tells us that was the menu of the first dinner that Sioc invited him to. Perch baked in mud. I found some wild onions today and put them inside. Delicious.

Now, if I only had some butter, some french fries, some asparagus or broccoli, a bit of good *vin blanc* . . . . Well, that's pretty un-Indian, isn't it? Still, why shouldn't Indians want good food? Good food is a part of the health of the world, isn't it?

I've got my books. The people now who are closest to the old world are the books. They often know more about the old days than living people do. How else, but through books, can we today know about how the whites got the Narragansetts to turn on the Pequots, or about Cooper's (maybe fictional) Mingoes and Mohicans and Hurons and Delawares.

How else can even an Indian find out some things? The old people couldn't write. So the closest thing we have to their own voices are the anthropological monographs by people like professors Kroeber and Barrett, who 70 and 80 years ago went into the bushes with their notebooks and primitive phonograph recorders and begged old Indians to talk.

They put down everything they heard, as nearly as they heard it, not trying to sift and analyze the data then. Just trying to get it down, because they thought their source was about to disappear. Even old Indians can't live forever.

Therein lies one of the contemporary Indian's dilemmas, as I see it. As he comes to know and understand more, as inevitably he must, he's going to be able to act less and less in primitive and instinctual ways. I'm not sure the traditionalists among us are going to like that. Books do that to you. Knowledge does that to you.

One of the things I hear speaking through those old pages is the vicious hatred the Indians felt for other Indians, just after they had been dispossessed. Maybe it was *because* they had been dispossessed and largely detribalized. "All the same as Coyote."

-< * >-

I caught more fish than I should have today. A big one after a couple of smaller ones. I really should have stopped with the two smaller ones, but I thought I had more hunger than two small fish would fill. Then I hooked this seventeen incher.

As I came up from the river, the old man with the black, stiff-brimmed hat was sitting on his apple box under his elm tree. I walked up, told him I had caught more fish than I could use, and offered the big one to him.

At first, he just nodded, almost imperceptibly. Can you imagine a picture of Wovoka, the Indian Messiah, nodding? It was kind of like that. A piece of a stone mountain tipping ever so slightly, wavering in the wind, then returning to its stasis.

He took the fish and seemed absorbed in looking at it. Read every scale on it. I didn't have anything more to say, so I backed up a couple of steps, then turned to go on toward my VW.

Behind my back, I heard him say, "Willy willock." It wasn't

soft, or muttered, but called out. I turned to look. He was smiling.

"*Wile wilak*," I answered and went on.

I heard him calling some of the women in his house, "Jenny, Jeanine!" I suppose he was going to give them the fish to cook.

This evening, he came and tapped on my VW window, not long after I had fired up my lantern. He had a piece of apple pie for me. I thanked him. Invited him in. Offered him some of those little pillow-shaped peppermints. He took a couple and sucked them with delight, while I ate my pie.

"You read a lot?" he asked.

"Yes," I admit. "That's my way of finding things out."

"I can't read much," he said.

So, without prelude or plan, I pick up a book and start reading to him a Patwin war story I studied not too many days ago. I've been pre-occupied with war lately.

> One time the Koru people went to Kusa and Sawa, two tule lakes west of Colusa, to gather grass seeds and catch some of the large perch that grew in the lakes.
>
> The Koru claimed these lakes and were angry when Saka people from down the river to the south came there to fish and let their women gather seeds. The Koru had already caught many fish when the people of Saka arrived. The Koru invited the southerners to take some of the fish and cook for themselves.
>
> After a while, a man from Saka heard one Koru say to another, "Can you shoot that crow in the tree?" Then the man from Saka thought, now the fight will begin.
>
> The second Koru said he thought he could shoot the crow. He shot one arrow at the bird, but missed. He took another arrow and shot again, but this time he aimed at a man from Saka. With that,

the one-sided fight was on.

The man from Saka was shot in the breast, but the arrow did not penetrate to the heart. He made for the water, dove, and hid under the willows, with only his mouth above water. He drew the arrow out and waited and listened.

Many of the Saka men were killed. Only a few escaped. When the Koru came back from chasing the men, the man from Saka who was hiding in the water heard them talking about him.

"We should find him and finish him," said one man.

"There is no need," said the man who had shot him. "I hit him in the heart. He is surely dead."

"What shall we do with these Saka women?" said another man, changing the subject.

"Let them go home," said one man.

"No," said another. "They will tell what happened."

"The men who escaped will tell that," said another.

"We should kill them."

"No. They are just women."

"Yes. They are just women. Let them go home."

"Yaiii," said the man who started the fight. "Let them go home, and they will breed more enemies."

"Yes," agreed some of the men "they will breed more enemies."

"Kill them."

"Kill them."

"Kill the breeders of enemies."

So the Koru men slaughtered all the Saka women, except one tall woman who outran the pursuing men and got home. Then there was wailing all through Saka, and the babies died for lack of milk.

Waikau and Hokum, the war leaders of the

Saka, were angry. They assembled the people in the dance house and told them all to bring arrows for hunting ducks in Kusa and Sawa. Then instead of going across the plains to the lakes, they went up the river. They found the Koru men fishing in one place and the women seed-gathering in another, below Kukui. They surrounded and killed all the women. Only one was spared to carry the news home.

Waikau said to her. "Tell them my name. I did it. I am Waikau. Tell them his name, also. He helped me. He is Hokum. Tell them we did it. We have made the counting of the dead even."

And Hokum said. "Yes. Tell them we did it. Hokum and Waikau did it. Tell them also, if they want to fight some more, they should come to Saka. We will fight them some more."

The old man just sits and stares. "Waikau?" he asks.

"Yes. The books say that Waikau and Hokum were not chiefs, but prominent fighting men of Saka. They also led the attack at a later time when the Cortina people were massacred at Pokmaton, a lake on Sycamore Slough near Grimes. The Cortina people had come there to meet the river people and fish.

"Waikau and Hokum sent a few men ahead, who reported that they had been spoken to unkindly. Waikau and Hokum waited with most of their men until all of the Cortina men, except their chief, were in the water. Then they surrounded them and killed most of them in the lake, like ducks.

"A few got out and ran away. Two Cortina brothers escaped because Hokum, who was leading the pursuit, had no more arrows. He ran alongside the lagging brother and called to him: 'Tell them my name is Hokum. I did it. Tell them we want to get more of you. We want to fight again. Tell them also his name is Waikau. He is with me.'"

The old man just gives me that sphinx nod of his when I

finish. He's not uninterested. I can see in his eyes that he's working me over, trying to figure me out. Not that his eyes are moving around a lot. It's just that they are so damned observant.

He wheezes a little, with his hands on his knees to sort of prop up his body. At last, he sighs, grunts, says, "I never heard about that one before."

Then he gets up and leaves. Just like that. Abruptly.

I'm curious— awfully curious— about that psychological transform that turns a man against his own culture and makes him hate his own kind. An Indian held Crazy Horse while an Indian guard bayoneted him at Fort Robinson. Indian police killed Sitting Bull. Indian scouts led the cavalry to Geronimo. Were the most vicious of slave drivers Negroes?

-< * >-

The old man in the black hat tells me his name is Bill Odock.

A magic name to me. Right away, I ask him, "Are you related to the Tom Odock who was the principal chief of the Colus Rancheria until his death in 1916."

Bill is hesitant at first. He rubs his nose, looks the other way. "How d'you know about Tom Odock?"

"Tom was the man who helped professors Barrett and Kroeber in 1906 and 1908 when they were recording and translating the Koru songs and the Hesi ceremonies that are now in the archeological archives at the University of California. He's the one who taught me, indirectly, what I know about the Koru language."

It turns out, yes, they were related, but Bill isn't sure just how. In those days, every adult male was an elder uncle. He remembers Tom as an old man, full of love for everyone, tolerant even to the children.

Bill knows who Doe-in-the-Dawn is, but doesn't remember her personally. He does remember Cia, though. I'm surprised to hear that, but he goes on to tell me that Cia lived until 1934. We had always assumed that she died in 1908, soon after sending Dawn into town, but Bill is quite certain about it.

Cia lived until 1934. She was blind from cataracts in her old age, as so many poverty-stricken Indians were. Are. She was adamant about refusing to speak English, although hardly anyone could speak Koru with her.

Bill remembers that she hid when the professors were here with their phonograph recorder. Not in the bushes. In the open. In the language. She simply refused to recognize that they were there. Refused to understand them, refused to speak to them. No question, she knew as much as anybody at that time, about the songs and traditions of the people, but she would not sing for Kroeber and Barrett.

"I was afraid of that old woman," says Bill.

"Why? What did she do to scare you?"

"Walked around, yelling and preaching in a language nobody could understand."

"Latin?"

"I dunno. Uncle Tom said she had a good education. Could talk English without any accent even. But I never heard her speak it. Don't know anyone who did, either. She was crazy, that old woman was."

I try to pump him for more information, but it turns out he has something else on his mind: "That story you told about the waikau. Is it true?"

"Well, I guess so. Somebody in Tom Odock's time told it to Kroeber."

"Read it again."

So I do. I add a little tidbit I've gleaned from another book: that Waikau once wanted to lead an attack on Hok, as the Indians called Sutter's Fort in Sacramento.

Bill seems interested. Those little stone-like nods. Absorbed. So I read to him about the Poné people who lived near Sites, in the foothills west of the river.

Once, when the Poné people had been hunting
in the plains and had set fire to the grass to protect

themselves from the mosquitos, the river Koru people from about Waitere saw the smoke, gathered their men, and came up to the hills. The Poné people had returned and had gone to the house of an under-chief to smoke and drink; he had mountain lion and bear skins to sit on. There they sat up until about midnight, then lay down to sleep.

With the first daylight, the attack came. The river people threw bundles of burning chamiso brush in the door and smoke hole and into the other houses also. Some of the Poné people succeeded in crawling out with their bows and arrows without being seen, by help of the smoke. When they got farther away from the blaze, the river people saw them and began to shoot at them. The river people called out: "Where are your brave men? Bring them out; don't hide them. We came to fight."

"Was that a waikau? Sitting on the bear rug?" asks Bill.

"No. Wrong tribe. These were Poné. Waikau was a Saka."

No response. He looks like Wovoka again. Enigmatic. Like he knows a lot more than he's saying. I'm about to ask him does he know any more about Waikau, did he ever hear about the man? But then an idea strikes me.

He asked, was that *a* waikau; he used the word as a general noun. I've been on the wrong tack.

"What does 'waikau' mean?" I ask.

"Crazy," he says, before he quite realizes he's said it. He looks at me and nods. "It was a kind of crazy. In the old days. I never knew anyone who went *waikau*. But when I was a little boy, I used to hear stories about it."

He acts embarrassed. Rubs his nose and refuses to look at me directly.

Ah, I understand; something I had forgotten. Ceremonial madness. I must have known the word once, for Cia surely went waikau.

A man or woman would dance until they went crazy—waikau. Kroeber interviewed people who said waikaus could run on top of the water. They'd run through the willows and sloughs. They'd scream and jump around like spirits. Sometimes, they'd come back after three or four days, and they'd have live snakes or ducks in their hands. They'd caught them while they were crazy.

"They were spirits," Bill goes on. "There was a time when men with strong medicine could transform themselves into spirits in the dance. They would dance and one of the great spirits, like Tsukui, the Grizzly Bear, would come and live in their body for a while."

I wait. He wants to say more.

"There was supposed to be a time when all the Spirits would return and live with the people. They were going to drive out the white men and give the world back to the Indians. It never happened."

I can't quite tell whether he's talking about the first Ghost Dance, the California Ghost Dance of 1871, or the one twenty years later, the big Ghost Dance that swept Indian country and resulted in the killing of Sitting Bull and the massacre at Wounded Knee.

Professor Kroeber thinks the first Ghost Dance caught on in California but not in the Plains, in 1871, because the California Indians had been more thoroughly dispossessed, detribalized, demoralized than the Plains Indians. After all, the combined Plains tribes decisively won their battle at Little Big Horn in 1876.

"Some men," says Bill, "would dress in grizzly bear rugs and go *waikau*. I never saw any. But I heard about some when I was a little boy. People always said it was a long time ago. They had a secret society, the Tsukui society. I remember one old man telling about himself. He put on a grizzly bear rug and laced the arms and chest up like a shirt. Then he attacked men on the path."

He glances at me, as if wondering how much he should

tell.

"One time this man said he caught two men on a slough, while they were fishing for perch. He jumped them and made sounds like a grizzly. He killed one of them right quick. Then he was cutting the other one, when he recognized him. It was his brother."

Bill pauses a moment. I wait, trying to be patient, not wanting to divert him from the story he wants to tell.

"He would have killed him if it hadn't been his brother. He dropped him and ran off, like a grizzly bear sometimes would. Lots of people in the old days, not just those that were in the Tsukui society, either, would kill their own relatives.

"Sometimes, too, a man would stab his own legs until he couldn't walk, and then say that a *waikau* had caught him.

"Some people would poison others, just because they had a grudge against them, or had been spoken to unkindly."

"All the same as coyote," I say, but Bill does not catch my meaning.

-< * >-

"Grandmother! Grandmother Doe-in-the-Dawn! I'm back!"

I yell, "I've discovered how Tseret died. He was murdered, just when he was beginning to get the tribe together again. Poisoned by another Indian."

Dawn is upstairs, working on another embroidery. "Indians have been killing each other from the beginning."

" Yes, and feeding the remains to coyotes. We've got to stop that."

I pull up a chair and sit.

"That's how Tseret was killed. About 1871 or 72, he led a hunting party to Onolai. Insisted on all the right things: you know, offering the first blood of the kill to the Spirits of the four directions. 'Forgive me, Brother Deer; for this is the way of living. Forgive me, Mother Earth; for this is the way of Nature.'

"They had killed several deer and had the meat drying. The women had found a good number of acorns and stored them in caches. They were going to be able to feed the people for another year. But not all of the party liked the old ways. Or maybe they were jealous of Tseret for being so effective in getting the tribe back together."

I stand up and act out this part: "Anyway, one afternoon while they were resting, a 'witch,' probably a discredited medicine man, slipped up and dropped something into Tseret's mouth, then kicked him so he would swallow the poison.

"Tseret coughed, trying to get the poison out of his throat, but it went on down into his stomach. He must have thought it was only a bug that flew into his mouth. In his sleepiness, he did not suspect any of the sleepers of a trick.

"In a week, Tseret was dead, and the hunting trip had disintegrated. Much of the food was left for the squirrels and buzzards at the base camp.

"And coyotes. The coyotes got a lot."

Dawn says, "All the same as Coyote."

19. Woman-Without-Basket

I have pieced together the turn of mind that came next: Cia's perceptions that caused her to send Doe-in-the-Dawn back into Colusa, to assimilate and acculturate, came to a head right after the San Francisco earthquake, April 18, 1906, and the Hesi dance at a village called Let in the Cortina Valley, May 5-8, 1906.

"We felt the earth jerk and jump where we were," says Dawn. "Some of our huts fell down, and it knocked down old people and babies. About three miles south of Let, it toppled a mountain off into a canyon on Cache Creek and backed the water up all the way to Clear Lake itself. After about four days, that dam broke and flooded everything below it, just three days before the Hesi.

"And the smoke. We could see the smoke, as high up as we could bend our necks. It looked like a distant piece of earth, turned up on end. And at night, the sky was red.

"We thought it was the end of the world. We thought it was the judgment day."

-< * >-

The oldest and wisest dreamer of the Cortina people, Sasa, went into a trance a few days after the quake and, in a dream vision, visited with Katit the Red-tailed Hawk. Not with Grandmother Turtle. Not with Old Man Coyote. With only one of the three forces of creation. The Red-tailed Hawk.

His dream told him to invite all the world to a Hesi. Everyone was to be saved. The Indians. The Chinese. The white people. All. All were to be invited to the dance. In addition to the River and Hill Patwin, there were people from the Pomo Tribe, some from the Maidu; all of the tribes wanted to be there.

And there was Professor S. A. Barrett, the anthropologist from the University of California, cranking a spring-driven phonograph, recording on primitive records and on paper as much as he could of what went on at that Hesi. Those records and a few photos are still in the archives at Berkeley. And there are bilingual transcriptions of Sasa's sermon.

The dance itself appalled Cia.

For his invitation ceremonies, the visual prayer, Sasa did not have a basket of the nation, to stand the leg-bone of a hawk in. He had an old tin can, jagged at its opening and crusted inside with rust and dried beans. Was this the universe he invited the spirit of our creativity to enter?

His skirt was not the beautiful feather-embroidered skirt of tradition, but a raveling burlap with colored strips of cloth and string tied to it. Was this the illusion we were supposed to believe?

His message, his sermon, was most repellent of all. Differences would dissolve miraculously, if we would only believe. There would be a return of all spirits past, and a world sufficient for all to live. It was an echo of Ghost Dance dogma.

Cia knew too much of Greek and Christian mythology, too much of western history, too much of the mental habits of the white man to be taken in by anything so easy. To her, his dream was fatuous.

Knowledge does that kind of thing to you: it makes it impossible to retreat from complexity into simplicity; it makes it impossible to accept religious solutions to practical problems.

"She left the ceremony in a terrible depression," says Grandmother Doe-in-the-Dawn, running her fingers along the arms of her chair, lost in old thoughts. "Right after that, we moved to a house. Not really a house. A shack. But it had a stove in it where we cooked in tin pots. It had a bed in it, on which we slept between sheets. It had a table in it, where we ate with forks and knives on old plates. Mother set about trying to retrain me. She was training me to be a white person.

"She taught me how to wear shoes and dresses.

"She taught me how to sit at table and serve the food.

"She tried to teach me to speak English, but she had been so strongly against it that she was a poor teacher and I was a very poor and reluctant student.

"For two years, she prepared me to enter the white world.

"People used to come to our house, Indian people, to ask her advice or opinion on all sorts of problems. Usually, they brought gifts: food, utensils, things like that. She never asked them for anything; they just brought them. And she listened to their problems, because they were people who were disturbed, because they were people who needed to talk.

"She never had any solutions. Sometimes, she would quote them a Latin proverb, or tell them a story of a Greek god or Saxon invader which their problem called up in her mind. She always touched their hands and said she was sorry, and they went away thinking she had told them something of value.

"My re-education was not complete by any means when Mother started having nightmares. She dreamed I was poisoning her.

"Or she would wake from thrashing in the bed and say that I had been biting her throat. In her waking moments, she knew better. But she couldn't quit dreaming that I was a demon.

"When she got sick, she wouldn't let me take care of her. In her fever, she thought I had brought the sickness on by poisoning her; so she would eat nothing that I cooked, nor take any medicine that I brought.

"One day, her mind was clear. She called me to her, and we had our last talk. She was mad, she said, and she knew it. She was coming to hate me, whom she loved more than anything else in the world, and she couldn't help it.

"We had talked of little else for the past two years than my entering the white world; now was the time to break. She dressed me in that white party dress with tiers and tiers of ruffles and sent me walking toward Colusa.

"Woman-Without-Basket, who had been mother, father, culture, universe to me— for I had known almost nothing else in my entire life— gave me her Latin journals and a letter of introduction, and sent me walking away, with instructions never to return; to start a new life.

"She had told me to give the letter to Mrs. Stonecrist. Sarah saved it and gave it back to me before she died."

My Dear Mrs. Stonecrist,

As you have shown compassion for individuals, I commend unto your mercy my only daughter, whose name translates as Doe-in-the-Dawn. She is also the daughter of P. B. Blanchette, once of Colusa.

She is the granddaughter of a Koru king, a product of a once-proud civilization that is no more. It has passed away. Please help my child, who is fair, to adopt the ways of the whites. Please help her to find happiness and satisfaction where her wants are realistic.

Because I was always aware that I was an Indian, I was never happy among your people. I journeyed long among you, so long that I could never be just an Indian again. After such a journey, what return is possible? So do not teach my Dawn to be Indian. Teach her to be white.

I am sick as I write this— and sad. But I see no future for Indian culture. What people of Indian blood survive are doomed to the fate of modern Greeks and Italians— to be the remnants of a dead civilization that is perceived only dimly in museums and old legends, themselves speaking a new language, living a new life, holding new values. Perhaps this is the inexorable march of progress. I know not. But I would commend my daughter to "the glory that was Greece and the grandeur that was Rome."

I can offer you nothing for this service, except the thought that compassion, if given freely, is its own reward.

Unto my death, which is imminent, I remain your   Woman-Without-Basket

Dawn goes on: "I have often thought since, that she was faking that illness, so she could drive me away."

"She may have been faking it then," I say, "but it was real enough later on. From what I learned at the Colus Rancheria, I'd say she grew progressively paranoid in her later life. And withdrawn, depressed, alienated. She had a hysterical fear about light, even after she went blind. The people still came to her for advice. She was their mad mother confessor and their *waikau ma-in,* though she spoke less and less Koru as time passed.

"People left her food, and she ate it, until she thought they, too, were poisoning her. After she went blind, she simply discovered food before her and ate it, until she became convinced that she was trying to poison herself. In 1934, she disappeared into the willows where you were born. Later, the people found that her bones had been scattered by coyotes."

"*Lu-mas.*"

Yes, she is dead. And I shout her name, CIA! CIA! CIA! to call up the evil that caused her death. Listen, you Daughters of American Rapists, Coyote has caught her. She roams the western plain. Cia, Woman-Without-Basket, is coming to haunt you.

As you walk along your streets or lie warm in your beds, you think you are safe, but she lurks in your conscience, ready to pounce.

You may think the dark about you is empty, but it is filled with your crimes.

You may think the silence about you is empty, but it is

filled with the anguished cries of vanquished nations.

Dead, did I say? She is not dead.

Her psyche, her genius, were the invisible gifts of the universe, the most precious of treasures. People came to her again and again and ripped from her what they wanted. Everyone recognized that. Otherwise, they would not have wanted to rob and ravish our Woman-Without-Basket.

20. Live, Little Rabbit

Lately, I have been troubled greatly by dreams. Awake, asleep. My own, other people's. It is my way of flagellating myself; my mind's way of scarifying my soul with a raw flint.

"That's what you get for copping out," says Grandmother Doe-in-the Dawn.

But I didn't cop out, Granny. My mind is still fighting.

"*Niathuau Ahakanith! Niathuau Ahakanith!* The Whites are crazy! The Whites are crazy!" sings the Sitting Bull in me.

The Indian is "a creature possessing human form," says the Custer in me.

"We do not want to be absorbed by a sick society," screams the Wallace Mad Bear Anderson in me.

"If the way of the Indian is to survive, it will have to use the ideas and techniques of contemporary politics," reasons the Clyde Warrior in me.

"If the world is to survive, we must treat the earth so as to provide for the seventh generation of our descendants," asserts the Earth Warrior in me.

My sympathies are split into a thousand shards by monomaniacal simplicity and juvenile overcompensation.

Then Mel Thom comes in to heal the split: "The enemy is [not the white man as such, but] the poisons of the dominant society. . . . These poisons are greed, abuse of power, distrust, and no respect for people who are a little different."

These and other things run through my mind. Awake. Asleep. I'm not surprised that conferences to enunciate one fiery purpose for the Indian Movement dissolve in shambles, so much tangle on the cutting room floor.

-< * >-

That's why I'm here, on Onolai, the sacred mountain of my Koru ancestors. Hoping that meditation, sensory deprivation, solitude will generate some peace in my blank mind. With a pouch of homemade pemmican; on my way to a vigil with my blanket.

It's Grandmother Doe-in-the-Dawn's idea, of course. She thinks a dream vision would transform me into a warrior for Red Power.

I can't help but feel a little foolish. Actively seeking a dream vision!

Through fasting and introspection, I'll try to make my psyche cough up— What? A vision to live by? A theory of the universe? A code of behavior that will include the earth, water, fire, and sky? Sounds foolish and pompous, even to me.

All afternoon, I have worked my way upward, without a specific goal. The young Crazy Horse knew he had to go to a particular rock for his vigil, but I don't. I have only a vague sense of climbing.

I cross ridges on game trails and climb gullies in old washes. I pick up sticks and toss them at tufts of grass, wondering if I'll scare out a rabbit. I look for elder bushes, remembering that Red-tailed Hawk and Old Man Coyote created men on these slopes from elder sticks.

Or was that a misunderstanding of the white man who wrote that myth down? Maybe the Indians said oak sticks, or manzanita sticks, and the interpreter misunderstood.

The myth had the geology pretty wrong. This mountain is the cosmic mud that Grandmother Turtle scratched up from the floor of the primal sea, but most of the rocks here are volcanic. Not anything that I'd want caught under my fingernails! I've seen some chert, good enough sometimes to make an arrowhead of. But not much mud. Not much sediment to make the wide earth's expanding corners of.

I stop to rest and crawl in under a short oak, next to a manzanita. I pull off my boots to let my feet cool. Lie back with my neck on my blanket roll, to take the weight off my bones.

I'm not much of an Indian. Can't stand the work, probably will whimper with the heat and cold, cry with the hunger that I plan to endure. The breeze moves the leaves of the oak, and they whisper.

I fancy I hear the sound of my ancestors striding along mountain paths. Which is both an idle fancy and a viable metaphor. The fancy does no harm, and the metaphor, if it expresses an inner truth, may be of great service to the psyche.

A sense of belonging. I suppose that's what Grandmother Doe-in-the-Dawn wants me to discover up here. She says I've been whitewashed too much by my urban background.

Ha! I protested. What about her? For sixty years, there hasn't been much sign of Indianness in her. Embroidering daisies on dish towels! For sixty years! Talk about whitewash!

But it was there, she says. In her blood. In her cells.

I was unable to respond to her, because I was of two minds. One said, Ah, yes. Collective Unconscious, that universal faculty of the mind that shows my dreams are brothers to all men's dreams. My other mind said, If you claim that is Indianness, if you claim this memory is peculiar to Indians, then you are as bigoted as the rednecks that killed our ancestors.

But I couldn't say those things. Instead, I said something like: So, you think my tithe of blood-and-cell memory is so diluted that I can't get my head on straight, eh?

That was precisely it. So here I am. To immerse myself in loneliness and introspection. She would like nothing better than for me to return to her and say: "I talked in a dream with Katit, our father." And if I came up with a chant like:

> Upright I walk.
> In wholeness I walk.
> Upright I walk to meet the future
> Under the Dawn Star,

she would be ecstatic. Because my white-man education taught me the principles of versification in Indian poetry, I can spit those chants out, almost without thinking.

-< * >-

I must have dozed a few minutes, for I awake aware of the earth. The afternoon sunlight strikes the rising slope almost squarely, casting misshapen little shadows under the trees and bushes. I put on my boots, get my blanket, and move out, climbing upward along a kind of clearing.

A small noise; a rabbit, hopping along, slowly, peacefully. He goes into a tangled dead-fall of manzanita that has sprawled over a rocky mound. A fine protected place for a warren. The gray, powdery branches arching over the mound even look a little like a hogan, or a dance house.

Quickened, I creep over to look. Through the web of branches, I see a little trail, a few droppings. There he is! I even see the rabbit, himself. Secure on his couch, ignoring me, huddled for a little nap of his own. I'll bet I could touch him with a stick, and he wouldn't move.

I look around for a reasonably straight stick to slide in his hole and twist into his fur. Then I can pull him out and kill him. Cook him. Have some real supper. But before I find a stick, I stop to think: Is that an Indian trick? Or redneck, pioneer trick? I can't remember now where I heard of it. If it's redneck, I'll skip it.

Maybe I could set a snare. Like my grandfathers did on this mountain. I look around, as if expecting to find a snare—ready also with instructions for using it. I neither have anything to make a snare of, nor know how to set one. I'm not much of an Indian.

I'll wait here at his hole, with a raised stick. And when he comes out, I'll whap him. I'll make it a ritual. I'll sprinkle his blood in the four directions: Forgive me, Mother Earth, for this is the way of nature. And I'll cook him over an open fire, aware of the bounty, aware that my soul as well as my belly is hungry, aware that the rabbit feeds both.

I find a good stick and brace my feet for a long, still wait.

To my left, a passage between the trees goes up the slope and across the ridge. It's not a game trail, by any means; nor is it a path made by Indians—

"Along paths made by Indians. . . ." That's how Will Green described his invasion of the Koru's river paradise. His imagined voice echoes in me.

As does Chief Seattle's, so like my own grandfather Sioc's that I confuse the two:

> When the last red man shall have perished from the earth and his memory among the white men shall have become a myth, these shores shall swarm with the invisible dead of my tribe. . . . At night, when the streets of your cities and villages shall be silent, and you think them deserted, they will throng with the returning hosts that once filled and still love this beautiful land.

I decide not to hit the rabbit. Presuming even that I was clever enough to do it.

Instead, I move uphill along the passage that opens before me. The line of manzanita does not quite grow up to a line of oaks. It leaves a sort of avenue in the low-slanting sunlight where the grass grows, not taller and sweeter, but shorter, sparsely. Here the animals may move, the wind and sun may pass. How right it seems. How right that I should be here.

This mountain is not mine. I own none of it. Have never climbed its slopes before. Yet, I feel like an owner, inspecting familiar holdings. Like a wolf, well within the round corners of my personal territory.

These oaks are mine.

These rocks are mine.

These hunting grounds are mine, for my ancestors gave them to me, as they gave them to you, to all of us.

To sustain us. To nurture us.

I fancy acorn-gathering families at their work. Deer hunters. Arrow makers. Each person doing his part, for himself, for me. Each one giving back to the earth, to the gods, a part of what the earth has given them.

The earth shimmers beneath me, quivers with power. I fancy I smell its fertility, feel its presence in my hands.

At every turn, I more than half expect to come upon some small group of people— arrow makers flaking chert, perhaps, or hunters gathered around a freshly fallen deer, shaking drops of blood on the forgiving earth.

A group of holes in granite boulders in a grove of old oaks does not surprise me. They are metates, where the women smashed acorns with a round post. Soggy, decayed leaves are in the holes now, but the chatter of the women seems to survive in the leaves of the trees.

All this déjà vu I do not take as evidence of my blood and cell memory. To do so would be credulous. Anyone who has studied as much about Koru as I have; anyone who has wondered a lot about this mountain, as I have; anyone who has invested his own loving energy in a piece of earth is sure to react to it with deep and powerful emotion.

The earth is not a mother, but a mirror.

Any piece of earth where I have beamed forth my mind will reflect back my passion. (It is an accident that I am on Onolai, not Paha Sapa, or Navajo Mountain.) It is the same for you: wherever you plant your heart, there your roots will grow.

The value and validity of the emotion is that it comes from inside us, not from anything mystic or magic about a physical place. Deep inside, in some dark and secret place, a silent ape crouches in us all and hungers. He hungers to be known. He hungers to belong to the known. He hungers to stand before the elements of the universe, before the Mother Earth herself, and give a creditable account of himself. SEE ME!

ME!

I AM!

And in the being, to become.

To transform from ape, to bear, to man, to prince, to—what? Not god, but something god-like. To something valid and valued in the inner-most secret caverns of our souls.

If I pour passion on the earth and hunger then for passion, the earth feeds it back to me. Nurtures me. But it is myself feeds myself.

Myself.

Nurtures.

Myself.

Most of the tribes fostered a strong sense of place in their people, a sense of what was appropriate, fitting, fair. And most places gave the individual a way to be. A way to belong. Ah, yes. We ate the health of the earth in those days. We must learn to eat it again.

I have made this mountain my abode. Here the stars are sure to be in their places. Here I will feel the emotions that will nourish me when I am hungry.

To put down roots. That's what I mean. In this sense, roots are not something one grows from, but something one puts down. Creates. If you are born amid the wealthiest traditions, but do not invest them with yourself, you will not grow from them. You cannot. Roots are an act of mind and soul.

The white tribe did not value roots, except possibly in isolated families. The pioneer mind was too much caught up in the grids of ownership and property, to notice that it might have inner needs that hungered. The white's psyche was moving too fast to be encumbered with roots.

Instead, his traditions were the poisons that Mel Thom named: "greed, abuse of power, distrust, and no respect for people who are a little different." These he has poured upon the earth, and it has reflected them back.

Do not mistake me: the Indian mind has no monopoly on roots. I'm talking about a human trait, not an Indian one. The Indian was not a paragon of virtues. Maybe it's natural to kill rabbits for fun— and rationalize the hunger afterwards.

One of the worst wars the Koru ever knew started as an

aggressive ruse— as arrow practice: "Can you shoot that crow in the tree?" asked one Koru of another, knowing the arrow would find a Saka man.

And didn't Plains Indians sometimes run whole herds of buffalos over the cliffs, to hear them bellow, when a few would have served their needs?

Documents show that the Iroquois traded the Dutch 30,000 beaver and otter skins in a single year, 1633, for guns, knives, strouds, and rum, and thus created an ecological catastrophe: a beaver desert. An Iroquois sachem told Governor Dongan of New York: "We war with the far nations of Indians, because they kill our people and take them prisoners when we go a beaver hunting."

There's at least a little greed, abuse of power, distrust, and lack of respect in such things.

I have read somewhere that, around 1934 or so, the CCC built a buffalo park in a canyon north of Allen, South Dakota. Then old men would come from miles and miles away, to stand silently for hours. Perfectly still. Staring at the buffalo. Some of them, after long hours, would suddenly raise their voices and sing a song to the air above the buffalo. Then they would turn and go away with tears in their eyes.

I don't want to claim a feeling as brave as that, but maybe I have a child's version of it.

Live, Little Rabbit, in your hogan, as I live in mine. This place is your place, too.

Your place shimmers around us, through us. We feel its quivering, aware of our roots, aware of our presence. Aware that there is nothing mystic about the way we nurture ourselves, about the way we give of ourselves to the earth, that we may be nourished.

In the failing light, I take from my beaded pouch the portion of the pemmican that I have allowed myself today and sit on a rock, looking west, to eat. It is good to eat. Eating today is an aesthetic act for me. I tingle as I taste the food, shiver with its goodness.

I take a little of my water. It is a communion. That I know

it is a communion, that I am aware it is an elemental health I drink does not weaken its goodness.

Red-Twilight-Sky-Boy is ending the day with a perfectly extraordinary sunset. What tribe is he from? I can't remember. No matter. I'm supposed to show him something white to ensure my good fortune. I have nothing but myself, eighty-eight percent of myself, that is white.

I remember the prayer chant that goes with the offering of myself.

  O, Red-Twilight-Sky-Boy,
 Make for me a cup.
Reach down from the sky to the water,
Reach down from the sky to the earth,
Reach down from the sky to the fire's ash,
Reach down from the sky to my breath;
Mix them all smoothly.
Mix them all to a fine clay.
Mix them all to fine clay coils;
Then roll for me a cup.

Make the base as round as the earth,
Make the walls as the sides of the sky,
Make the handles as the curve of a flame,
Make the inside as clear at the water.

  Then give it to me,
O, Red-Twilight-Sky-Boy,
That I may eat from it
  And be nourished.

21. Grandfather Loon

I awake with a passion for water. I'm such a lousy Indian, I can't stand the thirst, and I've used too much of my water already. Hardly half a canteen left. My mouth is parched. I take a swallow of water and hold it in my mouth. Force myself to hold it. Let it wet the parched membranes.

If I were a real Indian, I'd find some dew-covered grass and lick it till I had slaked my thirst.

The valley below is quiet in the dawn's semi-darkness and the dew is still settling. Wisps as distant as waves.

And I am a not-so-ancient mariner, marooned amid water, water, everywhere. He had committed some psychic evil, hadn't he? Refused to recognize some of the primal stuff within himself, and as a consequence got forever arrested at a stage in his development. Becalmed in adolescence.

What have I done to be marooned here? Failed to lick the grass? Failed to conserve what I have? Failed to have a goal? Well, I have a goal, today. I must find water. Or I will have to abort this mission and go home with a dry throat.

I roll my blanket and start up the first water-course I find. I climb over rocks and look for moist places where I might dig. Though I have nothing but my hands to dig with. I turn fallen stumps, fantasying virgin springs suddenly made to flow, clear and cool. I search for clumps of green grass which I might crush in my teeth for the trace of moisture. From my canteen, I take one small swallow, once an hour. That's my ration. One mouth-wetting, once an hour.

I serpentine my way up the little canyon that becomes a draw, then a gully, then a wash, with ever smaller and smaller, less and less growth beside it. About noon, I come out, not on a peak, but on a ridge. The water course had no water in it, only sand and pebbles.

I turn and look down it. I can see the wash whole now. It

Charles Brashear

winds back and forth, as I knew it did. This valley was, after all, the Cosmic Ocean from which Katit, Grandmother Turtle, and Old Man Coyote fished the world. The Universal amniotic fluid in which the Koru world was given birth. Not a fountain of youth, but the very fountain of life, the supporting energy and substance of the world.

The little, dry creek-bed is like a big snake, its head lying in the Cosmic Sea. Water is not only feminine and passive, the amniotic fluid in which our consciousness is born; it is also masculine and supportive, the semen of the great phallic snake that lies with his head in the sea.

Yes, I see it now.

Of course. Impregnate the earth with water, and it fructifies.

Water: both medium and matter of Being.

Would you reclaim the desert? Pour water on it.

Would you hold back the fires that consume life? Feed them with water.

Would you discover life on the stars? Show me the spectrograph of water-vapor, for life as we know it simply does not exist without water.

Water. The incomparable gift of the universe. And whether your needs are as modest as Old Man Wasp's or as greedy as Coyote's, the basket of the universe is always full.

Speak to the universe in the language of the basket that is always full. All morning, I have been trying, but the universe does not answer.

My throat hisses like a hurt horse, I must find water soon. Perhaps on the other side of the mountain.

I cross the ridge and walk on the eastern side. In the first wash, I find a soggy place and, not far up from it, a small spring, the size of a man's hat. Under a big rock. Scummed over with disuse.

Somebody probably has an appropriate aphorism for the situation. Don't drink from a muddy spring, or something like that. I resist the impulse to skim off the layer of disuse and fill my canteen. Who knows, I might contaminate all the remaining water I have. What would an Indian do in this situation?

I gather some dead grass and make a sort of brush to wipe the crust off the water. The water seems clear enough under the surface. No moss or algae to speak of.

I will take a small drink now and wait an hour. If I am not sick then, I will take a larger drink. If that doesn't make me sick, I'll fill my canteen.

My reflection in the pool, as I bend forward to kiss the water. Narcissus. He, too, fixated on a psychic stage. Fell in love with his own immaturity and sat there by the well, pining away. The human unconscious is the wellspring of our consciousness, under which are the deepest and truest things about ourselves. In the abyss of ourselves is our self. Narcissus never knew that, because he never looked beyond the surface.

But Loon knew it. Which tribe was Loon from? I don't remember; one of the northwest coastal tribes, I think. Anyway, an old man had paid so much attention to things-he-could-see that he went blind. He repented, but could not get his sight back. Then he heard the haunting cry of Loon on the lake, and he went down to visit Loon.

"What is it that you sing of, Grandfather Loon?" asked the old man. "What is so beautiful and so valuable, that you make such a beautiful song?"

Then Loon took the old man and led him under the water, under the stream, and told him to look inward.

Loon led him under the river to look inward. Loon led him under the pool of his home to look inward.

The old man's sight turned from black to gray, then from gray to white, then from white to clear. Each trip under his waters improved his focus, wiping away some of the illusion and darkness, until the old man could see again and value the things unseen of the universe.

In gratitude, the old man threw Loon his best shell breast-plate, but it broke and tumbled around Loon's neck and down his back.

And that's how Loon got his necklace! That's what we tell our children. In the old days. Now. A fairy tale of how Loon got his neck lace. And we don't mention the psychic parable of self discovery.

Idly at first, then purposively, I begin placing flat stones in the bottom of my little spring. I'll line it, as a well should be lined.

Then I tear out what I've done. I have to dig the spring a little deeper. I get out a lot of sand and dirt and rotten leaves, which muddies the water. No matter. It will be clear again by the time I will allow myself to drink.

I dig loose a little at the upper end, too, and the water begins to flow a little faster. Shall I make it into a flowing spring? Why? Would that be wasteful? Yes.

I'll just fix it according to my needs at the moment. That seems to me most appropriate. I line the little pond with shale. It is now a little well, fed by a spring in the earth.

Who do I see, now, when I look at my reflection in the little well I have built?

Who am I?

A person who believes in tolerance and patience?

"We all dipped in the waters, but our cups were different," said Chief Ramón.

That I am glad to be a person who believes in psychological progress?

That I am glad to know in my heart that the human soul is capable of changing for the better, or worse?

That I am glad to know that what we do and what we think determines which way our soul will grow?

"We participate in our own destiny, which is now," said my great-great-grandmother Sarah Stonecrist.

Our minds are the puppets of our soul; our souls, the puppets of something deeper and truer.

-< * >-

The afternoon has passed and the spring cleared without

my noticing. Nor do I feel especially thirsty just now.

It is colder. Clouds are coming on with the darkness. It's likely to rain. Yet I feel curiously warm.

Not warm enough to sit naked under a rain cloud. I'm such a tenderfoot, that would only invite pneumonia.

I tie one corner of my tarp to a small tree and peg down the other three corners, making a sort of half-tent. Sitting in it, wrapped in my blanket, I can see my little spring a little distance off.

I fill my canteen from the spring easily and drink a little. Then I am sitting in my tent, half-wrapped in my blanket, eating my ration of pemmican in the semi-darkness, when I see a deer come out of the manzanita brush and drink from my spring— our spring— without hindrance. He looks at me. Then is gone.

Do I wake? or dream?

I'll look for tracks tomorrow morning, I tell myself, knowing that the light drizzle that is setting in will make it impossible for me to tell new tracks from old.

Each day is but a sparrow that flies in the window, flutters a while in the light of the fire, then flies out again into darkness and illusion.

> O, Grandfather Loon,
> Make for me a new set of eyes.
> Take me under the water of life
>   and wash the mud from my sight.
> Take me under the water of my sight
>   and wash the scum from my mind.
> Take me under the water of my mind
>   and wash the sediment from my heart.
> Take me under the waters of my heart
>   and wash the darkness from my spirit,
> That I may see straight
> Where straight is to be seen,
>   O, Grandfather Loon.

                                       Charles Brashear

22. Tulcheris

I must kindle a fire, to drive the chill of the wet night from my bones. My tarp has kept me dry, but my blanket has not kept out the cold of the drizzle, though I've hunched and crouched.

Though first light is diffused through a mist and fog, I creep out, run a little, look for dry twigs and limbs under the thicker bushes and trees. I find a few, careful not to go too far from my tent, for in this morning mist, all directions look the same, and I am aware that I could lose myself very, very easily.

I scrape away debris right in the mouth of my little tent, trying not to get too near to the small tree I've tied my tarp to, and build a tiny fire. I huddle near it, holding up my blanket to embrace its two sides. In embracing the fire, I embrace Tulcheris.

Tulcheris was little, two-legged Root-Boy, then later old Dug-from-the-Earth, until his maiden mother showed him how all the people were sick and cold. They were sick at heart. Inside them, something thus was bad. They were dying, dissolving like clods; and the shamen, though they fasted and sweated, could give no help.

Then his mother sent Dug-from-the-Earth to the east in search of— in search of what? She hadn't the vaguest idea. Just "something."

"There must be something in the east," she said.

Tulcheris, too, was cold to the root, and he felt sick at heart. He did not want to go. But his mother said he must; it was his duty and destiny to go and find something for the people.

So Tulcheris crossed the first line of mountains and found only a forest. He was out of breath, and the forest invited him to stop and rest. But he was still cold, so he went on.

He crossed the second line of mountains and found a nicer forest. His legs ached with exhaustion, and he was even more out of breath. The forest beckoned him to rest, showing him shady places where the grass was soft, where a person could sleep undisturbed. But he was still cold, so he went on.

He crossed the third line of mountains and found again only a forest, lush and healthy, filled with game and flowing streams, and plenty of young trees to build good shelter. Delicious, edible roots and green, leafy vegetables grew all over the hillsides. Here a person like Tulcheris could live forever, with plenty on every side. But Tulcheris shivered with the cold in his roots and remembered the people were sick at heart, so he did not stop.

He crossed the fourth line of mountains and came to the cave of his father, the Sun. The warmth of the Sun scorched out the chill, and he spoke.

"Instruct me, Father," said Tulcheris, "for the people are cold and sick at heart, and none knows what to do."

But the Sun just grumped, "Don't bother me with such trivia, I'm a busy man." And he jumped through the sky, over the earth.

The next day, Tulcheris again waited at the mouth of the cave for his father. He had grown bigger and felt himself growing again, as his father the Sun came from the cave. "Tell me what to do, Father," said Tulcheris, "for the people are cold and sick at heart, and I must help them."

Again he was scorched, again he grew.

Again the Sun just grumped, "Don't bother me. I've got a duty to perform," and he darted off through the sky, over the earth.

The third day, Tulcheris was taller yet, almost as tall as a pine tree. When his father came from the cave, he asked again: "Give me something for the people, who are cold and sick at heart, Father, or we shall not live."

Again the Sun grumped, "Don't bother me. I've got a destiny to fulfill," and he darted off through the sky, over the earth.

Charles Brashear

Tulcheris sat down at the mouth of the cave. He could see now that he was going to have to do something more than just ask. For three days, now, his skin had scorched and turned reddish-brown. The sun no longer burned him, and he was growing stronger and taller with the warmth.

On the fourth day, as the Sun came from his cave, Tulcheris did not wait to ask the Sun for a boon, but leaped out and grabbed him. They wrestled all morning. First Tulcheris was on top, then the Sun was on top. They rolled over and over, as the day waited. At last, Tulcheris wrapped his roots around the Sun and tied him down.

"Let me go," said the Sun. "I must take the day through the sky, over the earth."

"Nay, Father," said Tulcheris. "First give me something. I am cold and sick at heart, and none but you knows what to do."

"Let me go," said the Sun. "You are keeping me from my job. A chill lies over the earth, and I've got to take the day through the sky to warm the earth."

"Nay, Father," said Tulcheris. "First give me something for my mother. She is cold and sick at heart, and only you know what to do."

"Let me go," said the Sun. "Darkness lies over all the earth. I've got to take the day through the sky, and light the earth."

"Nay, Father," said Tulcheris. "First give me something for the people, for they are cold and sick at heart, and none but you knows what to do."

"Let me go," said the Sun. "Ignorance and Darkness lie over all the earth, and I've got to take the day through the sky, and enlighten the earth."

"Nay, Father," said Tulcheris. "You must bless me with something for the spirit of the people, for they are cold and sick at heart, and none but you knows what it can be."

At last, the Sun relented. "Bend down that tree and flip me into the sky, Tulcheris, and I will leave you a gift in the tree."

So Tulcheris bent down the tallest of the pine trees, placed the Sun in a branching Y, and flipped him into the sky, over the earth.

When the Sun was gone, a fire burned in the tree. The Sun had left fire in the tree.

Tulcheris took the fire home, over the three lines of mountains, and gave fire to the people.

Mud, they were warmed.

Sweat, they were cleansed.

Tears, they were made conscious.

Tulcheris put some fire in each of the huts, and there it spoke to the people.

Like mesmers, it told them the color of their flesh, the color of their blood. And mesmerized by the tongue of the fire, they understood and were warm.

I, too, am warmed by the fire.

Like the young Sioux who, on his vision quest, was allowed a small fire each morning, I hear the voice. The shamen always said the fire was to light the seeker's ceremonial pipe for his morning smoke, but, I begin to see now, it was to teach the young man the language of the fire.

We are but mud-pies, made of cold earth and water, till fire speaks his warmth into us. He colors our bodies, he fills our veins, he heats this cauldron, our bodies, in which we cook the very stuff of our lives. Like lizards, we depend upon those loving tongues of flame.

Such understanding transformed the people. Transformed their cultures. Transformed them in the dialectic of adaptation, and, though no one especially noticed or cared, the old ways of cold and heart-sickness were lost. Lost in the adaptation which understanding had brought.

The cauldron will do that to us again.

The human mind will do that to you again.

Knowledge will do that to you.

-< * >-

My little pit of ashes is long since cold, for I have neglected it. That's what one gets for being lost in thoughts. No matter, I am not especially cold now anyway. The sun glows an eerie yellow in the afternoon fog and mist.

In the distance, above the fog, I imagine a porcupine tree. Porcupines like to climb pine and fir trees to eat the sweet bark a little distance down from the top. Sometimes, they eat a ring around the tree and kill the top. The terminal bud thus nipped, lateral buds begin to grow, and grow into new tops for the tree. Sometimes several grow at once— outward, then upward, so that a tree has four or five tops, sticking up like tines, or like a basket half finished. The tree survives by adapting. It is the way of nature.

I have seen forests, too, where fire has swept up the mountainside so fast it charred and scorched everything. From twisted charcoal stumps, I have seen old trees surviving, persisting, and new trees growing.

The Indian in America has been a forest invaded by swift fire. Both have survived by adapting.

The Indian was not annihilated. But neither did he persist unchanged.

The old ways were tried in the cauldron of a swift invasion— and found wanting. Why should we not admit it? The old culture was not sufficient to meet the multiplicity the Indian faced. The old ways disintegrated like the ashes of a fire, and then sprouted through the ashes. Something different. Something, perhaps, still not as strong as was needed. But something stronger. That, too, is a way of nature.

From the gnawed rings and ashes of our destruction, we sprout new tops.

You who hover your blankets around the ashes of the old ways, they will not warm you. They will not speak to you the color of flesh.

You who seek to rekindle the fire with cold ashes, they will not sustain you. They will not speak to you the color of blood.

You who cling to the old ways, you tend the wrong fire. You are forgetting the dominant quality of Indianness: its power to adapt.

Remember instead how Tulcheris was scorched brown by his bout with the Sun, but grew stronger and warmer.

Remember, too, how the boon he brought the people transformed them.

Remember: our strength is our capacity for psychic growth.

Remember: tie us to old ashes, and we will die.

Rolling mists of the valley cast a perfect rainbow against the evening sky. Is Rainbow male? Or female? Is it Rainbow Boy, or Rainbow Girl? I'm such a lousy Indian, I forget.

I remember the symbolism, though. Rainbow is half of the sacred circle. The universe's half. The completed circle is the symbol of unity. Good fortune. The universe supplies its half; I must make my life the other half. That is my kinship with the things seen and unseen of the universe: my psyche, my spirit, participates in and completes them. Makes them round and whole.

The rainbow persists as the sunset wanes, changing its shape and angle, as the sun changes its.

I eat my ration of pemmican and drink my bit of water, but can remember only a poor, limping poem for the prayer-chant today:

> O, Rainbow Boy, or Girl,
> Encircle me and my life
> As you encircle a Navajo sand painting
> That I may participate,
> That I may be round and whole,
> O, Rainbow Boy, or Girl.

Charles Brashear

23. Under the Dawn

One becomes aware of sky, in a dawning, and of the daybreak star, that bright herald of the new day. First, the familiar night stars set in the west; then the dark deepens, even on a bright night; then the head-dress feathers of the day-break star peek up over the eastern rim of the earth. He lifts his head, looks around a little, then climbs higher to usher in the dawn.

How very important the symbolism of the dawn sky has been to Indian holy men!

Deganawidah, the Iroquois prophet, said that the coming of the white man was a time of deep darkness for the Indian, a time of the whirlwinds of hatred, but that, someday, a marvelous bright star-chief would dawn in the east and drive the serpents of hatred before him.

Black Elk, holy man of the Oglala Sioux, dreamed in his vision that the people were doomed to travel the black road for a long time and that the sacred hoop of the nation would be broken and scattered. But eventually the day-break star would point the way to the tree of understanding, and the hoops of all nations would be joined again and made whole.

A Navajo prophecy tells that a new light is coming in the dawning, so quietly that those who live in the canyons, in darkness, will not know it, but those who live on the mesas with eyes open to know will see the nine-pointed star of the new day, herald of the Chief with twelve feathers which represent the twelve ways of brotherhood.

That is the uprising that is upon us, Sons and Daughters of America. It has less to do with Indian religion, than with such human realities as good will, health, warmth, nurture. Things we can do something about.

You may think the streets of your cities and villages are silent and deserted when you lie abed, sleeping. But know that they are not empty. Ideas stalk your doors, and some, like ghosts, will enter your dreams. Some will come on dimly, like dawning stars, getting a little stronger . . . a little stronger.

Did my white ancestors have a universe to speak to?

Did they have a Dawn Star that could speak to them?

I doubt it, considering all the aggression and bad faith on the white man's part. The roots of his guilt. Aggression corrupts, but deliberate aggression corrupts absolutely.

Why did my white ancestors consistently and deliberately shrink their souls? Why did the white man consciously make his psyche into a misshapen dwarf that is incapable of loving himself, others, or the world on which we all subsist? Why did he consistently and deliberately make his mind the puppet of his crowd?

Surely, the white man is not so simple. Surely, he knows that it is better to feel secure with wife, children, and friends around, to know that his neighbor's health contributes to his own, and to sleep peacefully with a quiet conscience, than to eat among enemies, continually suspect a plague, and sleep fitfully with a knowledge of his own smallness.

Surely, he knows the human spirit that dwells on trust and good will is healthier and happier than the one that is made up of suspicion and anger.

Today's Indian is no better off, with all his neo-tribalism, peyote cults, pan-Indianism, for those things are often made of mistrust, suspicion, anger. It is as if no tribe is culturally strong enough to furnish identity, and no substantial number of people are strong enough in themselves, so identity is sought in the act of seeking.

To seek— is that to find?

I doubt it, when I see a Tuscarora with a Sioux tipi, a Navajo blanket, and a Kwaikutl totem pole, selling Hong Kong transistor radios to Texas tourists in upstate New York. Superficial trappings. Of no ultimate consequence.

More important is the psychological irony: identity is defined as identity sought. The act becomes the end, the search becomes the product. So, one knows and is known by the postures he takes, not the principles he holds. Indeed, the holding of principles becomes a liability: to know is to cease to search; to cease to search is to lose identity.

Why should we be like the paleface youth cult? Defining themselves with things not unlike their fathers' Cadillacs and hula hoops, with trappings of headbands, moccasins, necklaces of Crow beads and turquoise; short circuiting their brains with drugs for a flash of personal identity. Defining themselves by the revolutionary postures they take, depending upon establishment rejection to define their code, surviving on the very resistance they elicit.

O, Grandmother Turtle, how much we are all brothers under the round sky! How little the human capacity for nobility of spirit plays in the affairs of men!

I've read somewhere the idea that, in the nineteenth century, the white man had four options of "what to do with the Indian"— he could exterminate, tolerate, ignore, or assimilate him. He tried all in varying degrees, in different places and times. He had the physical power to have accomplished any of them, had his mind been clear. But he had just enough decency in him to do none of them completely.

And the Indian had the choices of fighting back, surrendering, joining the whites, maneuvering a kind of hate-filled coexistence, or going underground. The only thing he couldn't do was persist as he was. Whatever he did, he was bound to transform his own psyche for the worse.

It has been hardly a month since I stopped at a gas station in Kayenta to fill up and asked the Navajo attendant about the activist newspaper, *Diné Baa-Hané*. He told me rudely it did not exist, but Grandmother Doe-in-the-Dawn got out of the car, went into the station, and bought a copy from the very attendant that had just lied to me.

There's at least a little suspicion and anger in that. And dwarfism of the spirit.

On such dreams is anomie built. And one feels the need

to go and visit relatives, for relatives are sympathetic and accepting. They nurture us, as we nurture them. The constellation of the extended family defines my place under the stars, until the stars, too, are cousins.

That is the prophet we await in the dawn— some psychically rich, elder relative, hallucinated in the dawn distance and approaching with his mesmerizing, transforming, fructifying gift. That is why we gaze for his headdress in the sky.

We sit on the rim of canyons and gaze until we populate the distance with our fantasies. Hoping to discover in distance the creative principle that will recreate us. Hoping to absorb our conscious mind in a day-break star, or the lazy circles of a red-tailed hawk, so that our unconscious can come up and speak to us.

For it is ourselves speaks to ourselves. Products of ourselves, which we feed the distance, that it may, in turn, feed us.

Hallucinations, if you will. Dreams. These visions are the language of what is deepest and truest in us. The voices of our essential identities.

These voices tell us who and what we are. These visions tell us how to live with the earth, water, fire, sky. Our minds are the puppets of our beliefs; our beliefs, the children of our psychic visions.

If we nurture the sky with honor, truth, compassion, we put a different set of puppet strings on our minds. It is ours to choose. With deliberation and consistency, we make our world what it is. Our spirit creates the world we live in.

Let us replace our greed, our need for power, our exploitation of property with a responsibility to use only what we need, what is our share, a responsibility to sustain the earth's yields, so that the seventh generation of our grandchildren have a world as beautiful as ours.

If we are provident, we make our world provident.

If we are mean, we make our world mean.

That is the message of spiritual unity the distance speaks

of.

Some are frightened; for distance, too, lays claim to a part of the soul. Fire tries to hypnotize, water to tranquilize, earth to enroot; but distance tries to capture a part of ourselves.

A huge prospect, come upon suddenly, startles an involuntary backward step and a breath jerked in. Protective gestures both. Preparations for an attack. But if we acknowledge those dreams, those hallucinations, those visions of ourselves, we can know.

And, in knowing, we create. Not just our world, but also our spirit.

With knowing, we create our own spirit.

We create ourselves.

By that creative principle in self-awareness, we create ourselves.

Yes, Red-Twilight-Sky-Boy, you are myself.

Yes, Grandfather Loon, you are myself.

Yes, Rainbow-Boy or Girl, you are myself.

Yes, Grandmother Turtle, who dug the primal mud from the primal sea and made the earth, you are myself.

Yes, Georgie Stonecrist, you are myself.

-< * >-

My time is passing. My quest is passing. I must roll my tarp and blanket and go back down the hill. Grandmother Doe-in-the-Dawn will be disappointed that I have had no dream, no vision. I come home with no story to tell.

Neither hunger, loneliness, nor meditation have short-circuited my psyche to hallucinate a distance, in which I could feed myself with visions flashing of "blue and purple horses . . . a house made of dawn," a dawn made of daybreak stars.

I'm afraid I have no blood-and-cell memory.

Yet, I have the earth, I have the water, I have the fire. And sky. I have the sky, too.

We all live under one sky, but in many houses.

We all are warmed by the fire, though our needs vary.

We all dip into the water, though our cups are different.

We all belong to the earth, the earth belongs to us all.

Yes, the human potential of the psyche belongs to everyone, and our symbols are but mirrors, reflecting what we are and what we can become.

I invent my own prayer today.

O, Grandmother Dawn,
Make me your arrow.
Make the shaft of a ray of knowledge.
Make the feathers of a flame of mystery.
Make the point of the earth, my foundation.
Make the binding of the oceans around,
    disseminated to all corners.

Then pluck the rainbow from the sky,
String it with my past,
Fit me to your design,
Aim me at your purpose,
And shoot me into the sky,
    Under the dawn star,
    O, Grandmother Dawn.

          Charles Brashear

24. I Won't Dance, Don't Make Me

Coming up the walk, I see a crowd of people through Grandmother Doe-in-the-Dawn's picture window. Another Red Power meeting. I duck back before any of them see me. Crouching near the front step, I am suddenly weary, weary, for I do not want to play their little games now. They are puppets, dancing on the strings of their own myths.

-< * >-

ESTABLISHING SHOT:

A group of modern Indians in Dawn Stonecrist's living room. GRANDMOTHER DOE-IN-THE-DAWN sits in her Sarah Stonecrist rocker in her usual place near the TV. She wears now an authentic buckskin dress, two silver necklaces, several bracelets and rings. On the color TV sits a basketry cylinder, where a plastic mountain hiding a TV light used to be. Above and to the right, the wall-hanging, "Home is where the Heart is," has been replaced by a poster of Chief Joseph saying,

The earth was created by the assistance of the sun, and it should be left as it is.... The country was made without lines of demarcation, and it is no man's business to divide it.... The earth and myself are of one mind. The measure of our bodies are the same.... Do not misunderstand me, but understand me fully with reference to my affection for the land. I never said the land was mine to do with it as I chose. The one who has the right to dispose of it is the one who created it. I claim a right to live on my land and accord you the privilege to live on yours.

The other people in the living room are: MARK ELLIS and MARY

BARNESFISH; Paul Allen, from Oklahoma, his wife, Joelle, from New Mexico, and their baby; the AIM leader who has changed his name to JAMES HAWK and his younger brother, CLYDE, together with three of their children, a teen-aged girl and boys ten and twelve; and BILL ODOCK, the old man from The Colus Rancheria, who always reminds me of Wovoka. A half-dozen EXTRAS. All wear beaded headbands or necklaces.

SCENE: JAMES HAWK has been reading a poem from *Akwesasne Notes*. He folds the paper carefully as he finishes.

-< * >-

Oh, I admit the problems they imagine themselves dealing with are real enough: dispossession of the land, detribalization, alcoholism and unemployment, anomie and rejection, cheating and chicanery on every side of the innocents, and with all, a disheartening unconsciousness in the surrounding, dominant culture. Without having entered, I feel I've been there before. I have no myths to dance to.

And I see that they are now a society equipped for persistence. With some elderly, some middle-aged, some young marrieds, children, babies. If they had a few horses and travois, they would be able to travel and persist as a band. Four able men to hunt, two young wives and a teen-aged girl to— Well, no— Joelle and Mary are much too well-educated to either deserve or accept that chauvinist division of labor.

Maybe what I shrink from is their modus of survival— suited to conditions of the remote past, when a hunting, gathering society could reasonably fulfill needs. But not suited to solving contemporary problems of sanitation, wages, identity.

For instance, Bill Odock has been teaching Koru basketry to the children. He hadn't made a basket in over fifty years, but it's something he didn't forget. It came back easily. They've made some remarkable specimens— ceremonial baskets with Hesi designs, some of them embroidered with woodpecker and yellowhammer feathers, some decorated with small shell sequins. Remarkable.

An anthropologist's dream, in every way, except that they were made today; last week. Something right out of the tradition: made with traditional materials, by traditional methods, by traditional artisans. And I'm left with a "so what" feeling.

Yes, of course; basketry is an art form, affording self-expression.

Yes, of course; basketry is an industry, capable of commanding a significant portion of the tourist dollar.

I agree with you when you tell me these things. But that's not what they are doing. They're making baskets to use in a Hesi ceremony, when the last Hesi was danced in 1906, and then, not by Koru, but by their cousins, the Hill Patwin. The retrogression of it is what sinks my sympathies.

Still, I suppose I have to go in sooner or later.

-< * >-

FULL LENGTH SHOT
GRANDMOTHER DOE-IN-THE-DAWN as she stands, falters, stands again, upon seeing her grandson enter the room.

DOE-IN-THE-DAWN
(excited)
Look! Look who's returned.
(turning to the others)
Get the things out. E-e-e-e Yo-o-o-o-o! All are invited. Get ready for a Bole Ho. Get ready for a dance.

-< * >-

"No, Granny. Don't," I say, staying out of her movie. "I'm not going to dance a Hesi. I have nothing to say. I saw no visions."

-< * >-

MEDIUM CLOSE SHOT
                    DOE-IN-THE-DAWN
        (unbelieving)
    What? What are you saying?
        (Pause, then more and more urgently)
    Why not? Didn't you have a dream? Didn't you
    have a vision? Didn't anything remarkable
    happen there on the mountain?

-< * >-

"No, I didn't dream. Yes, some remarkable things
happened. I saw a few deer, but they were real deer. I saw a
hawk, but he was a real hawk, flying his territory, hunting for
mice. Everything was just plain ordinary. I'm sorry. I'm a
lousy Indian."

-< * >-

FULL LENGTH SHOT
*DOE-IN-THE-DAWN, turning and going toward the kitchen to
make preparations for the dance.*

                    DOE-IN-THE-DAWN
    Oh, thank goodness. There for a moment you
    had me worried.
        (Calling to the others)
    Come! Let's get ready.

-< * >-

"No, Granny, there was no dream. I think I would have
known the symptoms. I kept looking for the heightening of
sensation. But I didn't feel Cia's chill bumps. I kept looking
for something like what happens in a fever, a wrinkling in the
interior abyss, perhaps, which flashes blue or purple, and
opens upon a vision of the center of the universe.
    "But nothing like that happened.

"It's no use, Granny. I won't dance."

-< * >-

CLOSE SHOT
DOE-IN-THE-DAWN
(turning again, confused)
What do you mean? What's wrong?
(ZOOM IN on her eyes, which get wider, unbelieving, as her voice quickens.)
You did dream, didn't you? ... Think hard. Maybe you didn't recognize it when the dream came. Maybe the remarkable things were the dream? Think. Tell us.

-< * >-

"I— speak only for myself, now, you understand?

"The trappings were a set of symbols. With symbols, a simple people could deal with psychic realities that they could not understand straight. Let's keep the psychic realities, but skip the drums and feathers.

"You see, every time you insist upon singing the old songs in the old ways, you fixate the psyche on a vision that is incapable of sustaining— I mean—

"Well, this is a part of what came clear to me on the mountain. Any time you define Indianness as the old dances and the old songs, even when they contain the real psychic realities, you are setting the Indian's head on backward. The message in Indianness is psychic progress; but when you cling to the old forms, you undermine the progress; you regress into a smaller, more primitive attitude. You dwarf the human spirit.

"Worse, you set up survival as an either/or syllogism. Either you have to persist as an apartheid Indian, convinced of your superiority and unwilling and unable to survive in the dominant culture, or you have to kick the feathers and stuff and assimilate. That's continual war.

"Don't you see? Don't you all see? War within yourselves. War with the whites. And there's no possibility for peace.

Either internally or externally. Either/or, and there's no in-between. No possibility for the Indian winning, either. That's what survival has been for us from the time of the first contact with whites. We've got to get beyond that. We've got to find a way to keep the psychic realities, even when—we have joined the dominant culture."

-< * >-

SMALL GROUP SHOT
DOE-IN-THE-DAWN, BILL ODOCK near the TV, and MARY BARNESFISH, beside him.

> DOE-IN-THE-DAWN
> Don't say that! You've got it in your blood and bones to see, the same as any of the rest of us. And look...
>> *(Crossing to the TV and picking up the basketry cylinder)*
> ... Bill — Mr. Odock — has made you a real basket-of-the-universe. And we've found a real hawk bone. See! We've even decorated it with the right symbols.

> MARY
> You can't stop now, Georgie. You've got to go on.

> BILL ODOCK
> You taught me to say "*Wile wilak*" again. You can't stop now.

> DOE-IN-THE-DAWN
> See. You've got to. You've got to dance Bole Ho. You've got to reaffirm the spirit.

-< * >-

"Oh, I'll reaffirm the human spirit. But not that way. Let's just skip the beads and feathers, the trappings and I'll—

"I speak only for myself—

"We've got to find a viable way to live. Even when we have joined the dominant culture. ..." I am aware that my voice trails off sadly. I am aware that the others are silent for a moment. I see in their Indian eyes their disappointment, a distrust, a sudden, new suspicion of me. They're wondering: have I sold out?

Paul Allen hesitates, then speaks: "It is possible — extremely difficult, but possible — for an Indian to survive now in American culture. It's possible for a person to be a productive member of society and still be an Indian in important ways."

Ah! A kindred spirit. He understands. I continue: "That's it. That's what I mean. The human psyche is capable of surviving on many different foods. It's foolish for us, today, I think, to pretend that the old Indian way was somehow superior.

"It's true, we have to insist upon a kind of genetic equality with the whites. Theoretically, there can be no real differences: all men have a capacity for growth, for health, for honor. They who have grown little, who are not healthy, who have little honor must be convinced of this. That's what we really mean when we talk about civilizing the white man, isn't it?

"But what we offer him is not Indianness; rather it is his own humanity.

"Neither of us is superior in that."

They are all flash-frozen. Baffled. And surprised. If they understood my words, they would be deeply hurt.

I can't stop myself. I tumble on. "As I say, I speak only for myself. But to me, it is foolish to pretend that our stone-age ancestors had an arm-lock on the problems of Being. We who stand on their shoulders and reach so much farther hesitate to claim as much.

"I think Indians should begin thinking of themselves, not as Indians, but as the fortunate product of a pluralistic background. They've had so many advantages! That's why they can be leaders now. Their background has allowed them to combine strengths that the rest of the world is groping for. Human strengths, now, not Indian strengths."

It's no use. They either do not notice what I am saying or choose not to see. Bill Odock keeps looking at me, looking away, then looking again, as if he is having trouble locating me. Joelle smiles her little Mona Lisa smile, waiting. Grandmother Doe-in-the-Dawn gazes directly at me, refusing to hear what I've just said. They hear what I say as a cop-out.

So, I'll have to sing and dance, after all. That's the language they are prepared to understand. If I want them to understand anything of what I say, I will have to say it in the singing. I will have to let my puppet speak to theirs.

25. Dancing Myself

If you look through the picture window, you will see my friends form a circle around me, ready to absorb the posture I take. That's what they want, not the principles I hold. They want to clap hands or beat drums. This is a role they are ready to play. They smile to one another confidently.

I place the basket-of-the-universe on the carpet near where I imagine a fire to be in a Dance House and put the leg-bone of Katit in it. Then I start shuffling around it, using the hesitation step so common to many Indian dances.

-< * >-

CLOSE SHOT, GRADUALLY BROADENING TO A GROUP SHOT:

Georgie STONECRIST
(picks up Bill Odock's basket-of-the-universe and the decorated leg-bone of a hawk. He makes gestures directly at the people in the room, as he chants:)
E-e-e-e-e-e Yo-o-o-o-o-o
All are invited.
I will sing of the spirit, yes.
I will dance of the spirit, yes,
I will affirm the spirit, yes.
All you girls there
All you boys, here,
All you men and women,
All you elderly,
Listen to me. Listen to me. Listen to me."

-< * >-

So far, so good. You out there will probably recognize that as the memorized formula of invitation. Now what do I do? Dance around a bit, I think. What comes next? I should remember. I've certainly studied the Hesi enough. Its structure should propel me along.

Oh, yes. The trip. Recount the interior trip.

-< * >-

> I went over to the mountain, there,
> I went down into the mountain, here,
> I walked all around through the mountain
> I said to myself: you must tell them something.
> I said to myself: you must sing and dance — to the north!"

-< * >-

Boy! Am I ever glad I thought of the north. A person gets into a crux where the form gives you slots to say things in, but nothing to say in them. Is that why some Indian poetry has gaps of vacancy in it? Can't get into that now; gotta sing to Grandmother Doe-in-the-Dawn. Singing to the north will give me a chance to dance around the "fire" four times. Give me a chance to think.

Let's see now. North. What does north represent?

Cold. Winter. The source of illness.

How can I say to them that the Indians' greatest illness, now, is not anything physical, like marasmus, nor anything psychological like anomie, though both exist and both must be eradicated.

No, the Indians' greatest illness now is nationalism. That same nationalism that dwarfed the spirit of the white man has now infected the Indian. When AIM campaigns to Indianize the BIA or to change the name of Custer State Park to Paha Sapa National Park, they are trafficking in either/or confrontations. Wars. Wars that polarize. Diminish.

Oh, I know, it's a flag to rally the Indian around. Identity. But if it dwarfed the white man's psyche, what makes you think it won't damage the red man's?

Maybe we ought to be colonizing instead. You know, open the tribes to everyone. Let white men become "Indians." Let them see for themselves what it is to be human and humane. Gain identity by keeping our cool. And by becoming articulate about that cool. Psychological individuation. Some of you outside the window would like that, wouldn't you?

But how can I say this in the dance? When we're all so puffed up with practical politics?

Puffed up. Katit was puffed up in one of the old Hesi songs. The illness. Rituals in the old days often dealt with curing an inside-me-thus-is-bad, puffed-up feeling. With a straw, the shaman sucked out the inside-me-thus-is-bad, and, with sleight of hand, displayed the shards of flint, the "pins" that caused the malady. I'll chant about that puffed-up feeling. Okay, here goes.

-< * >-

I was sick.

The people were sick.

All about me, the people were sick in the sweat houses.

So I went north.

I was all puffed up with illness, so I went north.

'It looks bad,' I said to myself. But I took out a reed straw and started sucking at the all-puffed-up within me.

Then I sucked something out of the puff and had to cough it up; it was a feather.

Then I sucked something else out of the puff and had to cough it up; it was a dance bell.

Then I sucked something new out of the puff and had to cough it up, too; it was a blanket.

'Okay,' I said to myself. 'You can go now, the puff's all gone.'

'Hey, wait a minute,' I said. 'I'm an Indian; you can't take my feather, my bell, and my blanket.'

'Nonsense.' I answered. 'Being an Indian is not feathers and bells.'

'Hey! Wait a minute,' I said. 'Give me something to take back to the people who are all puffed up in the sweat houses.'

'Can't do it,' I said. 'They gotta find their own selves.'

'But what'll I say when they ask me for their cure?'

'Tell 'em they gotta look for their own heads, themselves.'

Thus it was.

Thus it was when I was all puffed up.

Tcen-wer. Tcen-wer! (Come down. Spirit, come down!)

-< * >-

Well. That turned out a little more flippant than I wanted it to. But, you know, the old moving finger writes and moves on. That's Persian thought, isn't it? Or Heraclitian flux? Can't get into that now. Gotta dance to the west.

You see my friends around the room stare at me in amazement and disbelief. I can see that they don't understand or sympathize. They think I was explaining why I don't have on feathers and paint.

I shuffle counterclockwise around the "fire." Four times, I'll dance around it. Time to think. What am I going to sing? How can I make them see?

West. What does west represent?

Sunset. Autumn. Death.

Not bad death. Not the death that white men fear. The good death, the death after strength and good fortune. Fulfillment. Greatness in the past. Indians have a lot of greatness in their past— philosophers, peace-makers, psychologists, artists.

Deganawidah had more effect and more good sense than Christ.

Tecumseh is every bit the equal of Tom Paine; he just wasn't successful, that's all.

Chief Joseph is a non-imperial Napoleon.

Sitting Bull, a Voltaire or Rousseau, depending on your angle of vision.

There was a lot of strength and good fortune in that past. Now, it's clouded with a superficial gimmickry and a nationalism that disguises and disfigures it. How can we respect it and derive its strength for ourselves, without the crippling ancestor-worship?

Can we do it by being no less than they? Can we create ourselves in our own and their image at once? Can we, too, show most respect and derive most strength, by ourselves being great philosophers, peace-makers, psychologists, artists? That would require study. And study would mean knowledge. And knowledge cuts you off from simple answers.

Good grief. Once more around, and I'll have to sing. What am I going to sing about? When we're so hyped on dreams of traditions? Puppeted by the dead.

Coyote. He's on the western plain, waiting for the dead.

And an old Koru dream of dying, which Kroeber recorded in the '20s. Maybe I can remember enough of that— and get ancestors into it. Here goes:

-< * >-

Once I died. And went west.

Once I lay on my bed and nothing in the now-around-
    me interested me at all, so I died.

I went west, looking for Old Man Coyote.

I crossed the valley, but he wasn't there.

I crossed the mountains, but he wasn't there.

I crossed the ocean, but he wasn't there.

I crossed the sunset, and here he was.

Here inside me thus, he was.

He was hiding behind a cloud, reading the *I Ching*.

I said, 'Aren't you a little lazy and derelict. Aren't you
    supposed to be out chasing souls?'

'Oh, this arrangement works quite well,' he said. 'The
    little rabbit-like souls sneak through while I'm

reading and think they've triumphed.

'This arrangement works quite well,' he said. 'The strong ones always come looking for me and make me look up.

'They don't leave the living, you see? They stick around, to see if they can help the living, by their example or spirit.

It works out quite well, and I don't have all that running to do.'

'Where are they, then?' I asked. 'Where are the great dead?'

'Oh, they're here and there.

'Some live in old books.

'Some live in people's heads.

'Here's your great-great-grandfather Sioc, right here in your heart.'

He reached into my shirt and pulled out something.

He reached into my breast and pulled out something.

He reached into my heart and pulled out something.

And there was Sioc. Tall and strong. As ethical as an arrow.

And there was Sioc. Wise and good. Leading the people out of their illness and need.

And there was Sioc. Firm in his purpose, clear in his vision.

And there was Sioc. Defeated in his time, not by the white man, but by the dissolute tribe.

Then Coyote took Sioc by the heels and lay him upon me like a feather.

I was dead on my bed, and Coyote lay Sioc upon me like a bell.

I was sick of my now, and Coyote lay Sioc upon me like a blanket.

Then I awoke and stood up in a clear day.

My mother said, 'You were dead fifteen minutes.'

'No,' I said. 'I was out, grating my orbit in the willows.'

Thus it was. Thus it was.

Charles Brashear

Tcen-wer! Tcen-wer! (Come down! Spirit, come down!)

-< * >-

Well. That got a little heavier than I had expected. I was surprised and pleased, though, to get my blanket back. I didn't think I would be.

Oh, stop congratulating yourself, Georgie; you've got to dance to the south.

My friends are still baffled; but now, at least, they think I have good intentions.

South. What does south represent?

Warmth. Summer. Nurture.

Sustenance of the sort that kept the Indian soul from disappearing when the whites were killing so many bodies. In most tribes, young Indians were not men until they had gone off into the forest or mountain of themselves, had stretched out their sensations, spaced out their minds, until they hallucinated the vision which was true and eternal for that individual. That vision became the measure of truth by which the man lived his entire life.

His way of knowing was within himself. White men always had to verify their ideas with others, make sure others saw what they saw. Hungry for a sense of values, so hungry, they took their direction from others. But the Indian was always the inner-directed man. How about that, you Social Psychology Professors, outside the window? Have you studied the individuated Indian? Have you described his strength and good fortune?

Come on, Georgie. You've got to sing. What are you going to sing about?

I haven't the vaguest idea. How do you make a song about epistemology?

Apple pie. Why do I think of apple pie?

And Bill Odock! I once gave him a fish, and he brought me some apple pie. That's how we cultivated our mutual trust.

I'll have to dance around the fire a fifth time. Hope the

others don't notice. I'll tell them it's orders from Nurturing Woman.

Ah! Nurturing Woman!

-< * >-

I was hungry, so I went south in search of food.
I was dead in my dreaming, so I went south to be
    revived.
I saw nothing at the first turning, in harmony with
    the universe.
I saw nothing at the second turning, in harmony
    with the universe.
I saw nothing at the third turning, in harmony with
    the universe.
So, for the fourth turning, I went to a new tribe.
Just like that. I changed tribe.
Then I sat down on the earth, thinking I should
plant.
I walked near the sky, thinking I should cultivate
    my corn.
But I was lazy, and dead in my dreaming, so I went
    south to be revived.
Nurturing Woman came up while I was sleeping.
Up from my dream while I was sleeping.
Nurturing Woman came up, wearing a white dress;
Her breasts were full and her nipples made bumps in
    her dress.
She said, 'Eat,' and I sucked.
Nurturing Woman came up, holding out her arms;
They were lithe and warm, they were made for
caressing.
She said, 'Embrace,' and I embraced.
Nurturing Woman came up, rolling her hips about;
They were wide and healthy, they were made for
    bearing many children. She said, 'Emerge,' and I
    was born.
She took me up and shook me out like an old

buffalo robe.

She took me up and spread me out like a white
buffalo robe.

Nurturing Woman spread buffalo-robe-me on the
ground and prepared my food.

-< * >-

Now what? My mind is about as blank as it ever gets. And
you out there are not helping me one bit.

Why do I think of the Dawn Star? In the Navajo myth, it is
a nine-pointed star, a Sun Chief with nine feathers in his
head-dress. He ushers in the new age of peace and harmony,
the age of psychic health.

Ah, psychic health.

-< * >-

On buffalo-robe-me me were pictographs of
variables from the Minnesota Multiphasic
Personality Inventory:

There was hypochondria, depression, and hysteria.

There was paranoia, psychasthenia, and
schizophrenia.

There was anxiety, repression, and alienation.

Nurturing Woman placed a bowl on buffalo-robe-
me.

She plucked up each pictograph and plopped it
into the bowl.

She sang as she stirred.

Then she gave me from the bowl — a piece of apple
pie.

'I am your mother,' she said. 'Nurture me, as you
are nurtured.'

And I said, 'wile wilak.' (That means "good health to
you!")

Then she gave me from the bowl — a piece of apple
pie.

'I am your wife,' she said. 'Nurture me, as you are

nurtured.'

And I said, 'wile wilak.'

Then she gave me from the bowl — a piece of apple
    pie.

'I am your daughter,' she said. 'Nurture me, as you
    are nurtured.'

And I said, 'wile wilak.'

Then she entered me, and I enclosed her, in
    harmony with the universe.

Thus it was. Thus it was.

Tcen-wer! Tcen-wer! (Come down! Spirit, come down!)

Wile wilak.

-< * >-

Whew! I began to think there for a while I wasn't going to get through that one. My friends look at one another and nod. They think I'm trying to reinforce the myths they live by. But I want to cry out to them: That's not what I meant! That's not what I meant at all!

I'll have to try again.

Did you ever notice how these four-part rituals tend to take on classical symphonic form? First and second movements fairly standard allegro con brio and andante con molto; third movement different, vivace, comic scherzo, if not schizo; fourth movement, Largo, expansive, powerful. Kind of neat, though, how Nurturing Woman is really a part of my psyche, isn't it? Well, I can't stop to think about that now.

East. What does east represent? Daybreak. Spring. Creative knowledge.

Knowledge is power. Knowledge has clout. Knowledge is the key to winning the war of sentiment. When enough people know enough, they act. And act decently. With some honor. Knowledge is the source, the foundation, of our power, too.

Come on, *Akwesasne!*

Come on, *Eyapaha!*

Come on, *Diné Baa-Hané!*

Disseminate your knowledge.

Don't stay holed up, thinking only of horror stories for Indians.

The Indian, like the poor, is invisible, they say, because no one knows anything about him. Knowledge is visibility. Make the Indian visible. Make the white man visible to the Indian, too. Cure our invisibility, and we'll come to have power. Make them aware of our psychic realities, and they'll come to join us. Explicate the texts of our abundance, and we will win them over. For knowledge is power. Knowledge is freedom. Knowledge burns old bridges and opens new roads on every vista. Knowledge creates us.

As we create our world.

Out of the self-creation of our deepest and truest awareness, we transform the bridges before us.

Out of the humanity of our honest understanding, we nurture the tolerance that is all mankind's sustenance.

Out of our internal and external knowledge, we create the puppet strings on our minds and souls.

Come, my brothers and sisters, the future is ours to create.

-< * >-

Come up, there! Let us sing of the dawning.
Come up, here! Let us sing of a knowing.
Come, you boys, there.
Come, you girls, here.
Come, you men and women.
Come, you elderly.
All are invited. E-e-e-e-e Yo-o-o-o-o
All are invited to a knowing.

I went inside myself to the east.
I went inside myself toward the daybreak star.
I went inside myself toward the self made of dawn.
I walked out to the east and met Grandmother Turtle,

Met that part of myself that is Grandmother Turtle,
Met that part of myself that is the principle of self-
    creation,
Grandmother Turtle who creates her own dress,
Grandmother Turtle who creates her own
fingernails,
Grandmother Turtle who carries the world on her
    back.
'Three times,' she said, 'the world has been
    recreated bigger,
'Three times, people have been recreated better,
'Three times, the psyche has been recreated bigger
    and better.
'It is soon time to stretch the world again.
'I see by your coming it is time to stretch the world
    again.'
Grandmother Turtle—
That part of my self that is Grandmother Turtle—
Took a sack from her back,
Took from the sack four seeds:
'These are the seeds of understanding,' she said.
    'Take them.
'These are the seeds of tolerance, take them.
'These are the seeds of freedom, take them.
'These are the seeds of pluralism, take them.
'Plant one in the day, it will grow in the summer,
'Plant one in the sunset, it will grow in the autumn,
'Plant one in the night, it will grow in the winter,
'Plant one in the dawn, it will fruit in the spring.
'Spread them in the soil of tolerance and good will.
'Irrigate the sprouts with the waters of mutual
    sustenance.
'Cultivate the stalks in the sunlight of freedom and
    love.
'Harvest the fruits of pluralism in the dawn of your
    new world.
'In the world full of freedom for all.

                                                             Charles Brashear

'For you must know that every man and woman is
    capable of being free—
Free from his own stupidities,
Free from the darkness in his own soul.
'For you must know that every man and woman is
    capable of creating himself,
Creating his own soul as well as his dress,
Creating the direction and distance to his dawn.
'Tell all the boys, there,
'Tell all the girls, there,
'Tell all the men and women,
'Tell all the elderly,
'Go now with knowledge of a new dawn's light
'And you'll survive the darkness of this night.'
Thus it was. Thus it was.
It is finished.
It is transformed.
It is myself creates myself.
Tcen-wer! Tcen-wer! (Come down, Spirit, come down!)

-< * >-

My friends rush to me, applauding and hugging and kissing me with incomprehension. I offered the basket of the universe, but they received a dry, clay plate, a ghost of emptiness.

So it is my turn to stand amid a jubilant and moved audience.

And cry.

Not even Grandmother Doe-in-the-Dawn drank from my cup of fresh rainwater.

26. The Nottoway Dancers

After such defeat, after such knowledge, what forgiveness is possible? What's left but to fight? To rise up and fight back?

Granny, Sara Ann, and I are out on the road, traveling with the new uprising. About the first of March, AIM occupied Wounded Knee, and the government reacted, as we knew it would, in the most stupid way possible: "Awright! Y'all come on out o' thar with yer hands up!"

We travel from place to place in a little caravan. Two VW's and a Chevy van.

Our cover and gimmick is a dance-group. Mary Barnesfish, from Yakima— You remember Mary Barnesfish, don't you? She has brought along eight children, elementary school age, who dance in costumes when we get a crowd. They were trained at the Nottoway Indian Center in Carolina. They dance, and we sell posters or accept tips.

Our next stop is Lander, Wyoming, where we're going to work a three-day spring festival, a regular frontier days celebration. We're trying to raise money for bail and defense lawyers, as well as money to buy supplies for the Indians occupying Wounded Knee.

We figure if we can get as close as Rapid City, we can find someone who can run our supplies in to Wounded Knee. It's really neat the way our guys are getting in an out with food, rifles, blankets, just about anything they want that's smaller than a wigwam, even though the Feds have all the roads blocked and Wounded Knee surrounded.

Cops all over are apparently cooperating with the Feds and are stopping and harassing anybody with cheekbones, beads, or a slight tint to the skin, anybody that just might be on their way to Wounded Knee. Jailing a lot of 'em, too. For instance, ever since we crossed South Pass and started down toward Lander, highway cops have been swarming around us like wasps around tainted meat. They gaze in our windows, where our kids are playing with their feathers and decorated wands.

"Geez," says Sara Ann, "I feel like merchandise in a whore house, the way those guys are looking us over."

Out on the flats south of Lander, we meet a couple of new ones. Sheriff's Officers. In a Lander city car. As they zip passed me, I see that the driver is a big, handsome, Adonis of a fellow. Wearing big, pilot-style, reflective, rose-colored-glasses. No eyes. In my rear-view mirror, I see him flip a U-turn, throwing up dust, and come blasting back. He passes my camper without even tooting.

"He must be after one of the others," says Granny. They've gotten quite a way ahead of me.

Just at the city limits, we see they've stopped Rita and Taitchee's van. They have Taitchee out, standing back from the van, his feet spread and his hands on the side of the van. Real gang-busters!

Rita is struggling back. She's not very big, but she's tough as a bitch. Was trained in the Sioux tradition to be a "manly-hearted woman." Dark, Indian skin; heavy, black braids; strong-willed as the Hunkpapa she is. Her great-grandfather knew Sitting Bull, so she comes on strong.

The cop is pushing her, and she's scratching back. He's just about to slap her as I pull up behind, stick my head out, and yell, "Hey, what's going on here?"

Both the cops whirl around, their hands on their guns. Then they relax. To them, I'm obviously white. "Just a routine check," mutters Rose-colored-glasses. "Keep moving, buddy." He tilts his head so that all I can see is the reflection on his glasses.

Grandmother Doe-in-the-Dawn is already out of the camper on the other side and charging the cops in her gray shirtwaist. All she needs to be a stereotype out of some old movie is an umbrella.

She actually pushes the cops away from Rita and Taitchee. Swats at them with her purse. And they take it as meekly as whipped puppies. "You leave these people alone," she screams at them. "You hear me? They're with me. These are my friends!"

I tell the cops that this is a little Indian dance troop that I'm operating to make a few bucks, and they'd better leave my economic base alone. It works. They don't even ask for identification. They just take my word that I'm an ordinary, money-grubbing, Indian-exploiting Amurikan.

Sara Ann comes up beside me. In spite of the braids and necklace, she's obviously anglo to them. The cops look at us with a hesitant respect.

Just call us Tonto's revenge. Faithful white companions of the Nottoway Indian Rangers, who are doing the work of civilization. The Indians have humanity on their side. Justice. Compassion.

But, somehow, they're tragically flawed with a mask of tinted skin; just can't get through.

Can't ride into town.

So here comes faithful white companion to the rescue, for I possess (though deculturized) a marvelous *deus ex machina* to save the day. Tada-dum tada-dum tada-dum-dum-dum. We complete each other. Like yang and yin.

Oh, Grandmother Turtle, it makes me sick to know how little of man's capacity for psychic nobility is involved in the affairs of men!

The cops are caught off-balance. "Y' have t' have a license to dance here," says Rose-colored-glasses, his eyes shining like insect lenses.

"Fine," I say. "I'll get a license before we start to dance. We're not dancing yet."

Both the cops look around suddenly, as if to check that we aren't, in fact, dancing already. All the kids are practically pasted up against the windows, gazing out. Sara Ann slips her hand into the curve of my arm, so that we look like a couple.

Suddenly, Rose-colored-glasses drops the incident. Stalks off to his car. His deputy follows. They get in and roar away in a cloud of dust.

Rita and Taitchee look at me with a mixture of gratitude and hatred.

-< * >-

That cop has no idea, I'm sure, what a favor he did us, by letting us know we had to have a license. If he had waited, he could have arrested all of us legitimately! So, when we get into town, I leave the others parked on a side street, and Sara Ann and I go looking for a license.

Standard Western town. Bohunk cowboys boozing it up everywhere. Cheap steak houses. Stockmen's and cattlemen's bars and grills. Big, barn-like, piss-smelling beer joints.

But something about this town bothers me. Though there's an Arapaho Reservation nearby, no Indians around to speak of, and what few are around are sticking to the side streets, well away from the main drag.

We find the city hall and get the license. Not just one. I ask a lot of innocent questions. Get a license for selling posters. Soliciting door to door and on the sidewalk. Dancing. Camping. Just about everything they mention.

Then I find a printer. I want to get some little handbills printed which we plan to pass around. Not sell, just give to people. As public information. I had no end of fun writing them.

The printer takes a look at my first handbill: a cartoon of Yellow-hair Custer, talking to (you guessed it!) John Wayne. Custer is looking at the sky and saying: "Nice day to exterminate the Sioux, don't you think?"

The printer doesn't even answer. He glances disgustedly at Sara Ann, just lets the handbill fall away from him, then turns his back on us.

We go to an instant print shop. No questions. They don't even look at the handbills. Just put the money on the table, paid in full in advance, and they'll run them through the Xerox. I can pick them up in an hour.

We rejoin our friends and get ready to stage a dance on the street corner. Granny is tired and wants to nap in the camper. Sara Ann stays with her.

The town is filling up rapidly with people in new, bright-colored western outfits, mixed with grizzled men in faded Levi's and their plump wives in print dresses and too many, too-tight pin curls.

We choose a corner by The Cowpunchers' Bar and Grill. Taitchee, Rita, and John, who all look Indian, begin selling posters, while Mary and I hawk for the kids and beat the drum. I sense animosity in Taitchee, as if he thought I had given him the demeaning job, because he is more Indian.

First, Mary has the kids do one of those Aztec things where they are repeatedly getting into two small straight lines, then jumping out into a big circle. A sort of sunburst pattern.

It's an effective and amazing dance, but the kids aren't very good. Not many people stop to watch, and we get only a few nickels and dimes in the collection. I see, out of the corner of my eye, the Sheriff's car creeping by, ever so slowly, like a big cat, and going on down the street.

I see a rancher talking to Rita. He's stiff-kneed and the seat of his Levi's is faded in the shape of a saddle. He's fingering a poster Rita is showing him. Probably thinks it's pretty chintzy. He's right. We only pay twenty-eight cents each to get them printed. I see her lips form the word twenty. Then I see him take out a twenty dollar bill and give it to Rita. He takes two posters and hobbles away.

I give John the drum and go over to her, like I'm going to start an argument. Just stand there, looking at her. Silent. Stoic. Indian pose. She knows as well as I that even five bucks each is a rip-off we ought not to pull on even our best friends.

She understands. Picks up the twenty, fingers it, holds it.

I look away from the money. Look straight into her eyes.

Accusing. Doing my damnedest to be accusing. It's a question of honor. Dignity.

She shrugs her shoulders. The sign of no understanding. Quick, furtive glances at several things. Even looks for the rancher. At last, confronts my eyes. "Ha," she cries. "You guys have been stealing from us for 350 years. It's about time for a turnabout."

I say nothing. How can anyone say all that needs be said? Cheating always hurts the cheater more than it hurts the cheated. Because it damages his psyche; you dwarf your own psyche when you cheat. I want to cry out to all Indians in the movement, 'Don't imitate the white man. Don't fall into the trap. If you use chicanery to get your ends, you'll twist your mind. You'll shrink your spirit.'

Rita understands. I can see that in her eyes.

I turn to go, but she won't let it drop. She's so irrepressible. So straight Indian. Almost an advocate of Indianness Über Alles. I guess that's part of her Sioux training. You know, being told when she was a little girl that she couldn't do some things other kids might do, because, after all, she had to remember who she was. Real people don't act that way.

"What makes you so brash?" she demands. "What right do you have to come and tell a real Indian what to think and do? Sneaking around with your brash ears, listening to things that aren't meant for you? Even if you do have some Indian blood, that doesn't justify snooping."

Then, she suddenly adopts me. Gives me a name. "Here, Brash Ears, sell these posters yourself, if you're such a good Indian."

She tries to give me the posters, but I don't take them. Instead, I go back, take the drum from John, and do my best to be a real Indian. Here am I, standing on a street corner in an ersatz turkey-feather Sioux bonnet, a Zuni necklace, and a Sears shirt, beating a Kiowa rhythm on a Ute drum, besides which I have my heart and soul in the movement.

Heart and soul won't do, says Rita; it takes skin and

blood.

A pox on you, Rita, for your "chosen-people" bigotry!

-< * >-

Things are quiet for a while. I see Granny and Sara Ann at the edge of our crowd. Granny looks rested. I have the kids do a sort of ring dance. If they weren't wearing feathers and bells, you'd recognize it as Ring-Around-the-Rosy. Mary glares at me and curses silently, but it pays off better. We get about six bucks in the hat. I give the money to Taitchee to keep, and I can see he feels better.

Two drunks stagger out of The Cowpunchers' Bar and start bothering Rita. "Heyyy," says one, "Look it that purty, little squaw." His buddy says nothing, but leers at her.

"Hey, Honey," says the first one. "You open for business?" They both laugh and stagger around.

"You come on with me," says the first one, "Come on a my house 'n I'll show you what the cowboy did for Red Wing." As he speaks, he reaches out and paws Rita's right breast.

She doesn't knock his hand away, but reaches behind her with her left hand and brings around a huge haymaker that catches him square in the nose and mouth. His nose bursts in a splatter of blood. He staggers back, stumbles into his buddy, and they domino, plop, onto the sidewalk.

They haven't even finished falling before Rose-colored-glasses is springing at Rita from the corner where the side street comes up. Yelling, "Stay where you are. You're under arrest." But instead of grabbing Rita, he grabs the posters she's been selling.

"Don't anybody move," he yells.

Grandmother Doe-in-the-Dawn and I are already running, trying to get there before the herd of whites that are standing around starts crowding close, as they will in a moment.

"Let that woman go, Officer," yells Granny. "I saw it all. He attacked her."

The cop doesn't get a chance to look at her good before a plump woman in a print dress agrees. "That's right, Joe.

Charles Brashear

Harry started pawing the girl, and she hit him. Self defense."
A murmur of assent goes around the crowd.

Harry and his buddy are getting up. Catching the blood in
a big bandanna. Standing around sheepishly. Getting ready
to fade into the crowd.

Rose-colored-glasses glances around, not seeing anything
rosy, looks at Granny, notices for the first time that he is
holding Rita's posters. He stares at them long enough to have
read them, but I'm sure he didn't really see them. They're just
a black-ink silhouette of an Indian in a blanket, holding a
hatchet and a rifle, and below it, in white printing:

We have had some small Differences with the English, and during these Misunderstandings, some of their young Men would, by way of Reproach, be every now and then telling us, that we should have perished if they had not come into the country and furnished us with Strowds and Hatchets, and Guns, and other Things necessary for the Support of Life; but we always gave them to understand that they were mistaken, that we lived before they came amongst us, and as well, or better, if we may believe what our Forefathers have told us. We had then Room enough, and Plenty of Deer, which was easily caught: and though we had not Knives, Hatchets, or Guns, such as we have now, yet we had Knives of Stone, and Hatchets of Stone, and Bows and Arrows, and those served our Uses as well as the English ones do now. (Cannassatego to the Governor of Maryland, 1744)

Rose-colored-glasses lifts the posters into the air as if they are a stick of wood he is going to break across his knee, and yells, "You're under arrest for selling posters illegally."

"No! Hold it!" I shout. "We've got a license to sell them." And I thrust the paper in front of his eyes— over the posters which he still holds chest high.

He reads the license. Slowly. Slowly begins to let his arms down. Turns loose of the posters, slowly, so they peel off, like dive bombers, and drift to the sidewalk and gutter.

"Stop! You son-of-a-bitch," yells Rita. "You'll get them dirty." And she pushes him, so she can collect the posters again.

Rose-colored-glasses just looks down the street. A long way away. There's nothing there to see. He runs his tongue up on his teeth and sucks, as if to clear away something.

At last, he looks around. His shining eyes just brush past Rita, the kids in their feathers, Taitchee, John, Granny, Sara Ann, and settle on me. There's enough hatred in him to support a long war. "Awright, let's break it up, folks," he says. "Show's over. Go on home. Break it up."

Some of them came seventy miles for a three-day, Easter week celebration, and he says "go on home"!

Slowly the crowd drifts way. Newcomers asking what happened. Those who were there telling them what they thought they saw, as they head for a bar or beer joint.

27. Camp Fire Tales

We camp on Reservations or in public camp grounds when we can. Granny and Sara Ann cook food for the whole group. Rita and Mary feed the kids, then mother them into their sleeping bags, while Taitchee, John, and I gather firewood. We like to sit around a campfire at night and talk.

We bicker among ourselves over fruitless questions like "What was the most destructive thing the white man ever did to the Indian?"

Some will say giving him the pony and the gun were the worst.

Taitchee says, "The John Wayne mind was the worst."

Others will say "Removal."

Some will say, "Reservations," by which they mean prairie ghettos.

I, myself, think the Allotment Policy in the Dawes Act of 1887 was worst, for it tried to legislate American language, culture, economics, social organizations, political structure, religion, and values onto the Indians. Pretty big broom, that!

We fight and argue all the time, never agree on anything. Talk, talk, talk. That's the only thing we can agree on: that we all disagree. That's about the only thing all Indians have in common.

Tonight, talk drifts to tribalism. The New Tribalism of the current movement. The Pan-Indian movement is trying to unify different groups into one big tribe. Trouble is that a Sioux, remembering his wars, from New Ulm to Wounded Knee, has trouble sympathizing with the Cherokees' outrage at Removal, or the Long Walk of the Navajos.

The Navajos, in their turn, are very busy reviving Navajo religion and re-establishing as much of tribal custom as they can. Some Indians even want to go back to the blanket entirely. Have nothing to do with the white man; go back to hunting with arrows, living in skin lodges, worshiping the Great Spirits in the old way.

I maintain that there are very serious dangers in such tribalism. First, I say, it's a romantic delusion that we can go back. Not that we couldn't get rid of the material goods, but the knowledge would linger.

Suppose we went back to cooking with hot stones in a wicker basket, or even in a clay pot, and back to building houses with a stone axe. What would we do with the knowledge that brass kettles and iron hatchets exist in the world? And that they're better?

What would we do with the knowledge that it is not necessary to spend every second of our waking time scratching out a slim subsistence. What would we do with the knowledge that leisure exists, time to appreciate, time to allow our minds to create?

Knowledge complicates and makes back-tracking difficult. I do not live for the drudgery of making a living. It would be a sad culture that did.

Everybody jumps on me for this. Even Mary. Don't I know what tribalism accomplishes? Gives the individual a group to identify with, to find his security and sense of belonging and importance within. A group that preserves and perpetuates the culture, which in turn gives life to the individual.

"Suppose we accept the iron pot," says John. "First thing you know, they'll also want us to accept the stove that goes with it. And the indoor plumbing. And pretty soon, we're trapped in the same 8-to-5 rat-race as all the Anglos.

"And why? Just to support that stove and plumbing and the house that surrounds it and the mortgage that enslaves. Pretty soon, you'd have the Indian being the same as the white man. Indians don't want that 'sameness.' If that's the price of Progress, no thanks. Tribalism is a way to maintain cultural independence."

As we talk, Grandmother Doe-in-the-Dawn, who is the

only one of us who has ever lived beside an open fire and cooked with hot stones in a wicker basket, reaches across, touches my arm, and motions with her eyes.

After a pause, I let my eyes drift in the direction she motioned. Five or six faces in the edge of our firelight. Can't see what kind of clothes they are wearing. Just those faces. Not exactly surrounding us, but there. Watching. Sara Ann, who has been hugging my left arm, sees them, too, and moves slightly away to allow me free movement.

I get up on one knee, to tend the fire. I hand a big stick of firewood to John, whose back is to the intruders, and I select one for myself. I lay one out for Taitchee and flick him a glance with my eyes. Something in him understands. Almost too quickly. Then I stand up on one foot and one knee and call out loudly, without looking toward them, "Friends are welcome at the circle of our fire."

"The circle of the fire is the circle of the nations," says a voice in the dark. They come forward. Blankets, braids, black felt hats. Hands hidden in the folds. No shiny bracelets or necklaces, but when they get closer, I see that their faces are painted. Dull reds and earth colors. I guess them all to be about three-quarter bloods.

The leader squats by our fire, produces a beaded pipe bag, and takes out a long clay-stem war pipe. Fills it with pot from a plastic baggie. Lights it with a twig from the fire. Offers it to me.

It's good stuff. Getting harder and harder to get, I'll bet. But it's traditional. Even older than traditional. A necessary part of a conference.

When the pipe has gone the rounds, Chief Blanket speaks. "We heard about your scene in town." He passes the pipe over his shoulder to his buddies. "You got that cop mad at you."

I say nothing. Chief Blanket is playing a game. A role in a "B" movie. I can tell from his voice that he never learned his Indian language. Probably grew up in some suburb or small town, but turned sour on it. White boys got the paper routes, the carry-out jobs at the grocery store, all the opportunities at school. All he got was to envy the white boy all his symbols of affluence. As if to corroborate my thoughts, he adds, "They been mad at me all my life."

I say nothing, so he says, after a pause. "They been mad at a lot of people for a long time."

"Yeah," I admit.

"All o' the tribes," he goes on. "White men came on like they were the chosen people. Gave their solemn word, their utmost good faith, just so they could break it. They grabbed everything they could see, and then created welfare for the victims. Gaaa, they must've hated us."

I see Granny, Rita, Taitchee, and John nodding assent across the fire.

I say nothing still, but I agree with them. Only more so. It wasn't just hatred; it was insanity. The white man was simultaneously aggressive and paranoid. His collective behavior, viewed psychiatrically, shows a lot of hysteria and anxiety.

If such behavior occurred in an individual, he would be declared insane. Indian individuals may be depressed, paranoid, psychasthenic, withdrawn, anxiety-ridden, repressed, alienated, and isolated, but thank goodness "The Indian" isn't yet insane.

He gets his pipe back from his buddies. "They hate us," he mutters. "Hate. Hate." Sara Ann snuggles nearer my arm, as if seeking protection against him.

I realize I was wrong. He's not playing a game. He's deadly earnest. His eyes are screwing down to little points, not widening out, but screwing down, cutting out the available light. He must be going practically blind with rage. He starts talking loud.

"We're going get 'em, you hear? We're going to rise up against 'em, when the time comes, and kill every last one of them. We're going to wipe them off the face of the earth. We can hate, too. We can kill!"

Deliberately, he turns and starts crawling toward me. His blanket falls open, and I see he's carrying a quiver of arrows and a stone tomahawk.

"Listen," he says quietly, "You guys are on the right side. We can tell you. There's an organization. A secret organization. Only Indians. We're getting ready. Time comes, we're going to kill 'em all. Grab everything. Won't be any need for welfare afterwards for any of 'em. We're getting ready for the take over. Zap! Zowie! And there won't be anything left but Indians. Indians, you hear? Real Indians!"

As he's talking, he creeps closer and closer to me. I don't know quite what to do. Across the fire, Rita is puffing on the war pipe, watching and enjoying my discomfort and confusion. Taitchee is leaning forward, almost crawling.

Suddenly, car lights and spotlights and sirens blast on, maybe a hundred yards from our camp, and two cop cars come whistling up and start driving around us in circles. The bull horn on one of them barks out, "Awright! Y'all stay right where y'are. Don't anybody move." I recognize the voice of Rose-colored-glasses. After a couple of turns around us, they stop and four cops get out, guns drawn, and start moving in on us.

"Git yer hands up," says Rose-colored-glasses.

"What for?" I ask. "What's going on, anyway?"

"Shaddup. We'll ask the questions." He walks over toward our vans. "What y' got in them vehicles?" he asks.

"Children," says Mary. "They're bedded down in there." At practically every window, there's a little nose against the glass.

"Y' got any dope in there?" he asks.

"No," I answer. "Nothing at all." I glance, hoping Chief Blanket has hidden his baggie.

"Wal, I guess I'll jus take a look," he says and starts toward the nearest van.

"Better not touch that," says Sara Ann.

He stops. Turns around. "Who sez?"

"The law sez," she answers.

"And I guess you know," he says sarcastically.

"I'm a lawyer," says Sara Ann, unaffected by his bravado.

"First, we haven't seen any warrant that would let you look. Second, you're on an Indian Reservation, and even you know that you have no authority at all on an Indian Reservation. Federal law prevails here, and you're not a federal officer."

He stops. Tries a misinformed ploy. "That's only true when the criminals is Indian. We c'n go after whites wherever we want."

"That's not true either," I say. "But we're all Indian." I walk over, open the door to my camper, and stand there, displaying the kids in their pajamas.

He comes over, looks closely into my face, then looks away. Stares at something distant, in the dark, and sucks on his teeth. "So that's how it is, hunh?"

Rita touches his gun with the war pipe and says, "You'd better put that thing away before it gets you hurt."

Rose-colored-glasses flares up, ready to hit us.

Grandmother Doe-in-the-Dawn speaks up, for the first time in hours. "They're right, Officer. In fact, it's you that's trespassing. I'm sure no Indian or BIA official invited you onto this Reservation. And you don't have the right to come here, unless invited."

We're all slightly flustered for a few minutes, and when we look again, our blanket society friends are gone. Took their pipe and baggie, and drifted away into the darkness.

Rose-colored-glasses looks around. He's practically ready to whimper. Suddenly, he stuffs his gun in his holster and stalks off toward his car. "Come on, men," he barks. "Let's get the' hell out o' here."

28. The New Indian

I am awakened at dawn by a yell, "Hi-yaugh!" It sounds like men driving horses.

I get up on one elbow just in time to hear a rifle shot. The bullet slams into my camper and out the other side. I see fifteen men or so, coming up from the south, in a V-shaped, infantry attack formation. More shots ring out. Sara Ann and I scramble out of our sleeping bags. I grab my boots and crawl away, trying to get cover behind the VW.

"Knock it off!" I yell. "There are women and children over here!"

Just then, Grandmother Doe-in-the-Dawn swings open the camper door. She stands up almost straight in her white nightgown and yells, "Stop that! You hear! Stop that! There are children in here!"

The shots keep popping for a minute more, but I see that the men are pointing their rifles into the air now. So I walk out toward them. Take out my pocket handkerchief and wave. "Okay, okay. Knock it off," I yell. "We give up."

The attackers are all Indians, I see pretty quickly. All have short hair, some parted and combed; some, like the leader, in bristly, flat-topped crew-cuts. They wear different kinds of plaid shirts and leather jackets. They carry good, high-powered rifles.

John and Taitchee have pulled on their boots and come up close behind me.

"We're Indians, too," I say. "We're raising money for Wounded Knee and going from— "

Their leader cuts me off: "We know who you are!"

I stop. Taitchee and John probably think I talk too much anyway. Maybe even resent it.

The invaders probably know as much about us from the moccasin grapevine as we know about ourselves.

Charles Brashear

They're all well-fed, tending to paunchiness. Bedroom Indians. Live in some tract of three and four bedroom houses with attached garages and postage stamp patios, near the edge of the Reservation.

"We know who you are," repeats the crew-cut leader, "And we don't want anything to do with you. Pack up, and get on out o' here. And don't come back."

"Look, Man," says John. "We're all Indians, too. We gotta work together. Support the demonstrations at Wounded Knee an' all. We're just trying— "

"Trying to queer what we got going? That's what you're doing. We got jobs. We're living decently. Trying to be honest, law-abiding citizens. We go to church. Got friends in the white community. We're accepted.

"And here you guys come in with all your crap about fighting, and you queer it all for us. Our friends're gonna hold us responsible for what you do. You know that?" He pauses, looks around for assent from his army, gets it. "We're not going to stand for it, you hear? So pack your gear and get on out of here."

"But this is a Reservation," says Taitchee. "We can camp on a res— "

"No, you can't! Not this one! I'm the local tribal chairman, see? And most of the council is here with me. We've met and talked about this. Either you guys get on out of here peaceably, or we're going to give you knots on your heads you'll have to walk and push."

He lifts his rifle, sights, and puts another bullet through the metal part of my camper. I hear screams from inside the VW.

"Hey!" I yell, "don't kill the kids!" I start to lunge forward, but two guys put their gun barrels against my chest.

"These are Indian police, son," says crew-cut. "You wouldn't want them to see you attacking the tribal chairman, now, would you? Especially way out here on the Reservation, where the white cops ain't likely to come looking."

"But you just shot toward women and children; and

besides, you just put a hole through my camper," I protest. There are kids at every window, watching us.

"Yep," he says. "And in one minute, I'll put another hole through it. Maybe through the glass next time. One a minute, till you guys get your asses out of here."

I don't believe him, at first. So I don't move very fast.

"Fifteen seconds," he says. He's looking at an imaginary watch on his arm.

We decide he's really vicious, so we start running. Throw bags and tarp in on top of the children. Hop in. Get going. No breakfast.

"And don't come back!" he screams at us, as we drive away.

-< * >-

The dawn streets of Lander are empty and silent, except for a pack of dogs. Different shades of red and brown, a black, a dun-colored one that looks almost human. Sniffing around for a cat to kill, or something.

We stop in front of the bank, to decide what to do next. The dogs see us and come at once, so intently that I'm hesitant to get out of the van. No heads bobbing, no tails wagging; just straight, forward movement, like torpedoes with eyes. I tell myself that this is civilization; the fears I'm feeling are groundless.

But as I begin to step out, big red dog growls at me and bares his teeth; the roan and the dun begin to bark. We decide, by yelling from open car windows, to find the city park and fix some breakfast.

We have to settle on a place south of town where the shoulder is wide enough for us to pull off and set up a camp stove. Granny and Sara Ann again organize the cooking. Afterwards, several of us snooze in the morning sun, catching up on lost sleep. It's mid-morning by the time I suggest we pack up and go back into town to try our luck at dancing for another day.

"Geez. Let's skip this town," says Taitchee. "They got our

number."

"Oh, no," I insist. "The law is on our side."

Sara Ann nods her agreement.

"Lot of good that'll do us," says Rita.

We set up in front of the bank, thinking there we'll avoid drunks stumbling out of bars and beer joints. Taitchee and I each take one kid and a drum and go separate ways in the street to try to draw a little attention. Previews to drum up business.

My little dancer is Timmy Surrounds-it. He's half-blood Nottoway from North Carolina. He's wearing feathers like a Taos eagle and dancing a Hopi hoop dance. In a little while, he'll join the others in a Sioux war dance, part of the Cherokee Green Corn Dance, some Aztec patterns, greatly diluted.

I muse on these ironies as he dances. He's awkward. Still learning. Stops his rhythm when he has to roll a hoop up with his foot, so he can catch it on his toe, then picks up the rhythm again. The audience likes him. He gets applause, which he doesn't even acknowledge, but I know he's touched by it. As he grows up, he will adapt his Indianness to that applause, as so many of the people today already have.

What kind of Indian is he? He is not being raised with Nottoway traditions, but a little of everything. Stressing maybe the Plains culture. That's what being Indian has come to mean to him. Not wearing the turbans and tunics of his ancestors, but cheap imitations of eagle feathers and quill beads. Tipis for Tuscaroras! Absurd! He's growing up as fake in his way, as I did in mine.

What does it mean to be an Indian these days, when travel and television teach us so many idioms?

I nearly choke on the ironic bark with which Taitchee and I hawk up a fair crowd: "Come, see real Indian children, doing authentic Indian dances! Chance of a lifetime!"

In the hour before lunch, we do a pretty good business. We have the kids do the round dances, and the individual and pairs at hoop dancing again. The hit, as always, is the

Sioux War Dance. Full of whoops and feathers.

About noon, Taitchee and John are doing the drumming and I'm passing out the handbills I had printed, when I see Rose-colored-glasses in the crowd. He's standing near a lamp post, his right foot hoisted to rest on the cement foundation, like a wasp on a limb. He's just watching. When I pass near him, he says, "I suppose you've got a license for passing out them things?"

"Yes," I answer. "You wanta see it?"

"Nope."

I give him copies of the handbills I'm passing out.

He takes them. Reads the top one:

Charles Brashear

THE FIVE STEPS OF CATCH 22 — INDIAN VERSION

Step 1. A white man squats on Indian land and builds a cabin. "Wull, it wuz thar, 'n it's gov'ment land. Gov'ment land is free, ain't it?"

Step 2. Indians get the sheriff and take the case to court. The case drags on for 25 years, because the BIA is handling the Indian side.

Step 3. At last, the court says the cabin belongs to the Indians, because the land belongs to the Indians, and all the improvements on land go with the land. We all pack up our satisfaction and get ready to go home.

Step 4. But, says the court, it seems only fair that the Indians might compensate the white man for the cabin. After all, he put in his labor, sawed the lumber, dug the well, and so on.

Step 5. The only thing of value the Indians have is land. Therefore, title to 160 acres of prime land is transferred to the white man — and, of course, all natural resources like water, and improvements like cabins, go with the land.

IF YOU'RE NOT PART OF THE SOLUTION, YOU MUST BE AN INDIAN!

The kids begin the Navajo Childrens' pony dance, their little plywood horses hung on their shoulders with suspenders. The crowd loves it, especially the contrary little donkey. He's always getting lost, moving against the current, inventing his own direction— but, always, in the long run, re-joining the crowd of other ponies to become a coherent herd.

Without speaking, I show Rose-colored-glasses our permit for the kids to dance and solicit on the sidewalk.

Rose-colored-glasses, his lenses reflecting the sky, doesn't bother to read it. Says nothing. Just looks down the street, at that nothing in the distance he's so fond of.

29. The Battle of Wounded Thigh

After lunch, business dwindles. The semi-finals are going on out at the rodeo grounds, and most of the crowd has gone out to see them. Late in the afternoon, we decide to try it, too. Maybe we could stir up a little action in the parking lot.

But it's no go. The arena boss comes out. Tells us the drums are scaring the animals and would we please not beat them. We weren't getting any crowds or reactions anyway, so we decide to pack up and go. Rose-colored-glasses shows up, just as we are leaving.

"Where shall we stay tonight?" asks Rita.

Cockily, I ask Rose-colored-glasses if there are any parks, or public camp grounds, or other places we might pitch our camp.

He studies the distance again, sucking his teeth. Then he turns to me, his reflective glasses hiding his eyes, and says, "Sure. They's a place right out west of town. In the creek bottom. Sand creek. Fair number of trees and driftwood. Y'go three miles west, toward the Sink Canyon, and at that Coca-Cola sign turn right. Just follow the road to the creek. Y'can't miss it. The road don't go nowhere else."

"That's a public park?" I ask.

"No," he says. "But it's okay."

"Safe? Even from you?"

"Yep."

We don't go there. Instead, we find our own place, in a secluded creek bottom out east of town. We cook, eat, get the kids to bed shortly after dark.

We find a little wood, start an open fire, and sit round talking. Granny is ill and turns in early. When the wind has lain, and the day animals are silent in the dark, and the stars and the fire flicker, then that part of the human psyche that is most peaceful and honest and benevolent comes out and reigns. Ah, if only the world could conduct its political and economic affairs around an open fire at night, we'd have a happier present and future.

We try to decide what the Indian's most pressing need is.

"Food," says Taitchee.

"Jobs," says John.

"Training," says Mary. "How're people going to get jobs or food, when they don't have any training. Other than lifting, toting, sweeping, I mean. I think we need job training for the men and women who want to work, and other kinds of schools, too; literacy training, if they need it; and public schools that make Indian sense. I mean, what kind of jobs can Indians look forward to, when 60 percent of them drop out before they get through high school?"

A strange quiet settles over the conversation. I sense that they are all remembering their BIA schools on Reservations.

"What did the Pilgrim teach the Indian?" says John.

No one answers. But there is a kind of silence that says they all respond. I think every one of them had to write an essay on that topic in sixth grade.

"And feathers," says John. "Wear your feathers, so we'll know you're a funny bird."

I tend the fire. A few sparks go up.

"Worst? There is no worst! All these things are primary," says Rita. "They're all urgent. Jobs, food, clothing, housing, health facilities, school. They're all catastrophes."

Car lights approach. Speeding on a sand road. It's a new Ford pick-up with a cattle rack on the back. Out jumps an Indian. Trim. Muscular. Tailored worsted pants, plaid western shirt with mother-of-pearl snaps, new boots, a felt Stetson hat.

"Don't ask questions," he says. "Just pack and get out of here as quick as you can. That sheriff set a trap for you. If you don't get out of here damned quick, you're going to get your skulls bashed in."

Before we can ask questions, he's back in his pick-up and gone.

We bicker a little. That cop doesn't even know where we are.

Who's this guy kidding?

What is this? A "B" movie?

How melodramatic can you get?

But in a few minutes, we decide it's better not to take chances. So we pack and leave.

Just in time, too. The others are ahead, but I'm not quite out of the grove of trees, when a covey of horses bursts from the underbrush downstream. A herd of wild cowboys. All drunk. Most of them seem to be carrying a club about the size of a baseball bat.

"Get moving!" says Sara Ann, urgently. Granny and the children watch sleepily. I jam the gas pedal to the floorboard, but the first horsemen still catch up with me and run alongside, banging the top of my camper with their clubs and screaming "Hi-yaaah, Hooo-yeeee." Real war whoops.

I glance out my window. In the reflected glow of my headlights, I see one is keeping neck and neck with me. He draws back his arm and throws his club, but it drifts back and bounces off the tail of the bus.

In a quarter of a mile, we outrun them. Turn and head for town again. It's safest in town where there are people to see what goes on.

I come up behind the others, just inside the city limits. Rose-colored-glasses has stopped them with a road block. He and his deputies are rummaging through the vans, throwing things out. Breaking feathers. Ripping up costumes. One deputy is holding Rita's hands behind her back and has a gun pointed at the others. John is squatting on the ground, holding his arm, which is bleeding profusely. Taitchee is unconscious on the ground.

I protest, "You can't do that! What's going on here?"

Rose-colored-glasses just barks something about reasonable cause to suspect crimes and goes on breaking things. He's not gloating. Not even mad. Just methodical. Everything gets whapped with his lead-filled billy club.

Rita breaks loose and runs at him. One of the other cops grabs her, spins her around. Jams his billy club down the front of her blouse, under her bra, then pops her in the face at the same time as he gives the billy club a hard jerk. Her clothes are ripped off at the same time as the end of the club rams her breast bone and rib-cage up against her heart. Knocks her breath out.

She falls backward into the ditch. Blood on her face. Her mouth full of blood. She lifts her head, her arms and hands held up. Rolling her shoulders up, as if to pour out the blood, so she won't drown.

I am stopped by the sight: she is in the pose of Big Foot in death, after the blizzard at Wounded Knee.

Looking, pausing, was my mistake. A lead-filled club whaps my skull.

-< * >-

I awake when the sun is high. I'm in a jail cell. John and Taitchee are with me. Their faces are swollen and gashed. John has a big bandage on his right forearm. Blood has soaked through it. We don't move. Not even to pull the window shade to protect us from the brutal sun.

They don't give us anything to eat. We probably couldn't have eaten anyway. Early afternoon, the jailer comes for us.

Sara Ann has found a lawyer to submit a writ of habeas corpus. Turns out he's a white lawyer, who is retained by the Association on American Indian Affairs. He fights legal battles for the Indians in the area, mostly child-custody arguments with the welfare department who wants to take children away from poor parents and put them in foster homes. He prevents them from holding us without charges.

The judge is mad. We're keeping him from the finals of the rodeo. So he wants to make short work of this.

Rita can't make it to the court room. She's in the hospital. Bad cuts on the face and mouth, but no teeth missing.

Broken sternum and rib. Possible internal injuries in the solar plexus; she has almost constant nausea. The judge says he'll arraign her in absentia. I suspect that's not legal, but our lawyer says let it go. "Best to let him make up law as he goes along."

Really? Is that the way the AAIA works? As many battles as I've heard they win, and they say let the court be boss? Turns out, that's their local modus operandi for making deals. Even justice is corrupted by political deals!

Grandmother Doe-in-the-Dawn also says maybe it's best to accept the least of evils. They didn't arrest her, Sara Ann, Mary, or the children. They and the kids stayed in the Great Western Motel.

Rose-colored-glasses takes off his eyes and tells his story. We're charged with suspicion of possession of narcotics. Suspicion of possession of weapons. Suspicion of conspiring to cross state lines to participate in a civil disturbance. Resisting search and investigation. Resisting arrest. Assaulting an officer. Creating a disturbance.

Our lawyer is quiet, so Sara Ann and I protest. They didn't find any evidence to make those charges. They're all poppycock. We all know, even the judge knows, none of them will hold up in trial.

The judge comes down from the bench and takes on a fatherly, man-to-man tone. "I know you fellows can't afford a long trial," he says. "So I'll let you off easy. We haven't made any formal charges yet. So I'll tell you what you do. You plead guilty to inciting to riot, and I'll drop all the other charges and put you on probation, provided you get on out of town and out of Wyoming as fast as you can."

"Inciting to riot! Who started it? Who had the billy clubs? Who has the wounds this morning, and who didn't even get blood on his shirt?"

I see John and Taitchee trying to signal me to be quiet.

"You want to go to trial?" asks the judge. "Wait maybe three, maybe six months, before your docket comes up? It costs a man a lot to be out of work that long, besides cooling his heels in jail. I'm giving you a chance to get away free. Just so you get on away."

Rita wouldn't take it if she were here. She'd attack the wagon train one more time. I have to speak for her:

"No deal! This is a miscarriage of justice! Brutality is brutality. We're going to counter-sue. You slap us with those charges, and I'll charge you in Federal Court for intimidating witnesses and defendants, for false arrest, for making charges without a shred of evidence, for search and seizure without a warrant, for wanton destruction of personal property, and brutality. And we'll make 'em stick, too. You hear?

"Besides ourselves and our wounds, we've got Grandmother Stonecrist and eight children to testify. You know how judges and juries react to old women and children, don't you? Maybe you'd better consider accepting our deal."

To my own and Sara Ann's surprise, Rita's audacity pays off. The judge goes back up on the bench and dismisses the charges for insufficient evidence. Dismisses, too, our charges of brutality. Certain amount of normal violence in being a policeman.

At the sheriff's garage, they want to charge us fifty bucks for towing and storage of abandoned vehicles on a public road. We just tell them to charge it all to Rose-colored-glasses; he's the one who confiscated them without cause, stopped and searched us illegally, arrested us falsely and brutally.

"Shall I let 'em have 'em, Joe?" asks the attendant.

Rose-colored-glasses is looking off in the distance again. Like he didn't hear. The attendant just waits.

At last, the sheriff says, "Yeah," and lets his voice hang, as if he wants to say a lot more. The attendant waits. But when nothing comes, he turns our keys over to us. Granny has to be helped into the camper.

At the hospital, Rita is having a hell of a time. The x-rays don't show any internal damages, but she keeps retching with nausea. Practically tearing her broken rib out with dry heaves. Doctor says she should be better tomorrow; a kick in the stomach usually wears off in about thirty-six to forty-eight hours.

We pay the motel bill for the women and children and wonder what we're going to do next. We are free to leave this town when Rita can travel; we'll try our luck farther on, so we start preparing for it. Lot of feathers to repair and replace. Lot of costumes to fix. We park on a side street where a big tree shades the sidewalk, and put the children to work. It's a kind of school. We show them what to do, and they give it a try.

Up at the corner is The Cowpunchers' Bar. We hear hoots and laughter. Some of the cowboys prefer drinking to watching the rodeo finals. Granny is ill with exhaustion.

But mostly the streets are quiet and hot. It's almost a pastoral afternoon. Birds live in these trees. And squirrels. They chatter and scold us intruders. We hear from time to time the passing of a distant jet and the buzz of insects.

More Indians— ragged Arapahos— are around this afternoon, for some reason. They drive by in 53 Chevy sedans with broken windows and no seats, looking at us. They can't figure out why we're making drums and dance costumes.

From time to time, small clumps of cowboys burst from The Cowpunchers' Bar to fight on the sidewalk a little while, or just to get air. Occasionally, a small group comes down the side street, passes us on their way to visit somebody's wife. Sometimes, there are Indians among them, wearing their tailored worsteds, western shirts with mother-of-pearl snaps, and new boots.

One such group is passing, just as a 52 Buick stops at the end of the street. Two ragged Indians get out and try to entice a fifty-pound Labrador pup into their car. The cowboys see. But they aren't mad. That's just what they want Indians to do— prove continually that they are thieves. Animalistic heathens.

"Hey, Billy-Joe," says one of the drunks to one of the Indians, "How long's it been since you— " He breaks off. Runs on ahead to another drunk, says, "Hey, Jerry. How long's it been since you tasted a good dog stew?"

Billy-Joe, the urban Indian, suddenly turns, comes back to where we are, grabs up a stack of posters half as thick as a telephone book, and rips them in two. He kicks at the kids, swings at Taitchee and me. If he weren't so drunk, he would beat us up. The others are going on. Didn't even stop to watch him attack us. So he suddenly runs to catch up with them.

-< * >-

Late in the day, we move again. Go out to a remote corner of the Reservation. A barren, rocky place, near a dry arroyo, with a little hill that we hope will hide us from view. We cook and eat before sunset, so no one will see the light of our fire after dark. We don't even make a campfire, nor sit around talking. Just take our bruises to bed. Sara Ann stays in the camper with Granny, in case she needs help.

After a moment, Sara Ann comes out and say, "Granny's getting weaker."

"What d'you expect?" I say. "She's over 80. Maybe she shouldn't have come on this expedition."

"That would have killed her, to stay home. And you know it."

"Yeah, but I don't want to kill her with overexposure, either."

"Well, we could sure use a couple of days of rest. All of us could use a little recuperation."

"We can't leave until Rita is able to move," I say. "And we can't stay around much longer before Rose-colored-glasses figures out a way to get us."

She leans over and kisses me. "Yeah, I know. Maybe something will ease up tomorrow. Try to get some sleep."

"Yeah," I say and kiss her goodnight. But I can't sleep. I keep thinking about the Indian movement. Not in terms of tribes— that doesn't work any more— but in terms of John Birch Indians, Kennedy Indians, John Wayne Indians, bedroom Indians.

What is an Indian anyway? I keep remembering asking

Bob Sayre, if a person who looks Indian, but tries to be white is a Red Apple, what is a person who looks white, but feels Indian?

"A crab apple!" Bob retorted.

And now, so long after, I keep thinking of what I could have said back to him: When you render the juice of the crab apple, it's red. I keep shivering and throwing that back at the thin moon.

-< * >-

I am awakened at dawn by the thunk of something against the side of my camper and a clattering on my sleeping bag. It's an arrow. With a stone point. Then I hear a war whoop from the dry arroyo. Several Indians are attacking. Faces and chests painted with bars of bright color. Gray, nondescript, Goodwill pants. Moccasins. Bows and arrows. Blanket Indians!

I hop up, sweep up my sleeping bag, and race for the side door of my VW. I can see that Taitchee and John are jumping toward their vans, too, getting ready to cut out. Granny has swung open the door and is standing there, stooped over in her nightgown. Sara Ann is right behind her.

As I'm hurrying, an arrow hits me in the thigh. Fleshy part. Buries a flint point two inches deep and knocks me down. Wounded by the savagery in my background! I snap off the arrow as soon as I can and drop it. Another arrow clatters into the camper and breaks against the bunk.

I hear a wump-sound, like mud bubbling; Granny falls backward into the van, holding an arrow shaft with both hands near the bottom of her rib cage.

Sara Ann gathers her in her arms, screaming, "She's hit, Georgie! She's hit!"

I finally manage to scramble into the camper and get the door closed. Sara Ann and Granny are huddled on the bunk.

Without stamping into my boots, I dive over the driver's seatback and get the motor running and the VW moving. But not for very far.

Two cars come blasting over the little hill. One is a Federal car; the other, the Lander Sheriff's. They force me into a gully, which tears off one of my wheels and bounces Granny, Sara Ann, and the kids around. I look back, but already the blanket Indians are fading back into the dry creek bed.

In the Federal car is a Welfare Officer and the U.S. Marshall. They get out and show their authority, but Rose-colored-glasses does most of the talking. He's been deputized by the U.S. Marshall. Pulls his gun and motions me to get out. He rips my arms around behind me and cuffs my wrists, then shoves me roughly around to the other side of the VW.

"We're gonna lock you up and throw away the key, sonny," he says, enjoying himself.

I stand there, slightly faint. My pants-leg is soaked with blood. In the bunk, Sara Ann has her arms around Granny to hold her up. Tears are streaming down her face.

"Thought you were going to get away, didn't you?" says Rose-colored-glasses, his insect eyes shining in the dawn light.

He's gloating this time. Puts on his John Wayne voice. Sure he's got us on something. "Well, I got all the papers this time. See?"

He waves them under my face and enumerates them. "Warrant to stop and search. Court order to take custody of those children. How long you guys had them out of school, anyway? Well, no matter. We'll see they get nice homes with nice folks that can bring 'em up right. Thought you'd get away, didn't you? But you didn't reckon on meeting up with me, eh?"

I close my eyes. I don't want to see or hear any of this. I want only to go and visit my relatives in some peaceful, passed time.

Rose-colored-glasses walks over and bangs open the side door of my camper. He pays no attention to Grandmother Doe-in-the-Dawn, Sara Ann, or me. Three of the children are cowering in my van among broken arrows and feathers.

Sara Ann comes out of the camper, carrying Granny like

Charles Brashear

a bird from an oil spill. Granny is no longer holding the arrow shaft. Her head is lolled to the side. Her arms and legs drape down, like a rag doll's.

The bottom falls out of my consciousness. A tunnel of darkness surrounds the tube of my vision. I feel myself falling away. I hear Sara Ann, whimpering, "She's dead! Grandmother Doe-in-the-Dawn is dead."

The last thing I hear is Rose-colored-glasses cocking his .357 Magnum, and barking at the children, "Awright! Y'all come on out o' thar with yer hands up!"

About the Author

CHARLES BRASHEAR was born on the south edge of the Great Plains, the Llano Estacado in west Texas. Of predominantly English and Scots ancestry, he also has two branches of Cherokees in his family tree. At the beginning of WW II, the family moved to California and never got around to returning. Charles attended UC-Berkeley (B.A. 1956), San Francisco State (M.A. 1960), and holds a Ph.D. from the University of Denver writing program (1962).

He taught three years at the University of Stockholm on a Fulbright grant (1962-65), three years at the University of Michigan (1965-68), and 24 years at San Diego State. He retired in 1992 in order to devote full time to research, writing, and travel. He has published over twenty books, the most recent of which are a novel, *Killing Cynthia Ann* (1999) and three collections of short fiction, *Saving Sand*, Stories of a Prairie Culture During the Great Depression (2009); *Comeuppance at Kicking Horse Casino and Other Stories* (2000); and *Contemporary Insanities* (1990).

During his teaching career, Dr. Brashear published several textbooks, including *Creative Writing* (American Book Co, 1968); *The Structure of Essays*, (Prentice-Hall, 1973); and *A Writer's Toolkit* (1990; 2001). In 2001, he published a five-book series: *The Elements of Writing* and a biography of a distant cousin: *Brain, Brawn, and Will: The Turmoils and Adventures of Jeff Ross.*

Magazine credits include stories in *Michigan Quarterly Review, High Plains Literary Review, American Indian Quarterly, Studies in American Indian Literatures, Four Quarters, Fiction International, Crazy Quilt Quarterly, Returning the Gift, Ani-Yun-Wiya (anthology of Cherokee Writing), Cimarron Review, American Indian Culture and Research Journal, South Dakota Quarterly, Denver Quarterly,* etc.

Dr. Brashear is a member of Western Writers of America, Native American Writers and Storytellers, The Willamette Writers, and The Writers' League of Texas. Go to www.amazon.com > books > search > Charles Brashear for information on and reviews of some of his books, or visit his website: www.CharlesBrashear.com

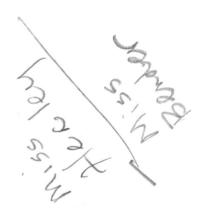

CPSIA information can be obtained at www.ICGtesting.com
Printed in the USA
LVOW010313151211

259361LV00006B/235/P

9 780933 362260